WAKES ON THE ALSEA

Greg Starypan

ISBN: 9781093535488 (paperback)
Imprint: Independently published

For Esther and John

PROLOGUE

Like most ten-year-olds, Skid thought summer was the best time of the year. Sure, school was out, and it meant twelve weeks of unbridled freedom. How could any kid not love that? But, for Skid, the best part about summer was that this was when he got to stay at his grandparents' farm on the Alsea River. It was a magical place, full of wildlife and endless possibilities for exploration. It was also his personal sanctuary where he could escape the verbal and physical torment he suffered the rest of the year at the hands of his abusive stepdad.

Skid was a scrawny, young man with steel blue eyes and a mophead of straw-colored hair. What he lacked in physical ability at his age, he more than compensated for in innate intelligence. This put him at odds with many of his classmates who were more athletic or who possessed greater social skills than him, but who lacked his mental capacity. With nothing in common, the divide between him and his classmates grew, and he increasingly found himself spending his free time alone. Perhaps it was just a defense mechanism, but he actually convinced himself that he preferred it this way.

Skid was born out of wedlock and never knew his biological father. The closest thing he had to a real dad was his maternal grandfather, Alfred Longbough.

Alfred was everything his stepdad was not. He was loving, kind, and nurturing. His stepdad was a mean, paranoid meth head who used Skid as a whipping boy to exorcize his own demons of self-loathing.

Alfred was a tall, frail man in his mid-seventies, who bore a striking resemblance to Jimmy Stewart. He had a thick crop of curly, snow white hair, which was reminiscent of the spun-glass angel hair used to depict snow or clouds in Christmas decorations. He loved his grandson, and Skid loved him dearly, or Pop-Pop, as he called him.

It was Pop-Pop, who had given his grandson the nickname Skid. Alfred was a fan of the show, *Hardcastle and McCormick*, a television series which aired on ABC in the early to mid-eighties. Hardcastle was a judge, and Mark "Skid" McCormick was an ex-con and race car driver, who drove a prototype sports car called the Coyote X. Together, they brought criminals to justice who had escaped conviction through the legal system. Alfred had recorded all episodes of the series on his VCR when they originally aired, and he introduced them to his grandson one summer when the boy first expressed an interest in cars.

It proved to be a bonding experience. The boy loved the show—especially the race car driver and the car—and the grandfather started calling the boy "Skid" as a way of building up his fragile grandson's self-esteem.

Skid was sitting on the sofa next to Pop-Pop with a bowl of buttered popcorn on his lap, watching "Rolling Thunder," Episode One, Season One of *Hardcastle and McCormick*. It was their ritual, the way they celebrated the beginning of each summer together. Grandma was in her recliner, knitting.

Suddenly, they heard a cacophony of loud and alarming cackles and squawks, coming from the chicken coop in the front yard. They knew what it meant. The raccoons were trying to kill their chickens.

Skid ran to his bedroom, grabbed the 10-22 long rifle his grandfather had given him the summer before and slowly opened his window. Alfred went to the kitchen as quickly as he could and turned on the outside light to frighten the raccoons and give his grandson enough light to see. As predicted, the predators withdrew into the shadows but did not leave, waiting to see what would happen.

Alfred grabbed a beer out of the fridge, opened it and walked slowly into his grandson's bedroom. Taking a sip of his beer, he grabbed Skid's shoulder and said, "Patience, son, that's the key. Wait until the varmints come out into the open and you have a clear shot. If you hurry and miss, you've lost your advantage, just scaring them off does nothing. They'll be back tomorrow."

Looking down his open sights, Skid said, "I know, Pop-Pop, I know."

"I know you do. It's just a lesson that's worth repeating."

Just then, two raccoons loped out of the shadows toward the chicken coop. One went to the near side of the pen, while the other went to the far side. The chickens, seeing the first predator approach, ran to the far side, screaming bloody murder, as they attempted to get as far away from the perceived threat as they could. They didn't know they were sealing their fate. As they pressed themselves against the fence, the raccoon, waiting on their side, extended his dexterous forepaws through the wire mesh and grabbed two hens by their necks, forcefully trying to pull them through the cage. Ripping off their heads, the predator started consuming one of them while the dismembered bodies of the two birds lay quivering on the ground in the run.

Two shots rang out, and both raccoons fell lifeless to the ground.

Alfred patted his grandson on the back and praised him. "Good shooting, Skid! We don't need any vermin on the Alsea. It's a constant battle, and I'm too old to do it myself. Thank God, Grandma and I have you!"

Skid ran outside, grabbed the two dead raccoons and carried them to the spot on the bank where he always left them for the vultures. He hadn't been on the Alsea for nearly ten months, so he didn't know whether the birds would be there in the morning. But he had confidence that it wouldn't take long for his "pets" to get habituated to his routine.

In the morning, Skid jumped out of bed like a kid on Christmas morning, eager to see whether Santa had come the night before. He opened the door and ran out on the deck. The vultures were there on the bank, eating the carcasses he had left them the night before. The boy was fascinated by their bare, red heads and found these birds beautiful in an odd sort of way. Standing there transfixed, he watched them consume the dead raccoons for nearly an hour with an almost reverential sense of wonder. He was joyous. Oh, how he loved the river.

WALDPORT, OREGON, 2010

Skid hated gym class and was thankful it was over. Entering the locker room, he quickly got undressed, grabbed his towel and headed for the showers. The warm water felt good on his tense body, and as he soaped himself up, he started to relax. Next week was the Prom, and he was going with Stacey Atwood. He still couldn't believe she had said yes when he asked her.

Stacey had luxuriant, black hair, and her light, green eyes were unforgettable. *They could see to your soul.* She ran track, so her body was lean but shapely. Her firm breasts weren't too big or too small. They were just right. He laughed to himself. *That sounds like something out of Goldilocks and the Three Bears,* he thought. He couldn't wait for the dance.

As he started to fantasize about her, he started to get a raging chubby. In a community shower with a bunch of guys, the last thing you want is a chubby. *They'll think I'm gay,* he feared. He rinsed himself off, shut off the water and walked briskly out of the tiled room. Grabbing his towel off the rack, he wrapped it around his waist to hide the evidence and walked back to his locker.

He deliberately took his time opening his combination lock to give his half erect penis time to subside before he removed his towel. As he started to put on his underwear, a muscular teen, who was nicknamed Hutch, opened the locker to his right and sat down on the bench next to him.

Skid couldn't help but see the colorful string of stickers on the inside of Hutch's locker door. He wondered what they meant.

"What's the reason for the stickers?"

"Oh, those? They're sort of like the pride stickers we get in football to recognize our offensive and defensive achievements on the field." Puffing up his chest and looking with pride at the stickers in his locker, Hutch said, "The difference is that these are meant to commemorate my sexual conquests." Pointing to the gold stars, he said, "You see these here? They represent the girls I tapped that were nines or better. The silver stars are for those who were either sevens or eights, and the bronze stars are for those chicks I screwed that were fives or sixes."

Pointing to the fluorescent green Mr. Yuk stickers that were positioned below the bronze stars, Skid asked, "And what do these represent?"

Giggling, Hutch said, "They represent the ugly fat chicks I fucked because I was drunk and they were easy." Changing the subject, the jock asked, "So are you going to the big dance next weekend?"

"Yeah, I'm taking Stacey Atwood," Skid said proudly. "How about you?"

"I'm definitely going to the dance, but I haven't made up my mind yet who the lucky girl will be." Admiring himself in the mirror on the wall at the far end of the row of lockers, Hutch laughed arrogantly. "When you're the school's star quarterback, you've got a lot of options."

"Well, whoever you choose, I look forward to seeing you at the dance." With that Skid finished dressing, stuffed his gym clothes in his locker and headed to his next class.

At the end of the school day, while Skid was walking to his car in the students' parking lot, Stacey Atwood came running up to him. She was obviously uncomfortable.

"What's wrong?"

"I'm glad I caught you before you left. I'm sorry, but I won't be able to go to the dance with you after all."

Obviously deflated, he asked, "Why not? I hope your family's OK."

"Oh, they're fine," she said dismissively. "It's just that Hutch has asked me to go as his date. I couldn't pass that up. You understand, don't you?"

Skid hung his head to hide his disappointment. "Sure. Thanks for letting me know."

Stacey flashed a big grin, relieved that the awkward moment she had been dreading was past. She gave him a peck on the cheek. "You're the best. I know you'll find another date for the dance." With that she left and ran for her bus.

On the night of the big dance, Skid stayed at home alone and played computer games. He put on Aerosmith's CD, *Pump*, and played the track "Don't Get Mad Get Even" over and over again. He smiled broadly as he plotted his revenge. He would make his move when the time was right. He didn't know how long it would take, but there was one thing he knew for damn sure. He would *definitely* get even.

ONE

ALSEA RIVER, 2015

As I paddled down the Alsea River in my kayak, looking for native wildlife to photograph, I watched a group of turkey vultures as they spiraled effortlessly skyward in search of a meal. With their six-foot wingspans, these birds are adept at catching warm thermal air currents to gain altitude and can soar for hours without flapping their wings. Although this is a common sight on the river, it is one I never tire of witnessing. I decided to appreciate the moment, stopped paddling, and let the current carry me downriver.

Turkey vultures are predominantly carrion eaters. They have keen eyesight and a superior sense of smell, which enables them to locate animal carcasses from as far away as a mile.

I floated about a quarter of a mile downstream when I saw the vultures beginning to descend rapidly. I guessed that they had found a fresh kill and were eager to get to the carcass before crows, coyotes, or some other scavengers could lay claim to it.

The bank on my left, which was heavily forested, rose straight up about five hundred feet. If the birds had landed there, I would not have been tempted to pursue them, but they were coming down on the bank on my right, which rose only about thirty feet before leveling off into what I knew was a large pasture.

While the height of the bank prevented me from seeing

exactly where in the field the vultures were landing, it was not enough to deter me from satisfying my curiosity. I wanted to know what it was the vultures had found for their morning meal. I paddled to the shore, hopped out and tied my boat to a willow. As I hiked up the sandy bank to get a better view, I tried to guess on what it was that the birds would be feasting.

Since it was mid-May, which is the birthing season for many animals, and I knew that both the rancher's cows and Roosevelt elk frequented the pasture, I thought it likely that one of these animals had recently given birth and that I'd find the vultures consuming the discarded placenta of a newborn calf.

When I crested the bank, I saw the avian scavengers huddled over a carcass in the middle of the pasture about two hundred yards from me. A half dozen or more birds obscured my view, and I couldn't tell on what they were feeding. I slowed my pace and walked as silently as I could in an effort to get as close as possible to these skittish raptors without scaring them off their meal.

I have always been intrigued by the unusual, and sometimes perplexing, names that have been assigned to groups of different animals. Because of their popularity with the public, most people are familiar with, and readily accept, the collective nouns used to describe charismatic megafauna, like wolves, lions and killer whales. A group of wolves is a pack, an assemblage of lions is a pride and a family of orcas is a pod. But there are many accepted terms to describe groups of lesser species that, in my mind, defy logic. Why is a group of crows called a "murder", for example, or a gathering of ravens called an "unkindness"?

As I slowly approached the turkey vultures, I couldn't help but think about this and had to grudgingly admit that I could easily see why these raptors were collectively called a "wake" while communally feeding on a carcass. Hunched over their prey, these two-and-a half foot birds, with their brownish-black plumage, were reminiscent of a group of mourners at a funeral home, dressed in dark, formal attire, with their heads bowed as they looked upon the casket of a loved one and said their last farewells.

However, as I got closer, it was apparent that this "wake" was not as solemn or as peaceful as it initially appeared. The vultures were grunting, growling and shoving one another as they jockeyed for position to get a better piece of the carrion pie.

Because they were in a feeding frenzy, the birds didn't detect my presence until I was about fifty yards from them. Then one bird raised its bare, red head, hissed at me menacingly and vomited on the ground before flying off. I guessed that by losing its meal, the bird was lightening its load in an effort to gain loft as quickly as possible. The others quickly took to the air, and I was finally able to see on what it was that they were feeding. It was the body of a dead man.

The victim was on his back, his throat was slit from ear to ear, and there were pools of congealed blood on both sides of the body. The vultures had already carved out his eyes and had used their powerful, hooked beaks to rip open his abdomen. His intestines were shredded and hanging outside the body cavity. Hundreds of flies were feasting on the blood meal. His skin was a purplish color, and his jaw and neck muscles were stretched tight, so it was obvious rigor mortis had set in.

The body gave off an odor of decay. It was the aroma of death. If you've ever smelled a dead animal on the roadside, you know what I mean. If you haven't, I really can't describe the odor other than to tell you that when you catch a whiff of it, it is a putrid scent that is unmistakable and one you will never forget. Although I now make my living writing nature books and articles for magazines, I previously worked as a naturalist in a 1,000-acre wildlife park for over ten years. If we didn't see an animal for several days, we'd tramp through the various habitats in the park, looking for it, and if it was dead, it was always this smell that led us to it.

Although the victim was badly mutilated, I was still able to identify the body. It was my neighbor, Harlan Gannet, who lived just two doors upriver from me. He and his friend had moved here from California only two years earlier.

I reached in my pocket, grabbed my cell phone and dialed 911, but the height of the surrounding hills blocked the call. No service. There was an old stone house on the top of the hill near the edge of the pasture, so I ran there to get help. It was the home of Edwina Risley, the ninety-year-old mother of the area's largest landowner and the Grande Dame of the Alsea. Although I had never met her, she had a reputation for being a crusty old broad and someone you wouldn't want to mess with. As I climbed the steps to her front porch, I hoped the stories I had heard about her were greatly exaggerated and that she'd prove to be a sweet old lady.

I rang the doorbell and waited for a response. I could hear someone slowly shuffling toward the door. After a few minutes, the door cracked open slightly, and a tall, frail woman with a thinning mane of long, snow white hair poked her head out and asked defiantly, "Can I help you?"

"You don't know me," I said, "but I live—"

She cut me off. "I know who you are. I know everybody on *my* river. What do you want?"

"Someone's murdered Harlan Gannet. I just found his body in your field. Call 911!"

I assumed the news would galvanize the woman to action. Instead, she opened the door and calmly invited me in. "So somebody finally killed that son-of-a-bitch. I wonder who it was, could have been anybody. You know nobody on this river liked him. He should have stayed in California where he belonged. We don't need the likes of him and his friend here anyway."

I was incredulous. "For fuck's sake, the man's dead. Call 911!"

Edwina was dressed in a faded, yellow housecoat and had pink bunny slippers on her feet. She took a drag off the cigarette she had in her right hand. Her clothes reeked from cigarette smoke. She was obviously a chain smoker. Her index and middle fingers were badly stained from nicotine and were yellowish-brown in color. "Calm down," she said. "I'll call the sheriff. It will be a while before he gets here, so why don't you come in and have some tea?"

"No! Somebody needs to protect the body. I've got to get back down there before the vultures come back and mutilate it even further."

The old woman chuckled and shook her head. "Suit yourself, but the buzzards have to eat too." She closed the door in disgust.

As I ran back to the pasture, I could see that the vultures had returned and were once again feeding on the carcass. I waved my hands and yelled at the top of my lungs to scare them off. They scattered as I approached and landed in the red alders that lined the riverbank—just far enough away to not feel threatened by me, but close enough to quickly return to the kill should I leave it unattended. I stood guard over the body for about twenty minutes until the sheriff arrived.

TWO

Two black cars with "SHERIFF" emblazoned on the sides in gold letters proceeded up the road that bisected the pasture and stopped about two hundred yards from me. Both drivers got out of their vehicles. I recognized the driver of the first car. It was Sheriff Whittaker. He was a balding, heavyset man in his mid-sixties. I guessed the younger driver of the rear vehicle was one of his deputies. He was lanky and had short-cropped, brown hair. After conversing for several minutes, the two men split up. The sheriff advanced slowly toward me, while his deputy walked over to the Risley place, presumably to question Edwina.

When he was about ten feet from me, Sheriff Whittaker stopped walking and placed his hands down by his sides. His right hand was only inches away from his revolver. I sensed he was subtly conveying the message that he was ready to take me out if I proved to be a threat.

"Are you the person who found the body?"

"Yes."

"Can I see some ID?"

I was nervous and quickly brought my right hand down to my back pocket to retrieve my wallet.

The sheriff barked, "Slow down! No sudden movements."

I raised both hands and said, "This is crazy. I'm the one who found the body."

"So you say. You are a potential suspect until I determine otherwise."

I slowly reached into my pocket and retrieved my wallet. The sheriff walked toward me, and I handed him my driver's license.

He read my name out loud, "Grady Riker." He looked at the picture and stared at me to be sure the two were a match. His change in posture told me he was confident I was no longer a threat. The sheriff handed me back my ID. "Mr. Riker, what are you doing here?"

"What do you mean? I found the body and have been keeping the vultures off it until you could get here."

"Yes, I know. But why are you here? How did you get here?"

"I was kayaking down the river when I saw the turkey vultures coming down to feed on something. I wanted to see what it was."

"Where's your boat?"

I pointed to the river. "It's tied up on the bank over there."

"So you're trespassing?"

"Are you serious? A man's dead, and you're worried whether I'm trespassing? I didn't see a sign. Is it posted?"

The sheriff ignored the question and bent down to inspect the body. "Well, well, it's Harlan Gannet. Looks like somebody slit his throat. Do you know this man?"

"Yes. He lived up the road from me."

"Then you know that in the short time he's lived here, he's managed to make a lot of enemies."

Wearing latex gloves and carrying two plastic evidence bags, the deputy walked up, and I glanced at the nametag on his shirt. It read R. Darby. The sheriff turned his attention to his junior officer. "What did you find out?"

"It all checks out," Darby replied. "The old lady confirms that this man is a local. He found the body and asked her to call us."

"Looks like we found our missing person," the sheriff said. He turned to me to explain. "Gannet's housemate called last evening to report him missing. He said his friend had gone out for a run. When he didn't return in several hours, he became concerned and went out to look for him. But it was dark by then, and he found nothing."

"Even if it had been light, I doubt he would have seen anything," Darby interjected. "The body's not visible from the road."

"Did you check out the surrounding area?"

"Yeah, after I left the Risley place, I started walking down the road and found these." The deputy held up the two plastic evidence bags. One had a pair of pink earbuds in it. The other had what appeared to be a small wad of black tape with something blue attached to it. "These were on the left side of the road. I noticed that the tall grass on that side was flattened down, so I checked it out. The victim was obviously drug across the pasture. There's a sporadic blood trail leading here."

"The earbuds are probably Gannet's," I offered. "He went jogging on the road every evening and was always listening to music on his iPod. With those earbuds, he was oblivious to cars approaching him from behind. On several occasions, I'd slowly pull up behind him and try to get his attention so he'd move out of the way. He was always in the middle of the road. I'd have to get my front bumper nearly on his butt before he'd notice I was even there."

"So it would have been easy for the murderer to sneak up on him from behind," Darby added.

The sheriff shook his head. "It all adds up. Well, Mr. Riker, we still have a lot to do here, but I think we can let you be on your way. Just let us know if you plan on leaving town for any reason in case we need to contact you for further questioning."

"I'm not planning on going anywhere."

"Good," the sheriff replied. "Deputy, go back to the car and get the camera so we can start documenting the crime scene."

I walked back to the river, untied my kayak and headed home. I thought that my involvement in this murder case was over. I didn't know how wrong I was.

THREE

When I got home, I was eager to put the morning's drama behind me. The best way to do this, I thought, was to follow my daily ritual. I got in my car and drove to Newport, a town of 10,000 people on the Central Oregon Coast. I went to the gym and worked out, stopped by the grocery store to buy something for dinner, and then went to my favorite watering hole, Brewers on the Bay, to have a couple of pounders of Old Crustacean barleywine.

When I got home around five, I was unloading my groceries when Harlan Gannet's housemate, Ryder Driscoll, showed up. We were casual acquaintances. I had been invited over to his and Harlan's place for dinner a couple of times, probably by default. There was no one else on the river that would have gone.

To a certain extent, I empathized with their situation. I've lived on the Alsea River for twenty years now and am pretty well accepted as a local, but initially, I had a difficult time fitting in. The people who were born here have an innate distrust of outsiders, and it takes time to gain their acceptance.

In defense of the locals, Harlan had done nothing to endear himself to them. If anything, he did just the opposite. He was against logging, initiated a petition to force the cattle ranchers to erect fences to keep their cows from defecating in the river, and reported every infraction his neighbors

9

committed. I knew why Sheriff Whittaker recognized his body. It was because Gannet had been in his face numerous times trying to have him arrest someone for some perceived offense.

The quickness with which Ryder showed up at my house told me he was watching and waiting for me to return. He was a tall, rawboned man in his mid-forties with an unruly crop of orange-red hair. He was visibly upset.

"I know you found Harlan's body this morning. Can I come in and talk to you?"

As I unlocked the door, I said, "Of course. Let me put the food in the fridge, and then we'll talk. Would you like a drink?"

"God, I'd love a gin martini!"

"You got it. Go out on the deck, and I'll join you there in a few minutes."

I put the food away, made two stiff drinks and headed outside. Handing Ryder his drink, I sat down at the table across from him. "I'm sorry for your loss," I said. "I know you and Harlan were close friends."

Shaking noticeably, Ryder grasped his drink with both hands and took a healthy swig. "I met him in grade school. We were like brothers. I'm devastated."

I hate awkward moments like this, so I tried to lead the conversation in a different direction. "What are you going to do now? Will you move back to California?"

"Eventually, maybe, but not before the killer is caught and punished. I owe Harlan that much."

"I'm sure the sheriff will do everything he can to find the sick SOB who did this."

"Oh, really? It's pretty obvious to me Whittaker won't do anything."

"How can you say that? You don't know the man."

Ryder became visibly angry. "I know him better than you. Harlan and I have dealt with him many times in the past year, and it's pretty obvious that he has a short-timer mentality. He retires in a little over a year, and he isn't going to do anything at this stage in his career to disrupt the tight knit community he's a part of. The killer has to be a local. Who knows? It could be a neighbor or a friend of his. Do you really think he wants to open that can of worms?"

"With all due respect, I think you're upset and not thinking straight. Give the sheriff a chance to do his job. If there's a lead out there, I'm sure he'll pursue it."

"I don't intend to let Harlan's murder go unavenged. That's why I came over to talk to you. I'm hoping you'll help me find his killer. I have no one else to turn to."

"That's crazy. I'm not a detective and neither are you."

"No, but you are a trained scientist."

"I'm a nature writer with a PhD in zoology."

"Whatever. You're a left-brain thinker. You're analytical. You know how to gather data, evaluate it and base your conclusions on facts, not preconceived notions. I'm an artist for God's sake. I'm right-brained. I'm more intuitive and rely on my gut feelings to make decisions."

I tried not to laugh, but I couldn't help myself. "That's a pop psych myth. It's an outdated, oversimplified view of how the brain works."

"See, you just proved my point. You're a smart guy. You know a lot. If I'm going to find Harlan's killer, I can't do it alone. I need your help."

"I'm sorry, Ryder, but I have to say no. The locals wouldn't talk to us anyway. I admit I've lived here longer and am, perhaps, more well-received by some of our neighbors than you are, but they won't talk to me either. If we go out asking a whole lot of questions, they'll just clam up, and it could hurt the sheriff's chances of finding the real killer."

Ryder finished his drink and got up to leave. "Well, I'm sorry you won't help me. It's no secret no one else on this river will. I guess I'll just have to pursue this on my own. Thanks for the drink."

As I escorted him out, I could only feel pity for the man. He had lost his best friend today and had nowhere else to turn. I wanted to call out to him to come back, but I knew my refusal to help was the right decision. I said nothing and closed the front door.

FOUR

I love my younger sister, but she and I are totally different in so many ways. I'm sure the fact that I'm twelve years older than her has something to do with this. I've always been independent and actually enjoy my solitude. My sister, however, has always been emotionally needy and requires the constant company of others to validate her worth.

A year ago, when she told me she was getting divorced from her husband after seventeen years of marriage, I knew she would devolve into a nervous wreck. It's probably why I've avoided speaking to her since then. I didn't want to be dragged into her emotional drama. I should have known my luck would eventually run out.

As I headed into the kitchen to start dinner after my meeting with Ryder, the telephone rang. If I had caller ID, I would not have answered, but my home phone is just one step above a rotary, so I made the fatal mistake and picked up the receiver. Of course, it was my sister.

"Hello, Grady. I hope I'm not catching you at a bad time."

After removing the phone briefly from my head so I could emit a heavy sigh without my sister hearing it, I tried my best to sound genuine. "Hi, Sis, it's good to hear from you. How's everything going?"

How's everything going? Are you kidding me? That's an invitation for her to go off on a diatribe about how everyone has abandoned her and no one loves her anymore! I looked at my watch so I could time her harangue.

"Oh, I wish I could say everything's great, but my life has been falling apart since Lou and I got divorced. All of our mutual friends are avoiding me like the plague. They probably blame me for the breakup."

Trying my best to reassure her, I said, "They're probably doing the same to Lou. You know, because they don't want to take sides. It's normal. Divorces can be messy. Just give it time and everything will get back to normal. You'll meet another guy, fall in love and forget all about Lou."

She started crying. "I wish I could believe you, but I don't see any light at the end of the tunnel. It's all black."

That's the way I feel about this call. "You're just depressed. It's to be expected." In an effort to change the subject, I asked, "So how is Spencer doing?"

Sobbing loudly, she said, "Oh, you must be a mind reader. He's the reason for my call. He was always a happy boy. He's changed since the divorce. You know how much he idolizes his father. I think he blames me for the split. I'm sure Lou is trying to turn him against me."

"No. I know Lou. He would never use Spencer as a weapon against you. He's a good man."

"So you're taking his side too?"

"No, I'm *not* taking his side! I've been through a divorce myself so I know what I'm talking about. You and Lou are both good people. You just fell out of love. It's unfortunate, but it happens sometimes. Nobody needs to be the villain here. So tell me more about Spencer. How has he changed?"

"He used to love his mother, and now he never talks to me. He has new friends, and I think they are a bad influence on him. He used to be a straight-A student, and his grades have been going down all year. This semester he got only one C and all the rest were D's. He'll be a sophomore next school year, and if he continues down this path, he won't get accepted by any good

14

colleges. I'm at my wit's end. I don't know what else to do. He's always looked up to you. He'll listen to you."

"I can try talking to him if you want, but I can tell you it won't do any good. He's at that age where he's rebellious and questioning authority. It's normal."

"No! I'm his mother. I know it's more than that."

"So what do you want me to do?"

"He's just completing his freshman year. I want him to go live with you for a year so you can turn him around. He needs the influence of a strong male figure in his life right now."

"Why can't he go live with Lou? Have you raised that possibility with him?"

"Have you not heard anything I've been saying? Lou's changed. He's not the man you think you know."

"I heard you. I just don't agree with your assessment."

"I'm telling you he'd brainwash Spencer, and I'd lose him forever. I'm not going to let that happen. Are you going to help me or not?"

Arguing my case, I said, "I've never been a father. I don't have any kids."

"No, and that's a shame because you would have been a great father. You have a chance to do something good for your nephew."

"You know I love Spencer, but I think it's a bad idea. At his age, his friends mean everything to him. Tearing him away from them and placing him in a new environment will not produce a good result. Trust me."

"He's flunking out of school! How could going to live with you be any worse? You're his only hope. I'm begging you."

"And what happens at the end of the next school year?"

"If he likes living with you and gets good grades, I hope you'll let him stay until he goes off to college. If you can't turn him around and his grades continue to go south, then you can send him back to me."

"What does Spencer think of all this?"

"He's against it, of course, but he doesn't have a choice in the matter."

"Great," I said, letting out a heavy sigh while I played for time. *So what do I do now? I want to say no. I'm an old man set in my ways. I enjoy living alone, and the idea of a teenager sharing my space scares the hell out of me, but she has me boxed in. If I say no, I contribute to her emotional downfall and look like the bad guy for not coming to my nephew's aid.*

Grimacing, I said, "Again, I don't think this is a good idea, but I'm willing to give it a try. When will you be sending him down?"

"In June. School starts after Labor Day, so he'll have a few months to get adjusted and have a chance to enjoy his new life on the beautiful Alsea River. I'll send him down on Amtrak, and you can pick him up at the train station in Albany. I'll send the rest of his stuff down later."

"Just give me a heads up a few days in advance so I can make sure my schedule's free."

Hanging up the phone, I sat on the chair in silence for several minutes, trying to comprehend the enormity of my decision and how it would affect my life in the coming year or longer. Failing to come up with anything positive, I settled on the obvious. *I'm screwed.*

FIVE

When I got to the Amtrak station in Albany, I walked up to the ticket counter and looked at the melamine white board which listed train departures and arrivals. Having commuted on a regular basis on trains from this station for over seven years when I was working up in the Puget Sound region, I knew that delays were more than a possibility; they were an all too frequent occurrence. Since Amtrak doesn't own the tracks their trains travel on, the movement of freight takes precedence over passenger travel, and Amtrak trains are frequently delayed because of this.

As I searched the list of arrival times, I braced myself for bad news but, instead, was pleasantly surprised that the train my nephew was on, the 505 Amtrak Cascades, was on time and scheduled to arrive in ten minutes. *I won't have to cool my heels in a waiting area devoid of a television or WIFI after all.*

I walked outside and sat down on a bench next to the tracks where I knew the passengers would unload. As I waited for the train to arrive, I wondered how much my nephew had really changed and whether his attitudinal or behavioral metamorphosis would manifest itself in a striking alteration in his appearance. Would the clean cut boy I knew with short, flaxen hair now have a neon green faux hawk or would the lean, athletic lad who had always worn name brand apparel now have jet black hair and be dressed as a Goth and be decked out in black clothes and big industrial boots? The anticipation was killing me.

Suddenly, I became aware of the sound of a chugging train slowly approaching. I looked to my left and saw the locomotive coming around the bend as it circumvented the field of empty freight cars that sat motionless on parallel tracks some distance in front of me. The iron horse came to a stop, and the conductors opened the doors and placed stools on the ground out in front of the steps.

As I waited for the stream of passengers to begin to disembark, I thought, *What if I don't recognize Spencer? I should have asked my sister for a current photo of him so I would be able to identify the kid. That's stupid. You haven't changed, and he knows what you look like. Get up and make yourself visible.*

I stood up and walked back into the parking lot not that far, but far enough away, so that passengers, getting off at multiple doors on the train, would be able to see me. My head shifted back and forth as I scanned the series of doors, hoping to catch a glimpse of my nephew.

Then I saw him. He was coming down the steps of the third car from the front of the train. He had his skateboard under his right arm and carried his suitcase in his left. It was definitely Spencer, and he didn't look any different. He had short cropped, pale yellow hair, wore a Trailblazers T-shirt, Nike running shorts and white Air Jordan basketball shoes.

I ran over to greet him, opened my arms wide and gave him a big bear hug. "It's good to see you," I said. "I'm happy you're here."

He reciprocated by hugging me back. "Not as happy as I am to be here!"

His answer took me aback since his mother had said he was against the move. I tried to hide my reaction. *Where is the troubled youth my sister made him out to be? Is this just an act on his part? Is he fucking with me?* Grabbing his suitcase, I said, "Let me take this." I pointed to my truck. "My pickup's right over there."

Spencer laughed. "Oh, yes. There it is. Uncle G's old Ford Ranger. How many miles does it have on it now?"

Smiling broadly and puffing up my chest, I said, "350,000."

I placed his suitcase in the bed of the truck, and Spencer put his skateboard in there as well. We both got in the truck. As we left the parking lot, I asked, "Are you hungry? We can stop and get a pizza if you want."

Shaking his head, Spencer said, "No, I ate on the train. The food's not great, but it's OK."

"Yes, it's better than McDonalds, but it's pricey."

Looking at me and laughing, he said, "Yeah, you're a captive audience. What choice do you have? It's either this processed shit or nothing. If you're hungry, you go for it. If not, you say I think I'll pass."

This doesn't sound like a kid who is having an emotional crisis. It doesn't add up. I wanted to ask him why he was doing so poorly in school, but I thought it was too early to broach this subject. I decided to make small talk as we got onto Highway 20 and headed home.

"Is this the first time you've been on a train?"

Spencer turned to me and looked incredulous. "Are you kidding me? Dad and I used to take the train from Portland to Seattle to go to Mariners' games all the time. Two of his buddies would go with us. Mom would drop us off at the train station and pick us up when we got home. Dad and his friends would drink on the train and at the game. They'd get snockered, but nobody was driving so nobody got hurt." Looking wistfully, he said, "I miss those times."

As we turned left onto Highway 34, going toward Waldport, I said, "I'm glad your train was on time. Did you and your Dad ever have any times where you were late to a Mariners' game?"

Shaking his head, Spencer said, "No."

"Well, then you were extremely lucky. Maybe it's because it was a fairly short trip. I've had a host of bad experiences on Amtrak. Do you want to hear one?"

"Sure. Why not?"

"OK, so I was commuting from Albany to Tacoma. It was about 10 o'clock at night, and we had just left the station in Olympia when we ran over something big on the tracks. It ripped out the holding tank in the last bathroom on the train, and the rear wheels of the car came off the tracks. It was obvious that we weren't going anywhere. The obstruction also had taken out the water lines, so there was no water to flush the toilets. Amtrak, in its infinite wisdom, decided to give us free coffee and tea, which are diuretics. Do you know what that is?"

Laughing, Spencer said, "Yeah, it makes you piss more."

"Exactly. We sat there for hours waiting for the train coming from California to come up on a parallel track to rescue us. I was in the Bistro car, and it smelled like shit. A fat woman came out of the can and said, 'Don't use the toilet, I just filled it up!' We sat there in that stench until two in the morning when the California train finally came up beside us, and we were loaded onto that train. We had to stand the whole way because there weren't enough seats."

Spencer slapped his knee and shook his head. "Uncle G, you always have the best stories."

As we weaved our way up the two miles of tight switchbacks, leading up to the Alsea Summit, I decided I had to confront the elephant that was pregnant in the room.

"Spencer, you seem so normal. Your mother told me you had changed. I don't see that. You seem to be the same happy kid with a good head on his shoulders that I knew before your folks got divorced."

"I'm not going to lie. I wish my parents were still together, but a lot of my friends' parents are divorced. It's not that big a deal really."

"So what's your problem? Why are you tanking in school?"

Spencer bowed his head and exhaled broadly. "To get away from my Mom," he said. "I wanted to go live with my Dad, but he said if I did that, my Mom would be devastated. I know they're divorced, but my Dad still cares about my Mom. He doesn't want to hurt her."

"So that's why you're coming here to live with me?"

Spencer shook his head.

"You're OK with that?"

Spencer grimaced. "If I can't live with my Dad, then you're my next best choice. My Mom has been driving me crazy. I can't live with her."

"And so your poor grades are just a cry for help?"

"Pretty much. If you can stand having me around, I guarantee I'll do a lot better."

Laughing and shaking my head from side to side, I extended my hand to Spencer and said, "I've got to admit that you're not what I expected. You're a lot older than your years."

Spencer squeezed my hand and said, "You grow up fast when things get tough. It's called life, Uncle G."

SIX

When Spencer and I got back to my place, my next door neighbor, Dave McConnell, who is a mechanic by trade, was in his driveway, painting a silver 2010 Honda Civic SI. Dave was short in stature, had dark brown hair and sported a well-trimmed, thick, full beard. At age forty, he was twenty years younger than me.

Spencer jumped out of my truck and ran next door. "That car's sick!"

I yelled to Dave. "You've met my nephew Spencer before, right?"

Looking up at me, he said, "Of course." Dave then turned to my nephew, and they shook hands. "Good to see you again, Spencer. I heard you are going to be living here for a while." Gesturing toward me, he joked, "You know your uncle's getting up there in age. He needs somebody to look after him in case he falls down and can't get up by himself."

Spencer laughed at the joke made at my expense. "Where'd you get the cool rice burner, Dave?"

"It's not mine. It belongs to a customer. I'm just doing some body work on it."

I saw that there was a FOR SALE sign in the rear window of the vehicle. Pointing to the sign, I said, "So how much is he asking for the car?"

"The bluebook on the car is $4500, but he's asking $2500,

which is about right for the condition the car is in. It needs a new timing belt, cooling flush and transmission service. Other than that, it's a good little car."

"How many miles does it have on it?"

"170K."

I could see that my nephew obviously loved the car. "Spencer, I'll make you a deal. I'll buy the car now, and if you get all B's or better this next school year, I'll give you the car."

Spencer's eyes grew wide. "Really?"

"Yes, really."

"Can I rice it out?"

Laughing, I said, "You can do anything you want to it once it's yours. What do you say?"

"Heck yeah!"

Dave tapped Spencer on the shoulder. "Well, you better go over and seal the deal with a handshake before your uncle changes his mind."

Spencer ran over to me and shook my hand vigorously. "It's a deal!"

Looking over at my neighbor, I said, "And I know a guy who can help you do the work that the car needs to get it in tip top shape for when it's yours."

Spencer turned to my neighbor. "Will you help me, Dave?"

"I'd be happy to." Dave looked over at me and smiled broadly. "I do free shit for old farts all the time. I guess I can help out a fine young man like you."

I shook my head and said to Dave, "You're an ass." Turning to Spencer I said, "No, seriously, Dave's helped other teens with their cars before. It pains me to admit this in front of him, but he's a good teacher and a good role model. You'll learn a lot from him."

SEVEN

I hadn't seen or heard from Ryder in months. Through the grapevine, I knew that he was making good on his promise to try to find Harlan's killer but getting nowhere. As predicted, the locals weren't receptive to what they considered was his prying in their affairs, and he was mostly met with front doors being shut soundly in his face.

Our local paper, the *News-Times*, also had nothing to report, which suggested that there was no movement in the murder case. Whether this was because there were no good leads or whether Ryder had been right and the sheriff was reluctant to pursue the case, I could not tell. Either way, the end result was the same. I got used to having a teenager in my house, and each day was pretty much the same, which is the way I like it.

Then Ryder came back into my life.

It was in mid-October, and I was in my upstairs study, working on an article about wolverines when the doorbell rang. When I opened the door, I could tell immediately that Ryder was distraught. He was shaking visibly. "Can I come in?"

"Of course. You look like you've seen a ghost. What's wrong?"

"Someone tried to break into my house last night. I think it was Harlan's killer and that I'm going to be his next victim!"

"Calm down. Let's go into the kitchen and talk."

Ryder sat down at the breakfast nook as I walked over to the coffee pot.

"My nerves are shot," he said. "I haven't slept for days. Coffee is the last thing I need right now. Can we have something else?"

"Sure. What do you want?"

"Got any whiskey?"

I looked at the clock. It was 10:00 a.m. A little early even for me, but Ryder obviously needed a drink and, more importantly, a friend to turn to. *What the heck,* I thought, *Hemmingway famously once said, "Write drunk, edit sober." If I am lucky enough to get back to work after Ryder leaves, maybe my creative juices will be flowing.* I grabbed a bottle of Scotch, a tray of ice cubes out of the fridge and two rocks glasses out of the cupboard and joined my neighbor at the table.

As I handed him his drink, I said, "So tell me what happened."

Ryder quickly downed his drink and made himself another. "It was around three in the morning. I was in bed, trying to fall asleep, when I heard someone trying to open the front door. Thank God, it was locked! I jumped up and walked over to the window as quietly as I could and slowly pulled the curtain back slightly to peek out. My neighbors had their floodlight on, but the fog was thick, and all I could see was the dark silhouette of a man silently coming down my front steps. He avoided the light coming from the neighbors and soon disappeared in the heavy mist."

"Did you call the sheriff?"

"Of course, but they didn't even send a deputy out this time to investigate."

"What do you mean *this* time?"

"This is the third time in the last two months I've heard someone trying to break in. It's just the first time I actually got a glimpse of him."

"Then how do you know someone was trying to break in? Were there scratches between the door and the frame as if someone was trying to use a crowbar to jimmy the door open?"

"No. Deputy Darby could find no evidence of an attempted break-in either time."

"So they did come out to investigate the first two times?"

"Yes."

"Well, for fuck's sake, Ryder, that's why they didn't come out this time. You've cried 'wolf' one too many times, and they don't take you seriously anymore."

"Come on, Grady, I'm not imagining this. Someone was trying to break in. I know it."

I downed my drink and got up. "OK, let's go over to your place and check out the front door."

I led the way, and Ryder followed close behind. I inspected the lock and checked the area around the door and the frame to see if there was any evidence of an attempted break-in. I could find nothing to support Ryder's claim.

"Look," I said. "By your own admission, you're sleep deprived, and this can affect your mental state. Maybe you're not thinking clearly. It's understandable. You've been under a lot of stress lately."

Ryder's demeanor changed quickly, and he snarled, "I'm not crazy. I know whoever tried to break in last night was after me."

"Let's say you're right, and the intruder last night was Harlan's killer. Maybe killing you wasn't his motive. Maybe he just wanted to scare you enough to get you to leave the area and to stop asking questions. If he's tried to break in three times without success, he's either totally inept or just trying to rattle your chain. In either case, I don't think you have anything to worry about. I'm not trying to blow you off, but I have a deadline that's fast approaching and need to get back to the article I'm working on about wolverines."

Ryder looked dejected. I couldn't leave him like this, so I asked, "How is your detective work going by the way? Have you gotten any good leads?"

Ryder calmed down and let out a heavy sigh. "No, you were right. Nobody on the river has been willing to talk to me. But I'm tenacious like the badgers you're writing an article about."

"They're wolverines," I corrected him.

Ryder waved his hand dismissively. "Whatever. You know what I mean. The point is I'm not giving up. You do know Harlan was an investigative reporter before he retired, don't you?"

I nodded in agreement. "He mentioned that a couple of times when I came to your place for dinner."

"Well, he was also a big fan of the true crime genre. You know what that is, right?"

"Yes, I'm not a fan myself, but I know what it is."

Ryder scowled. "You say that like you think it's trash. There are some very respectable and highly acclaimed true crime non-fiction works like Truman Capote's—"

I cut him off. "Yeah, I know. Capote's *In Cold Blood* and Bugliosi's *Helter Skelter*. What I think about the genre isn't important. Tell me why you think Harlan being a true crime fan is important."

Ryder calmed down. "Well, when he retired, Harlan started researching local murders and hoped he could find one that he could write a book about. Something like Michael Finkel's book, *True Story*, which deals with the Christian Longo murders. You know what I'm talking about?"

"Yes, I was living here when that scumbag killed his wife and three kids. It was in December of 2001 if I'm not mistaken."

"That's right. Well, before he died, Harlan said he had found a local murder case he wanted to focus on, and he started to schedule interviews with people who had intimate details of the case."

"What case was it exactly?"

"I don't know. Harlan was very protective when it came to his work. He'd never let me read anything he was working on until it was finished. It was just his way, and I respected that. I'm the same way when it comes to my artwork. I won't let anyone see a painting I'm working on until it's done."

"So you think him starting to ask questions about this murder case had something to do with his death?"

"I don't know. You probably think I'm grasping at straws, but it's the only thing I can think of that makes any sense."

"There's nothing wrong with considering all possibilities," I assured him. "So what have you learned so far?"

"Nothing. After his murder, the cops got a warrant to search the house. They seized a bunch of stuff...our computers and flash drives and Harlan's paper files, so I'm at a standstill."

"Have you told the sheriff about your theory?"

"Of course, but he just brushed me off. He said they'd check into it."

"Well, I'm sure they'll review the files thoroughly. If there's something there, they'll find it."

Ryder swayed slightly back and forth as if he was drunk. I guessed that his lack of sleep magnified the effect of the alcohol he had consumed at my place. He definitely needed some rest badly.

"Look, Ryder, you've done all that you can. Right now, you need to get some shut-eye. No one is going to come after you in broad daylight. You're safe."

Ryder stepped forward and embraced me. "You're the only friend I have left."

"Trust me," I reassured him. "You'll be fine. Just get some sleep."

EIGHT

Skid put on his black nitrile gloves and looked at his watch. It was two in the morning, and time for him to make his move. He strapped on his shoulder holster with his Thompson 22 LR pistol, donned his hooded fleece, put on his backpack and went outside. He grinned as he turned on his flashlight for he knew it was a perfect night for what he had planned. It was a new moon, so it was pitch-black outside. A dense fog had settled in, and even with his light, he could only see a few feet in front of him. It was high tide, so he wouldn't have to traipse through a lot of mud when he got to his victim's house.

Skid walked down to his dock and got in his boat. To make as little noise as possible, he didn't fire up his outboard but turned on his electric trolling motor instead. Hugging the shore, he slowly made his way upriver, confident that his movements would go undetected.

When he got to his destination, Skid tied his boat up to the dock and hiked quietly up the bank. There was a solitary light on in the house, and from his earlier reconnaissance missions, he knew it was in the living room. He turned off his flashlight, put it in his coat pocket and slowly climbed the stairs up to the deck, crouching low as he went, to keep from being seen.

There were three large picture windows, overlooking the river. When he got to the first one, Skid peered through the window and saw Ryder sitting in his recliner. The sound on the television was blaring, and an infomercial on acne treatment was on the tube. There was an empty glass and a half-drained magnum of red wine on the end table next to him.

Skid chuckled to himself for it was obvious that Ryder was passed out. *This is going to be easy,* he thought to himself.

Skid made his way to the sliding glass door, tried to open it and, as expected, it was locked. He removed his backpack and took out two butter knives. He placed one on the runner, picked up the door and stepped on the knife, sliding it over the tracks. Then he used the second knife to keep the rollers up, while he pulled the door off its track. Setting the door aside, he put the knives away and removed a coil of polypropylene rope before putting his knapsack back on. He placed the rope over his shoulder, grabbed his gun from his holster and entered the house.

The living room was carpeted, so it was easy for Skid to advance toward Ryder without making a sound. As he cautiously moved ever closer, he stared intently at the back of Ryder's head for any sign of movement. There was none, and as he got closer, he could hear Ryder snoring.

Confident that he was in control of the situation, Skid started to relax, put his gun back in his holster and removed the coil of rope. Tying a slip knot on one end, he passed the rope through the loop and made a lasso. When he was directly behind the recliner, he quickly placed the lasso around Ryder's upper torso and chair and cinched it tight.

Ryder awoke immediately and started to scream. Skid grabbed a rag out of his pocket and stuffed it in Ryder's mouth to silence him. Ryder struggled to free himself, but it was futile. Skid already had another loop of rope around his neck and the chair. He then bound Ryder's hands and feet to prevent any chance of escape.

Skid grabbed a chair from the adjoining dining room and placed it directly in front of Ryder with the back of the chair facing forward. Straddling the chair, he rested his arms on its back and smiled menacingly at his captive.

"So we finally meet. You don't know me, but I'm sure you know who I am."

Ryder started sobbing.

"I'll make you a proposition," Skid said. "If you promise not to scream like a little girl, I'll take the gag out of your mouth so we can talk. The moment you start to scream, it's going back in your pie hole, and I'm going to kill you. What do you say?"

Whimpering and shaking violently, Ryder slowly nodded his consent.

Skid reached out and removed the gag from his mouth. "Good, that pleases me. I need to find out what you know and who you've talked to."

Ryder beseeched him, "Why are you doing this? I don't even know you!"

Skid jeered, "You don't know me, because you and your friend never took the time to get to know any of us locals and our ways. You never cared about us. You came here and tried to change the way we live. I grew up here, and I don't want life on the river to change. It's perfect the way it is."

Ryder was wide-eyed. "So that's why you killed Harlan?"

"Yeah, he tried to californicate the Alsea. We all knew he was the agitator. You pretty much kept to yourself. It wasn't until you started asking questions that you became a target. Why did you have to become a nosy neighbor anyway? You know, I never really tried to break-in. I just wanted to scare you and get you to move back to Cali. Your repeated calls to the cops just fed into my plan. The authorities stopped taking you seriously. I know the sheriff didn't send anyone out the last time you called, and you and I both know that nobody's showing up tonight."

"Fuck you!" Ryder screamed. "Kill me and get it over with you sick son of a bitch!"

Skid patted him on the knee. "Calm down little camper. All

I want from you is a little information. Tell me what you know, and I'll let you go."

Ryder looked hopeful. "Then you'll let me leave Oregon?"

Skid shook his head slowly. "No, it's too late for that. I'll let you go to your Maker." He looked at Ryder incredulously. "Do you actually think I would let you leave here alive?"

Ryder cried, "I don't know anything. Nobody's talked to me, I swear. If you let me go, I won't call the cops or tell anyone about tonight. I'll leave in the morning, and you'll never see me again."

Skid barked, "Ryder, don't insult me! I didn't go to Stanford or USC, but I wasn't born yesterday. If I let you go, you'd squeal like a stuck pig. Don't be stupid. You're going to die. It's just a matter of how quickly. Tell me what I need to know, and I promise that I won't make you suffer."

"Look, I swear. I don't know anything. I admit that I've tried to get my neighbors to talk, but they've told me nothing. I asked my neighbor Grady to help me, but he didn't want to get involved."

"How much did Harlan tell you about the murder case he was so interested in?"

Ryder was taken aback, obviously rattled by the question.

"Oh, so you didn't think I knew about that? I know a lot more than you think. I know Harlan was sticking his nose in my business."

"What business is that exactly? Murdering innocent people?"

Skid laughed derisively. "I prefer to call it human garbage disposal services. I'm ridding the river of unwanted trash like your buddy. He would have been better off letting sleeping dogs lie. Instead he started asking a lot of questions, trying to dredge up something from the past that is better off left alone. So let's cut to the chase. What did he tell you?"

"Nothing, I swear. He just said he found a murder case he wanted to write a book about. That's all he told me."

"Do you know who else he may have talked to about the case?"

Ryder didn't say anything. He just shook his head in the negative.

Skid leaned in close to Ryder's face and looked directly in his eyes, trying to gauge whether he was telling the truth. Ryder tried to turn away, but Skid grabbed his face and held it firmly in front of him. "Look at me!"

Ryder acquiesced and stared into the eyes of his captor for what seemed to him like an eternity. When Skid was satisfied Ryder was telling the truth, he released his grasp, leaned back and patted Ryder on the head. "Good. I believe you."

Skid stood up and said, "OK, you told me what I needed to know, so now I'll give you what you want." He grabbed the wine bottle on the table next to the recliner and read the label. "Napa Valley, California. I should have guessed. Did you know the Willamette Valley is noted for its pinot noir?"

Ryder shook his head in the negative.

"No? It's a pity you won't ever get to try some." Skid filled the glass. "Would you like one last drink before you go?"

Ryder didn't say anything. He just shook his head back and forth.

"Suit yourself, but it's a sin to waste good wine." Skid grabbed the glass and downed the contents. Opening his backpack, he removed a mason jar, containing three reddish-brown salamanders and held it in front of Ryder's face. The amphibians were sluggishly trying to scale the glass, revealing their bright orange undersides in the process. "Do you know what these are?"

"I've seen a lot of them in the river," Ryder answered. "They're newts, right?"

"Yes, very good, rough-skinned newts, to be more precise."

Skid brought the jar up to his face and stared inquisitively into the yellow iris of one of the newt's eyes. "I love their eyes. You can see the universe in them. They're quite mystical." Returning his attention to Ryder, he asked, "Do you know why they are so plentiful in the river?"

Ryder closed his eyes and sighed. "I have no idea."

"It's because they are extremely poisonous. The glands in their skin produce a powerful neurotoxin. It's the same toxin found in Japanese puffer fish, blue-ring octopus, and some species of South American frogs. There's no known antidote for the poison. But I'm sure your neighbor friend, Grady Riker, could tell you that. You know, with him being a scientist and all. Anything that tries to eat a rough-skinned newt dies. Well, that's not totally accurate. Garter snakes can eat them, but they are the only animals I know of that can do that and survive. You're not a garter snake, are you Ryder?"

Ryder bowed his head and started to cry convulsively.

"Come on, be a man. I'm sure one of these little guys would kill you, but I don't know how long that would take, and I have to leave before it gets light. I think three should hurry things up, don't you? I had planned on shoving them down your throat, but I noticed you have a blender in the kitchen. A newt 'Slurpee' will be easier to swallow, and the cause of death won't be immediately obvious. Make the cops earn their pay, that's what I think."

Skid got off the chair and headed to the kitchen. "You know, I really feel bad about doing this."

"Then don't kill me! I swear I won't say anything. The cops wouldn't believe me even if I did."

"Oh, I'm sorry, you misunderstood me," Skid said mockingly. "I have no problem killing you. I feel bad about sacrificing the newts. They haven't done anything wrong. But if they can help me clean up the river, I feel they're serving a higher purpose."

Skid dropped the newts in the blender, added a little water from the faucet and turned it on. In seconds, the salamanders were transformed into a dark, mud-colored suspension. He poured the slurry into a plastic cup and walked back to the living room. Inserting his fingers in Ryder's nose, he pulled his head back severely and force-fed him the poisonous liquid.

The toxin burned severely as it went down, and Ryder moved his head vigorously back and forth, coughing violently in an effort to eject the noxious substance from his throat. Skid grabbed the top of Ryder's head and lower jaw and held them shut until he stopped fighting.

When Skid released his hold, Ryder's mouth dropped open and vomit drooled out of the corners of his mouth. He was still conscious, but paralysis was setting in, and he was struggling to breathe.

Skid poured himself the last of the wine, looked down at his watch and said, "It's 3:00 a.m. Let's see how long this takes." Sipping the wine slowly, he sat there looking at Ryder as he waited patiently for him to die.

NINE

It was several days since I had talked to Ryder. Given how distressed he had been, I was concerned for his welfare. I tried calling him several times, but all I got was his voicemail. His vehicle was in his carport, so I knew he was home.

I walked over to his place to make sure he was OK. I rang the doorbell, and when there was no response, I banged on the door and listened intently for any sign of movement inside. There was none.

I went around to the back of the house and climbed the steps to the deck, which overlooked the river. The curtains were open, and I saw Ryder in his recliner. His back was to me, and he was facing the television, which was off. If he was asleep, I didn't want to wake him, but I got a sinking feeling in the pit of my stomach that something was wrong. I rapped on the glass door several times, and when he didn't wake up, I became alarmed.

I tried the door, expecting it to be locked, but it slid open easily. Entering the living room, I shouted, "Ryder, are you OK?"

He didn't move.

With my heart pounding wildly in my chest and adrenaline coursing through my body, I ran to face him. He was obviously dead. His eyes were open and hollow. His mouth was agape, and a dreadful expression was frozen on his ashen face. He had obviously died a painful death.

Shaking violently, I grabbed my cell phone from my coat pocket and dialed 911. As I struggled to get the words out, stuttering somewhat incoherently as I answered the operator's questions, I couldn't take my eyes off Ryder's face. I wanted to look away from the hideous sight, but I just stood there, transfixed with guilt. I remembered the last thing I had said to him: *Trust me. You'll be fine. Just get some sleep.* Ryder had come to me, looking for help, and I had let him down. And now he was dead.

Suddenly it felt like the room was closing in on me, and I had to get some air. I ran out on the deck, leaned out over the railing and started vomiting. When I was through barfing, I closed my eyes and tried to relax. I don't know how long it took, but after a while, I felt my heart rate lessening and my breathing slowly returning to normal.

When I was once again in control, I opened my eyes and noticed there were footprints in the mud, leading up from the river. I walked down the steps on the opposite side of the deck from where I had originally entered the house and inspected the tracks, being careful not to obliterate any with my own footprints.

The marks were evident in the soft substrate. The tread design on the sole of the left foot was clearly visible in all the prints I examined. Although this told me nothing, I hoped the cops would be able to identify the boot maker from the pattern.

When I looked at the right tracks, I became excited. Only the back half of the tread on the sole registered in the mud in all the impressions I examined. The front of the footprint was smooth, showing no pattern at all.

TEN

Just then, I heard two cars pull up in the driveway. I assumed it was the sheriff and his deputy. I entered the house, ran through the living room, unlocked the front door and waved them in.

They entered the house deliberately with their hands near their sides as if they were expecting trouble. They didn't draw their revolvers, but I could tell by their demeanor that they were ready to do so. As expected, the sheriff took the lead.

"Well, well, Mr. Riker, we meet again under unfortunate circumstances. Found another dead body, did you?"

I was rankled by his off-putting remark. "Oh, I'm sorry. Did my 911 call take you away from your donuts and coffee?"

Deputy Sheriff Darby stepped forward like he meant business and barked, "Hey, have some respect! This is the sheriff you're talking to."

"Yeah, well you're talking to a law-abiding citizen who pays your salary. I've done nothing wrong, and I've been through a lot today. I don't appreciate you or your boss's attitudes. Respect is a two-way street, sonny."

Sheriff Whittaker patted his deputy on the shoulder. "It's OK. I can handle this. Go outside and look for evidence."

As he left, Darby scowled at me and said, "Sure thing, Sheriff. Just let me know if you need my help."

The sheriff turned his attention to Ryder and spent several minutes examining the body. "The medical examiner is going to have to determine the manner and cause of death, but I can tell you it wasn't from natural causes or suicide. There are abrasions on the victim's wrists and neck, like he was tied up and struggling to get free. This man was murdered, that's for damn sure. So, Mr. Riker, how did you come to find this body? Were you trespassing again?"

"What's your fixation with trespassing? That's the second time you've asked me that. Don't you have more important things to worry about?"

"Just answer the question."

Sighing heavily, I said, "No, I wasn't trespassing. Ryder came over a few days ago freaked out because he thought someone was trying to break into his house. He told me he called your office, but nobody came out to investigate."

Whittaker became defensive. "The man was delusional. He called us every few weeks to report an imaginary intruder, and we never found any evidence to substantiate his claims."

"I know. He told me that. He asked me for my help, and I told him I thought he was just sleep-deprived and imagining things." I broke down and started sobbing. "I told him everything would be all right and to just get some sleep. And now, look at him. He's dead because none of us took him seriously."

"Let's cut the shit," the sheriff sneered. "You didn't like these two guys any better than the rest of us. I heard about your run-in with them over that stupid preacher goose they brought up here from Taylor's Landing a while ago."

"Yeah, they pissed me off. They brought that goose up here and didn't have a dock at that time, so they fed it on my dock and my neighbors' docks to encourage it to stay upriver. That stupid bird shit all over the place and would start honking at five in the morning. It was a nuisance."

"So you and your neighbors got wrist rockets and started peppering the bird with lead until you drove it downriver."

"Yeah, but we didn't want to kill it. We just wanted the goose to leave, and it did."

"Sort of the way we all felt about Harlan and Ryder. Sounds familiar, doesn't it?"

"They were a pain in the ass, but neither of them deserved to die. Ryder was an acquaintance, not a good friend. But after Harlan died, Ryder needed someone to turn to, and I wasn't going to walk away from him when he asked me for help."

"But you did. Just like us, you didn't take him seriously."

"You're despicable! Finding his killer is your job, not mine. You're the one who's culpable here."

The deputy entered the house from the deck, interrupting the exchange. "There's an inch of peeled aluminum on the bottom of the door casing as if someone had placed something flat under the rollers to lift the door out of its runner. I also found muddy footprints coming up the steps. I followed the trail of prints down to the river. Looks like whoever broke into this house last night came by boat."

"Tell me more about the tracks," the sheriff replied. "Is there anything unusual about them that could help us identify the killer?"

"Yes," I blurted out. "The tread design on the sole of the boot shows clearly in the left tracks but the pattern only registers for the back half of the sole in the right imprints for some reason."

Whittaker's face became blood red. "And how do you know this?"

"When I found Ryder's body, I felt like I was going to get sick, so I ran outside to throw up. When I was done puking, I noticed there were footprints in the mud, so I went down off the deck to inspect them."

"So you're telling me you contaminated the crime scene."

"No," I protested. "I didn't step on any of the tracks."

"It doesn't make any difference. By leaving the deck and checking out the tracks, you contaminated the crime scene."

"What about my puke? Is that OK? I'll save you the trouble

of having that analyzed. I ate two breakfast burritos: one egg, jalapeno and cheese and one egg, applewood smoked bacon and cheese. Does that help?"

Darby started to come toward me, but the sheriff fended him off and asked him a question to defuse the situation. "Deputy, in your expert opinion, can you tell anything else by looking at the footprints?"

Darby was livid and wanted to kick my ass, but he looked at the sheriff and knew, if he did, he'd be the one in trouble. He took a deep breath to calm down and exhaled loudly. "By the size of the tracks, I'd guess the perp's boot size is probably a ten."

The sheriff looked down at my feet. "What shoe size are you, Mr. Riker?"

"Eight and a half, or nine, depending on the shoe. You can't seriously be considering me a suspect?"

"You've found two dead bodies. What are the chances of that happening? At this stage, I wouldn't just say you're a suspect, I'd say you're our Number One suspect."

"If I was the killer, why would I report the bodies? It makes no sense."

"Oh, really? Some arsonists set fires and then report them because they get off watching the firefighters battle the blaze. It gives them a perverted sense of power. Maybe you're like that. Maybe you think you're so much smarter than us that you get your jollies watching us stupid cops fumble around trying to catch you."

"Now who's being delusional?" I asked. "Ryder said you were a short-timer and wouldn't do anything to jeopardize your retirement. I didn't believe him at the time, but maybe he was right. If you're looking at me as the killer, you're either stupid or just going through the motions and not serious about solving these crimes. Which is it?"

"Don't push me, son."

"Or what? Are you going to shoot me?"

Whittaker glared at me menacingly. "I don't have enough

evidence to justify arresting you now, but I'll be watching you closely."

"Maybe you should spend your time looking for the real killer. Do you have anything else you want to ask me or can I go now?"

The sheriff turned away. "Yeah, you can leave."

"Gladly." Turning to the dimwitted deputy, I said mockingly, "Don't get up. I'll show myself out."

ELEVEN

As I walked back to my house, my neighbor, Dave, pulled into his driveway. I needed moral support right now, and I was happy to see him.

Dave got out of his pickup, lifted his fourteen-year-old, black cocker spaniel, Roscoe, off the bench seat and placed him gently on the ground. Roscoe came over to greet me, his docked tail wagging vigorously.

As I bent down to pet the old dog, Dave turned to me and said, "Hi, Cramps. (He said Cramps instead of Gramps, thinking he was funny.) What's going on over at the neighbor's place? Why's the sheriff there? Is Ryder seeing ghosts again?"

"No. Someone's murdered Ryder! I went over to talk to him a few hours ago and found him dead in his living room."

"Are you shitting me?"

With a disgusted look, I barked, "Why would I kid about something like that?"

Dave's face grew serious. "I'm sorry. You caught me off guard. How are you holding up? Are you OK?"

I started sobbing. "No, I'm not OK. Ryder came to me for help a few days ago, and I blew him off."

Dave grabbed my shoulders firmly to get my attention and calm me down. "Listen to me! What ever happened, it wasn't your fault. I want to hear all about it, but first, let me get some wood to start a fire in the stove. Go home, get some beer and come back."

I walked over to my house, went into the kitchen and uncorked a bottle of merlot. Grabbing a glass out of the cupboard, I picked up the wine and headed to Dave's garage. He had just gotten the fire started, so the shop was still cold. I nestled in next to the old stove. "It's cold in here," I groused.

Sitting down in his recliner, Dave shook his head slowly back and forth. "Give me a break. I just got the fire going." He looked at the bottle of wine in my hand. "What? No Coors Light today?"

I sat down on the sofa next to the stove, poured myself a glass of wine and put the bottle on the cement floor. "No, I decided I needed something stronger."

"Probably a good idea," Dave confirmed. "So tell me what happened today."

Because I see him most evenings after work to share a beer, Dave knew about my prior meetings with Ryder, so little explanation was necessary to bring him up to speed.

"Did I tell you Ryder came over my house earlier in the week and was worried that someone was trying to break into his house?"

"Yes, go on."

"Well, when I hadn't heard from him in several days, I tried calling Ryder but got no answer. I saw his car was there, so I became concerned and went over to see if he was all right. I found him dead in his living room. At first, I thought he might have overdosed on sleeping pills and alcohol, but there were abrasions on his wrists and neck like he was tied up, so the sheriff thinks he was murdered. And now that asshole thinks I'm a suspect."

Dave burst out laughing. "Well, you did find both bodies."

"So you think I'm the killer?"

"No, of course not. All I'm saying is the fact that you found both Harlan's and Ryder's bodies would be a red flag to any cop. You have to admit it's highly unusual. I know this whole ordeal has been stressful on you, but it's over now. You have nothing to worry about. Just let it go."

"No, I can't! I feel guilty that I didn't do anything to help Ryder. He came to me twice asking for help, and the last thing I said to him was, 'Trust me. You'll be fine. Just get some sleep.' I can't get those words out of my head. It haunts me. When Harlan was murdered, Ryder said he owed it to his friend to find his killer. I know it's weird, but I feel Ryder has passed that burden onto me. The only way I'll ever get some peace is by finding out who murdered them."

"That's crazy. You're not a detective."

"I know, but at least I have to try, and I know the sheriff isn't going to pursue the case. You're the only one who can help me. You're a true local. You were born and raised on the river. People who won't talk to me will talk to you."

Roscoe crawled up into Dave's lap, and, as usual, my neighbor used that as an excuse to stay in his chair and not get up to get his own beer out of the fridge. He held up his empty can of Hamm's with one hand, while pointing at the old dog with the other.

Shaking my head in disgust, I got up to fetch his beer and said, "You're lame. I'm doing this for Roscoe, not for you."

Handing him his beer, I asked, "So are you going to help me?"

Dave stroked his beard thoughtfully and said nothing for several minutes. He then leaned forward in his chair and said, "OK, if we are going to do this, there is only one way I can see this working. We can't go knocking on our neighbors' doors and asking questions. We'd get the same response Ryder did when he tried that. It doesn't matter how long you've lived on the river, locals don't like anyone messing in their affairs. The only way they'll talk to us is if their guard is down."

"How do we do that?" I downed my wine and filled my glass up again.

Dave smiled broadly. "A week from now is our annual Halloween party. You've been there. You know that just about everybody on the river shows up and gets drunk and stoned. In that setting, they'll be more likely to talk candidly. If anyone knows anything about these murders, it's our best chance to find it out."

I was excited. "I like it. It's worth a shot. Let's do it!"

TWELVE

Looking at my reflection in the mirror through my purple, John Lennon sunglasses, I tied my red bow tie and donned my green, velvet tailcoat before finally adjusting the oversized, matching felt top hat on my head. Underneath the jacket, I wore a yellow and black checkered satin vest. My trousers were jet black, and I sported white spats over my black, patent leather shoes. I was pleased with the look. I *was* the Mad Hatter.

I went into the kitchen, grabbed two beers, opened one and placed the other in my coat pocket. As I left the house, drinking my beer, I heard the telltale sound of a church bell tolling loudly as AC/DC's "Hells Bells" began blaring on my neighbor's stereo. The night was cold but clear. Dave's driveway, as well as mine, was packed with cars.

A group of people in costumes were milling around outside. A blue-gray cloud of smoke hovered over them, and the unmistakable smell of ganja was heavy in the air. I walked past them unnoticed and entered the garage.

As I expected, the place was packed with people. Along the far wall were several tables filled with a variety of local favorites, including salmon, crab, venison, and elk. There were also countless salads, pasta dishes, large bowls of chips and dips, numerous bottles of hard alcohol and mixers, and coolers filled with beer.

I scanned the room, trying to locate Dave, but there were too many witches, zombies, vampires, and overweight super heroes blocking my view. I knew I'd have to wade into the sea of people and slowly work my way around the room, trying to find my friend.

Luckily, the first person I encountered was Dave's girlfriend, Chloe. Dressed as Dorothy from the *Wizard of Oz*, she had a wicker basket filled with joints and was passing them out to people as she slowly made her way around the room. Roscoe was by her side with a sign hanging around his neck which read TOTO.

Roscoe greeted me with a tail wag, but he didn't look pleased. Reaching down to pet him, I couldn't help but laugh. *Not the image I remembered from the movie*, I thought.

Chloe offered me a reefer.

Shaking my head, I said, "You know I've got to stay focused."

"Lighten up, Cramps. I was just fucking with you."

"So where's Dave?"

"Where else? He's rooted to his recliner."

"Of course, I should have known."

As I slowly made my way to the far left corner of the room, a tall man, weighing 280 pounds, blocked my path. In his mid-twenties, he was dressed as a Minion, a character from the computer-animated film, *Despicable Me*.

His bald head, face and neck were covered in bright yellow make-up, and he wore white, round swim goggles, which were held tightly around his head by a black rubber band. He was clad in a yellow sweatshirt and denim overalls and had black combat boots on his feet.

I recognized him immediately. It was Jasper, a not-too-bright kid who I've encountered many times in Dave's garage. I started laughing because his costume belied the image he tried to portray. He wanted people to think he was a skinhead, so he shaved his head and spewed racial epithets, but everyone knew it was all bravado and that he was just harmless and stupid.

"What are you laughing at, Hobbit?" he asked.

"You, of course," I retorted. "I was going to say I was surprised you knew what a Hobbit was, but then I remembered Peter

Jackson made movies about them. I couldn't image you reading a book. You do know how to read, don't you?"

Jasper grabbed the wide label of my jacket. "Don't push me, Short Shit! I'll fuck you up."

There were a couple of birds trapped in the garage that were flying overhead, trying to find their way out. A feather from one of them fell down and landed on Jasper's sweatshirt. I lifted it off his shirt and said, "Oh, it's not fat. You're filled with feathers!"

It took a few seconds for what I had said to sink in and then Jasper picked me up, lifted me over his head and started spinning me around like he was a wrestler in the WWF.

"Don't spill my beer," I yelled.

Everyone at the party stopped to look at us, and Dave jumped off his chair and screamed, "Jasper, put him down!"

Jasper stopped in his tracks and gently lowered me to the floor. "We were just playing," he said. He looked at me as if I had better back him up. "That's right, isn't it, Short Shit?"

With the room still spinning and me, pacing back and forth in a futile attempt to get my land legs, I said half-heartedly, "Yeah. No harm, no foul."

Dave came up to me and whispered, "Nothing like keeping a low profile."

I looked at his costume. Dave had a bicycle helmet on his head and had a skateboard under his arm.

"So that's your costume?" I asked.

"Yeah, I'm a skateboarder."

"Could you have spent any less time on your costume?"

Dave waved his right hand around the garage. "Look at this place," he said, pointing out the fake cobwebs, orange and black LED lights, skulls, carved jack-o-lanterns and other Halloween-related paraphernalia that graced the floor, walls and ceiling of his garage. "Who do you think did all this? Chloe?"

With a big smile on my face, I said, "No, I know you don't vacuum this place very often or, more accurately, *never*. I thought spiders were responsible for the cobwebs."

Dave gave me a dirty look. "Who invited you to the party anyway?"

Pointing my index finger at him, I said, "That would be you."

With a disgusted look on his face, he asked, "Why do you always have to be such an ass?"

"I guess I have a need to live down to your expectations."

Coughing and laughing simultaneously, Dave choked out the words, "Well, you don't disappoint."

"So," I asked, "are you going to answer my original question or not?"

"What was that?"

"Could you have spent any less time on your costume?"

With an exasperated look on his face, Dave screamed, "Oh, for fuck's sake. I didn't have the luxury of spending a lot of time on my costume like you did. OK?"

"I wasn't trying to piss you off," I said defensively.

Shaking his head, Dave said, "No. I know you weren't trying. It just comes naturally to you."

When he calmed down, he gave my costume a second look and said, "Nice duds, by the way. Come to think of it, you always go all out on your costumes. What's up with that?"

Looking up, I rubbed my chin and grinned. "I never thought about it before now, but I guess it's because I was traumatized as a kid. When I was in grade school, maybe third or fourth grade, my Halloween costume was Buzzy the Crow."

Dave had a quizzical look on his face. "Don't you mean either Heckle or Jeckle?"

"No, they're cartoon characters too, just like Buzzy, but they're magpies. Buzz the Crow is, duh, by definition, a crow."

"Jesus! Everything with you always comes back to zoology. Just tell me, long story short."

"You know I don't do long story short. A story should be as long as it needs to be."

Dave looked up at the ceiling and rolled his eyes. "Whatever. Just get on with it."

"OK, so I was dressed as Buzzy the Crow, and, like all kids' costumes, it was cheaply made. The mask was plastic and stamped out on a press, which meant that Buzzy, with his long beak, couldn't be looking forward. He had to be looking either right or left. In my case, he was looking left."

Dave was incredulous. "Do you actually think they made right and left Buzzy the Crow masks?"

"No, of course not. Do you think I'm that stupid? Come on. My point was that Buzzy could either be looking right or left but not looking forward. I thought you wanted long story short. If you keep interrupting me, it's only going to get longer."

Dave waved his hands. "OK. Go on."

"So I was wearing my left-facing, Buzzy the Crow mask on Halloween…" I paused to see if my left-facing comment would, as I hoped, elicit a response from Dave.

To my chagrin, he didn't take the bait, so I continued. "And I went up to this house with my friends to get some candy. In those days, you could go out as kids by yourself without your parents. It wasn't like now."

Interrupting me, Dave was nearly apoplectic. "Stay focused. So what happened?"

"This woman came to the door. She had obviously been drinking and reeked of alcohol. She surveyed all of our costumes and then bent down and zeroed in on me. After a long look, she straightened back up, turned her head toward the living room and, in a gravelly voice, yelled to her husband, 'Hey, Bob. You have to come here and see this *fucked up* costume.' Bob was a fat slob with a big beer belly, and he was wearing a wife beater T-shirt. He came waddling over to the door and looked down at me and started laughing. So did the bitch. She put candy in our bags and then closed the door. As we went down the steps, the other kids, who were with me, were laughing their asses off. Then one of them started chanting in a nasally, singsong manner. 'You have a *fucked up* costume. You have a *fucked up* costume.' All the other kids joined in, and those little pricks didn't let up until we got to the next house and rang the doorbell. I was mortified and scarred for life."

Dave was crying, he was laughing so hard. "So now you don't wear fucked up costumes. It's only the person inside the costume who's fucked up."

"Fuck you! Why do I come over here anyway?"

Dave chuckled. "If I knew, I'd change what I'm doing so you didn't."

"Oh, really?"

"Oh, lighten up. I'm just kidding. You know we love you, warts and all." Changing the subject, Dave whispered, "So while you were stirring things up with Jasper, I was talking to people."

"What have you learned?"

"You see that tall, skinny guy over there, who's dressed like the Joker from Batman?"

I shook my head. "Yeah, so what?"

"That's Dax. You know him. He's a bartender at the Flounder Inn in Waldport. He told me Buster Jenkins came into the bar one night in a foul mood."

"So what's so unusual about that? When's Buster not in a bad mood?"

Dave laughed. "That's what I said, but Dax said he had never seen him this angry. He said Buster found out that his wife was having an affair with Harlan."

"How did he find out? Did he catch them together?"

"No, his neighbor told him he saw them come home together several nights when Buster was fishing in Alaska."

"When was this?"

"A couple of months before Harlan was murdered. Dax said Buster got drunk at the bar and started shooting his mouth off and said he wanted to kill that son-of-a-bitch."

"Everybody knows Libby Jenkins is a slut," I said matter-of-factly. "She's cheated on Buster before, and he's known about it and done nothing. Why was he so jacked up about it this time?"

"Because he thought Harlan was gay. Apparently, he thought

that made him look bad, that it reflected negatively on his manhood in some way."

"That's crazy."

"Maybe, but we're talking about Buster here."

"Why did he think Harlan was gay?"

"We all did," Dave said.

"I didn't."

"Well, then you're the only one who didn't. Two older guys living together? Come on."

I laughed. "You think everyone is gay."

Dave snickered. "No. Not everyone, just you and the two dead guys from Cali."

I shook my head. "You're an ass. You're so backwater."

"Better a backwater local than a liberal dandy from New Joisey," Dave retorted.

"Did Dax tell this to the cops?"

"No, he said he's no snitch, but he thinks the sheriff knows about it anyway. You know how loud Buster gets when he's drunk. Dax said there were at least three other people at the bar who heard him say it. Look, it may be nothing, but at least, it's a lead. Go work the room, and I'll do the same. We'll compare notes later. Right now, I'm going outside to get some wood for the fire."

I downed the last of my beer and grabbed the one I still had in my coat pocket. Opening it, I took a swig and started to make my way to the buffet table. The partygoers were obviously having a good time, and I could tell that most of the people I talked to were already lit up.

The *News-Times*, which comes out on Wednesdays and Fridays, had run front page stories on the dual murders in Tidewater both days this week, so it was easy to strike up a conversation on this hot topic without arousing suspicion.

About half the people I talked to thought the killings were horrible. The other half showed no remorse and actually said they were glad the two were dead. But all of the people I surveyed expressed the sentiment that the river was better off without them.

When I got to the buffet table, I finished my beer, grabbed another one out of a cooler and loaded a plate with smoked salmon, cheese, crackers and a healthy portion of Dungeness crab dip.

When I turned around, a man dressed as Freddie Krueger was standing in front of me. At six foot five, he was considerably taller than the actor who played the serial killer in the *Nightmare on Elm Street* films. Despite the foam mask, because of his height and build, I recognized him immediately.

It was Otis, a neighbor who lived up the road about a mile from me. He had a 16-ounce plastic cup in his hand, which was filled with his favorite libation, Black Velvet and Coca Cola on the rocks. He raised his cup to toast, and I did the same with my beer.

"Enjoying the party?" he asked. "I know I am."

"Yes," I replied. "Chloe and Dave have gone all out as usual."

Otis bent down, leaned in close and placed his right hand on my shoulder. I knew he meant this as a comforting gesture, but it made me feel uneasy nonetheless. He had a leather glove on his hand, and excluding the thumb, the other four digits had six-inch long razors, coming out of them. They were just plastic blades, but they looked real and they gave me the creeps.

"So, Little Big Man," Otis asked, "how are you holding up? The newspaper says you found both bodies. Are you OK?"

"Yeah, I'm fine, I guess, at least as good as can be expected. Thanks for asking."

"Look, I'm sorry those two guys are dead, but you know they didn't belong here."

"That's what everyone says," I replied.

"It's because it's true. Just ask Scooter. He's in hot water right now with the Feds for killing a harbor seal."

"Scooter McCracken?"

"Yeah, it was Gannet who turned him in."

"How do you know that?"

"Scooter told me himself. He said Gannet was out fishing near his place when he shot the seal from his deck. No one else was around. It couldn't have been anyone else. That S.O.B. called the NOAA Enforcement Hotline and turned him in."

"Wow, that's a stiff penalty."

"Yeah, I know. If convicted, Scooter could be fined up to $100,000 and go to jail for a year."

This was a good lead, I thought. Scooter stood to lose big if he was convicted of violating the Marine Mammal Protection Act. With Harlan out of the way, there'd be no witness to implicate him, and the case would be dropped for lack of evidence. I struggled to hide my excitement. Knowing Otis was a NASCAR fan, I changed the subject. "So, are you still rooting for Jeff Gordon in the Chase?"

"Oh yeah, he's retiring after this year, and I'd like to see him go out with another win."

"Don't tell that to Dave," I joked. "You know how much he hates Gordon. He calls him the Cry Baby."

Otis laughed heartily. "It's Davey who'll be crying when my driver ends up winning the Championship."

Just then, Otis' wife came up and grabbed his arm. She was thirty-five years his junior. Dressed as the Little Red Riding Hood, she was an attractive woman with large breasts and long, curly black hair. She had harlequin-colored, green eyes and white, porcelain skin.

Looking at this beautiful woman, I couldn't help but think Otis had failed miserably with his costume choice. He should have dressed up as the Big Bad Wolf. It would have been perfect in so many ways.

I gave her a hug and said, "Are you enjoying the party?"

"Of course, we look forward to it every year. We wouldn't miss it for the world."

I gestured toward the table. "Look at this spread. Let me get out of the way so you guys can get some food."

Using this as my excuse to leave, I turned and slowly made my way across the room, back to the far corner of the shop, where the wood stove was and where I knew Dave would be. I was eager to let him know what I had learned from Otis.

When I got there, Dave was standing with his back to me, star-ing at the TV, watching the two young mechanics who work for him, Darwin and Jacob, play Guitar Hero III: Legends of Rock.

Darwin and Jacob were casual friends who rented a house together a few miles downriver from where we live. From what Dave had told me, Jacob spent most nights at his girlfriend's apartment, so Darwin pretty much had the place to himself. Not that it was any business of mine, mind you, but it seemed like a good deal for Darwin, if you ask me.

Although Darwin and Jacob were roughly the same height and build, in terms of personality, they couldn't have been any more different. Darwin was intelligent and unassuming. Jacob, on the other hand, was one-dimensional and cocksure to a fault.

Darwin was dressed as a South American killer bee from an old *Saturday Night Live* sketch. He wore a black and yellow striped vest over a black flannel union suit. Over his shoulders and chest, he sported a leather bandolier filled with shotgun shells. A black sombrero hung on his back, held there by a leather strap across his neck. On his feet, he wore brown cowboy boots, and a black, skull cap beanie hid his scalp of thinning hair. A black plastic headband completed the look, supporting his antennae, which were two long springs ending in yellow ping pong balls.

Jacob was dressed as Alex DeLarge, the protagonist from the Stanley Kubrick film, *A Clockwork Orange*. A black bowler hat sat on his head, and he sported long, fake eyelashes only on his right eye. He was dressed in a white, collarless shirt and white carpenter pants, which were held up by white suspenders. He had black US Army paratrooper boots on his feet. But, without question, the most noticeable feature of his costume was the cricket codpiece he wore over his pants.

Darwin had the guitar-shaped controller. Jacob was by his side, watching him enviously as Darwin easily hit the barrage of notes that were scrolling on the screen. Because of the back-ground noise of the crowd and the music playing on the stereo, I couldn't tell what song it was that Darwin was challenging until

I got immediately behind him and Jacob. Then it was unmistakable. It was "Raining Blood" by Slayer.

I stood there for a minute watching Darwin work his magic. I had seen him and Jacob in Dave's garage countless times before, playing this PlayStation Game. I knew Darwin was a master at the game and that Jacob didn't have a chance of beating him.

I knew Jacob knew it too. I waited until Darwin finished the song and Dave got to see his friend's score before approaching him. Darwin had racked up 211,000 points.

I grabbed Dave by the arm. "Jacob can't come close to beating that score. No need to watch his humiliating defeat. Come talk to me."

Dave congratulated Darwin and patted Jacob on the shoulder. "Good luck, man. You'll need it to best that score."

Turning back to me, Dave said, "Let's go outside where we can talk. I need to get more wood for the fire anyway." I followed him out to the wood pile. "So what have you learned?" he asked.

I recounted what Otis had told me.

"That's interesting," Dave said, but he didn't seem sincere.

I was deflated. "Scooter clearly had the motive to commit the crime. You don't think that's something?"

"No, I do. It's just that Scooter has been caught red-handed before. I know for a fact that he's been caught selling halibut to businesses that weren't listed on his commercial fishing license. I thought he'd go to jail for that, but he got off that time like he's done for other infractions in the past. I don't know if he has someone in the agency on the take or if he just hires the best lawyers to get him off. Either way, I find it hard to believe he'd resort to murder. Look, I could be wrong. It's just my humble opinion. So what's your next step?"

I had a disgusted look on my face. "I guess I'm going to have to pay a visit to my buddy, the sheriff."

THIRTEEN

To save himself a trip upriver, the sheriff agreed to meet me at the City Hall in Waldport. Unlike most municipal buildings in larger cities, which have grandiose façades, this modest building is dwarfed by the large fire station to which it is connected and is easy to miss if you don't know where it is.

When I walked in the front door, a receptionist greeted me and directed me to a small room in the back. The carpeted room was devoid of furniture except for one eight-foot, folding table and four chairs. Two indoor flag poles, one with the Stars and Stripes and the other with Oregon's State flag, were positioned against the far wall directly behind the table.

I had seen enough press conferences on television to know that government officials always have the flags to their backs, so I took a seat at the table facing the flags. It was not long before Sheriff Whittaker and Deputy Darby entered the room and took their seats at the table across from me.

"So, Mr. Riker," Whittaker said, "when we talked on the phone this morning, you said you had some information which might be helpful to our investigation."

"Yes. I've been doing some investigating on my own and think I've uncovered a couple of good leads. I wanted to share them with you in case you aren't already aware of them."

Whittaker looked irritated but struggled to maintain a

conciliatory tone. "We are always grateful for any input we can get from citizens in solving crimes, but when did you become a detective?"

Looking him directly in the eyes, I retorted, "When you made it clear you thought I was a suspect. Look, I'm not here to waste my time or yours. I'm trying to be helpful. Do you want to know what I've learned or not?"

Whittaker's face reddened noticeably. "And I don't have the time or the inclination to verbally joust with you, Mr. Riker. Just tell me what you know."

Letting out a heavy sigh, I said, "OK, let's start over and try this again. I don't have anything to back it up, but I've heard through the grapevine that Harlan Gannet was having an affair with Libby Jenkins. Apparently Buster found out about it and was mad as hell one night when he was drunk at the Flounder Inn. He said he wanted to kill Gannet."

The sheriff chuckled. "Yes, several people who were in the bar that night heard him say that and reported the incident to us. I questioned Buster, but as expected, it turned out to be nothing. In high school, we used to call him 'Bluster' Jenkins. He's always been all talk and no action. What else have you heard?"

"That Gannet allegedly saw Scooter McCracken shoot a harbor seal and called the NOAA Enforcement Hotline to report him. I know it's a stiff penalty if you're found guilty of violating the Marine Mammal Protection Act. I figure with Gannet out of the way, there'd be no one to testify against Scooter and the charge would be dropped. It seems like a good motive to me."

The sheriff shook his head in agreement. "Again, it's something we're aware of. The seal killing is not my concern; it's the Fed's problem. I will admit that it would have been a good reason to want to kill Gannet. The problem is Scooter has a rock solid alibi for the day Gannet died. Earlier that day, Scooter went to Moby Dick's in Newport to tie one on. He got in a brawl with another patron, and they busted the place up pretty good. My deputy here was the one who brought them in. I know for a fact that, at the time of the murder, Scooter was cooling his heels in jail."

Obviously disappointed that both my leads were a bust, I said, "Well, Sheriff, it looks like I wasted your time." I started to stand up, but Whittaker motioned for me to remain seated.

"No apologies necessary," the sheriff replied. "You haven't wasted my time. I was actually going to contact you anyway. Do you mind if I ask you a few questions while you're here?"

"No, not at all."

"I know you are a nature writer. You know a lot about animals. Am I right?"

"I research my subjects thoroughly beforehand, so I'd say I'm very knowledgeable about the animals I've written about."

"And what animals would those be?"

"Wildlife native to the Pacific Northwest, predominantly."

"Do you know much about rough-skinned newts?"

"Actually I do. I've written a couple of articles on them. One was about how poisonous they are and another had to do with the evolutionary battle between rough-skinned newts and garter snakes. How garter snakes have evolved a resistance to this salamander's poison."

"What makes them so deadly?"

"Their skin secretes a powerful neurotoxin called tetrodotoxin." Pausing momentarily, I asked, "Why are you asking me about this? Was Ryder poisoned? Is that what the autopsy report says?"

"I'm not at liberty to reveal anything about an ongoing investigation. I'm sure you can appreciate that."

"Of course," I said as I cracked a half smile. The sheriff didn't have to say anything. I knew the answer to my question. There was no other plausible reason why Whittaker would have asked me specifically about rough-skinned newts. Ryder died from tetrodotoxin poisoning. I was sure of it.

"I have one last question for you, Mr. Riker. Would you consent to let us collect a DNA sample from you today?"

"Do you have a warrant?"

"No, not yet. I was hoping you'd be cooperative and make that unnecessary."

"So you found the killer's DNA at the crime scene, but it doesn't match the DNA you have in your genetic database. Is that it?"

"Again, I'm not at liberty to confirm or deny this."

Laughing out loud, I said, "You don't have to. There's no other reason why you'd want a DNA sample from me if you didn't already have a sample from the killer to match it to."

Whittaker smiled at me, but his dagger eyes betrayed his true feelings. "If you are not guilty, you have nothing to worry about and we'd then be able to eliminate you as a suspect. It would actually help our investigation. I can't see why you'd refuse."

"Oh, really? You can't see why I wouldn't want to give up my constitutional right to privacy?"

"So is your answer no?"

I thought for a second and then said with a smirk, "No, what the heck. I'll do it under one condition. If there's no match, I want my sample destroyed and I want your word my DNA profile will not be entered into your or any other law enforcement database."

Whittaker shook his head. "That's a reasonable request. I give you my word if you're exculpated, we'll expunge your sample. Have you eaten or drank anything in the last hour, Mr. Riker?"

"No, nothing."

"Excellent." Whittaker turned to his junior officer. "Deputy, go out to the patrol car and get a DNA kit."

As Darby got up from his chair and left the room, the sheriff said, "The buccal swab test is a simple procedure and won't take long. We're going to—"

I cut him off. "No need to explain, Sheriff. I'm familiar with the test."

"How silly of me," Whittaker said sarcastically, "of course you are." The sheriff stood up and motioned for me to get up as well.

"As I'm sure you know, Mr. Riker, we like to have the person being tested rinse his mouth out before we collect the sample. So if you'll follow me, I'll take you to the breakroom where we can get you a glass of warm water to rinse with."

I followed the sheriff's directions and when we returned, Darby was in the room waiting for us. The sheriff stopped at the doorway and said, "I've got another appointment, so I've leave you with the deputy. There's a consent form and pen on the table. Fill it out, and then the deputy will do the cheek swab test."

While I completed the form, Darby donned a surgical mask and nitrile gloves and opened a package containing a sterile, cotton applicator. Removing it, he inserted it into my mouth and gently rubbed and rotated the swab against the inside of my right cheek.

After placing the applicator in a dry transport tube and labeling it, he removed another swab from its packaging and performed the same procedure on the left side of my mouth. Once this swab was in its container and labeled, he placed both tubes in an envelope and said, "I still have some procedural work to do here for chain of custody purposes, Mr. Riker, but we don't need to take up any more of your time. Thank you for your cooperation."

The deputy chewed on his lower lip in frustration as he watched me leave. He had expected me to refuse to submit to the DNA test and was surprised, and disappointed, when I assented to the request. He thought I was a little prick and secretly wanted me to be guilty. I knew he'd send the samples to the forensic lab for analysis and await the results, but I also knew he knew what the outcome would be. There would be no match. He knew I wasn't the killer he, for some reason, so fervently wanted me to be.

FOURTEEN

Leaving City Hall, I got in my car and looked at my watch. It was 4:45 p.m. I was anxious to tell Dave what I had learned. Since his place of business was nearby and I knew he was about to close up shop for the day, I stopped at Ray's grocery store, which is just a block away from his garage, and bought two six-packs, Coors Light for me and Hamm's for Dave.

When I got to the shop, I parked in the back, grabbed the beer and entered the side door that opened into the last bay. A mechanic was lying on a creeper underneath a Jeep Cherokee, servicing the transmission. I knew it was Jacob. Getting out from under the car, he stood up, grabbed a rag from his back pocket, wiped his hands and said, "I'm done for the day. I'll finish this job tomorrow."

Jacob was in his mid-twenties. He was just shy of six feet tall, had blond, short cropped hair and a scraggly goatee, but his most noticeable feature was his very prominent nose. He had a long, narrow proboscis that even a tapir would envy. If he had been sensitive about his snout, I wouldn't have kidded him about it, but Jacob was proud of his nose and actually liked the attention he got from it. I remember one time at a party, when I took a slice of a dill pickle and placed it on my nose and asked, "Who am I?" and everyone yelled, "Jacob!"

"Hey, Jacob," I said. "I liked your costume last night. I remember that scene from *A Clockwork Orange* when Alex put on that long, fake rubber nose and violated that rich, middle-aged lady while he made her old husband watch. You know, while he was singing that Gene Kelly classic, 'Singing in the Rain.' It's a powerful but disturbing moment in the film. I can't believe you went there."

Jacob had a confused look on his face. "What are you talking about? I was dressed as Alex. I wasn't trying to depict him from just one scene in the movie."

"Oh, I'm sorry. So that wasn't a fake rubber nose?"

Jacob finally saw where I was going with this. "Ha-ha, very funny. You're just jealous. You know what they say, big nose, big hose,"

"Yeah, well, it's all subjective. It's like a guy, telling a fish story about a whopper he caught. He holds up his hands a yard apart and says, 'That fish was huge. It must have been twelve inches!' What one guy thinks is a kielbasa, is just another man's Little Smokies sausage."

Jacob guffawed. "I forgot how much I hate you. What are you doing here, anyway?"

Holding up a six-pack in each hand, I said, "I'm bearing gifts. Where's your boss?"

"He's in the front of the shop, closing up."

Just then, Dave entered the bay, followed dutifully by Roscoe. "Hey, Cramps, what are you doing here?"

Holding up the beer, I said, "I'm here to grace you with my presence."

Dave laughed. "What have you been smoking? We'll take the beer. You can leave."

"No. It's a package deal. I come with the beer."

Dave lowered his head in mock disgust. "Damn it!"

I handed Dave a Hamm's and took a Coors Light for myself. Jacob asked, "Do you have one for me?"

"Of course. What do you want?"

Looking at the choices, Jacob said, "A Rolling Rock if you want the truth, but I'll take a Hamm's."

Handing him a beer, I shook my head in disapproval. "You're just kissing up to your boss."

Dave joked, "Good choice, Jacob. You can keep your job." Turning back to me, he said, "So how did your meeting with the sheriff go today?"

"About as good as you'd expect. He still has it out for me." As I recounted the meeting, I could see Dave's eyes widening noticeably.

"Wow! The Old Grady would never have agreed to take a DNA test," he said.

I pursed my lips. "I *am* 'The Old Grady.' It's 'The Young Grady' that would have told the sheriff to fuck off. I'm smarter than that now. The sheriff was looking at me as the killer, and this was clouding his judgment. If I didn't eliminate myself from the equation, he wouldn't go beyond me and pursue other suspects. Science is replete with accounts of researchers who are so wed to their hypotheses that they discount their own data and try to rationalize why it doesn't fit their model."

Dave shook his head and looked at me as if what I had just said was spoken in some foreign tongue. "Well, Cramps, you gave it your best shot, but it looks like it's time to throw in the towel."

"I'm not ready to call it quits just yet. Thomas Edison once said, 'Our greatest weakness lies in giving up. The most certain way to succeed is always to try just one more time.'"

Looking at Dave with a puzzled look on his face but pointing at me, Jacob blurted out, "Where does he come up with this shit?"

Dave chuckled. "Oh, one of his egghead friends gave him a desk calendar as a gift last Christmas, which has a different quote from a famous person for every day of the year. He throws these out in conversation whenever he can shoehorn them in. He thinks it makes him look smart."

"It sounds dumb if you ask me," Jacob responded.

Shaking my head slowly, I said, "I should have known better than to try to have a serious conversation with you guys."

"Give it up, Cramps," Dave responded. "You're not a detective. You're wasting your time, and at your age, that's a precious commodity. I know you have an overabundance of confidence in yourself, but you're not Sam Spade or Sherlock Holmes, and you never will be."

Jacob piped up, "No, but he kind of looks like Columbo."

Dave got a big grin on his face. "Personally, I try not to look at him. But you're right. He sorta looks like Peter Falk. He's short like him and has that squinty-eyed look."

Looking at Dave, I countered, "I'm the same height as you, asshole, and I don't have a glass eye."

"Maybe not," Jacob argued, "but if you were wearing a trench coat, you'd be a dead ringer for him."

Dave leaned forward and pretended to examine me closely. "No, on second thought, I have to disagree with you, Jacob. Look at those jowls of his. If Cramps was wearing a trench coat, he'd look more like McGruff the Crime Dog."

Jacob burst out laughing, and Dave did too. I tried not to join in, but I couldn't help myself. Getting up to leave, I said, "You yahoos are about as funny as a crutch. I'm out of here." I left the Hamm's but grabbed the rest of the Coors Light and headed out the door.

FIFTEEN

As I drove home from Dave's shop, it started to rain heavily, and a strong wind ripped through the valley, pummeling the red alders and big leaf maples along the highway. The trees let loose a shower of yellow-hued leaves, which rained down around me. An occasional splash of brilliant, red leaves from vine maples in the understory cartwheeled hurriedly across the rain-soaked highway in front of me.

As I made my way around the winding turns, leading up the river, I thought back to my last meeting with Ryder. He told me Harlan started asking questions about a murder case he was researching. Is it possible that this had something to do with his death?

When Ryder suggested this as a possibility, I, admittedly, didn't take him seriously and assumed it was just a desperate move on his part to keep his hope alive that he would be successful in finding his friend's killer.

I wanted to race home to get on the internet and see what I could learn about Harlan as an investigative reporter, but the torrent of water hitting my windshield made it difficult to see the road clearly, and I couldn't go above twenty-five.

When I got home, I ran to the house and bounded up the front steps, but by then I was already drenched. Unlocking the front door, I headed upstairs, jettisoned my wet T-shirt and grabbed a towel from the bathroom to dry off. I then went straight to my study and turned on my laptop.

I googled Harlan Gannet's name and found he had been a reporter for a supermarket tabloid. He wasn't an investigative journalist. He was a smear-monger. He had made a living writing sensational crime stories and scandalous articles about celebrities' private lives. Now it made perfect sense. No wonder he was a fan of the true crime genre. To me, these novels, like the tabloid he worked for, cater to the basest level of the human condition.

Most people won't admit it, but they get some vicarious pleasure from the suffering of others. We've all experienced it when there's an accident. The traffic slows to a crawl, and often, it's not because the wreck is blocking the road, but rather because the people passing by are slowing down so they can rubberneck. They want to make sure they have a ringside seat to someone else's misfortune. I find that sick. So Harlan Gannet was even more of a scumbag than I thought. I had to ask myself, why was I looking for this guy's killer anyway?

I knew the answer to my question. It was guilt, pure and simple. I wasn't doing this for Harlan. I was doing this for Ryder. But as much as I wanted to avenge Ryder's death, without a new lead to pursue, I was at an impasse. I finally had to face the truth and be honest with myself. Dave was right. My mission to find the killer was a foolhardy endeavor from the very beginning, and it was time to call it quits.

SIXTEEN

As Skid waited for the young female barista with the unruly blond hair to make his Americano, he scanned the front page of the Wednesday edition of the *News Times*. Nothing caught his interest. The two main stories were the extended delay of the December opening of the Dungeness crab season because of high levels of domoic acid in the tissues of this commercial shellfish species and the Newport City Council squabbling over whether to spend money on what was probably another hare-brained, local improvement project.

Skid watched the barista grab a plastic scoop, put a few ice cubes in his molten java, gingerly set a plastic lid on the top and then place a cardboard sleeve over the container. When she called his name and he grabbed the cup, he knew that it was still too hot to drink, but he felt he had to taste it if he was going to go off on the girl.

Skid took a small sip. *Dammit! I knew it.* With his tongue still on fire, he handed the coffee back to the clueless girl and asked, "What is it about lukewarm that you people don't understand? I asked you to put enough ice in it to make it lukewarm. If it's so hot to the touch that you need to put a cardboard sleeve over the cup, then it's not lukewarm."

The young girl seemed unfazed by his anger, which made him even more enraged. "I'm new here," she said, "but during my training, I was told we have to heat the coffee at a certain temperature to enhance its full flavor."

By now, he was nearly apoplectic. "That's brewing it, not serving it, you dolt! Put more ice in it!"

Her hands shaking, the girl grabbed the cup and opened the lid. She filled the plastic scoop with ice cubes and held it over the drink. "Tell me how many to put in."

Skid shook his head, held out his hand and barked, "Give me the cup!"

The girl handed him the Americano. He pulled the cardboard sleeve off the cup and handed the drink back to the girl. "OK, now put in a few ice cubes until it's still warm but not too hot to the touch."

The girl did as he directed. She then gave the cup back to him.

Skid took a sip and smiled. "Perfect! Now was that so hard?" With his drink and newspaper in hand, he went to a small table at the back of the room.

Sipping his now lukewarm Americano, Skid opened up the newspaper and leafed through the pages until he found an article that caught his eye. He read it with disgust:

Five Rivers Man Arrested on Animal Cruelty Charges

Responding to a call from a concerned neighbor, a Lincoln County Animal Services deputy went to Lenny Scott's home on Five Rivers Road and discovered two severely malnourished horses in their stalls. According to the deputy, it was immediately obvious that the animals hadn't received proper care in a long time. The horses' ribs, hip bones and spines were clearly visible, and their hooves were tangled and unusually long. The horses also exhibited labored breathing, which authorities said was likely exacerbated by the three feet of manure, which was found in their stalls.

After obtaining a court order to seize the emaciated animals, authorities transported the horses to an equine veterinarian for examination. The horses will remain under the supervision and care of the veterinarian until the court case is adjudicated.

Scott was arrested and charged with two counts of animal abuse in the first degree, which are Class A misdemeanors. Additional charges could be filed once the results of the veterinarian's examination are finalized. Scott was released on $2,500 bond and given a court date of January 25th in Newport.

Skid clenched his fists. *How could anyone abuse a defenseless animal? I'll take care of that son of a bitch. I'll give him a taste of his own medicine.* Shaking uncontrollably in anger, he jumped out of his chair, folded his paper, put it under his arm, grabbed his coffee and stormed out of the store.

SEVENTEEN

Returning home, Skid got on his computer and searched the internet to learn as much as he could about his next victim. From Lenny Scott's mug shot, he knew that the man looked like "Boss" Hogg from *The Dukes of Hazzard*. He was short, bald, overweight, and was all chin. His bulbous head seemed to melt into his shoulders, and he appeared to have no neck. From court filings, Skid knew that Scott's wife had divorced him a year earlier and that the couple had no kids and that he lived alone. *Perfect!*

Skid got in his truck and drove past Scott's place to scope it out. There was a dense stand of Douglas fir on both sides of the driveway, concealing the farmhouse, but at the entrance to the driveway, there was a sign that read:

GMC '69 K20 Camper Special
$10K OBO
45,000 miles
541-867-5309

Skid's mouth expanded into a toothy grin. He now knew the ruse he would use to get close to this SOB so he could kill him, but he still had to do his due diligence. He spent the next several nights doing reconnaissance outside and immediately around Scott's house. The nearest neighbor was a quarter-mile away.

When he was confident that he hadn't overlooked anything, he placed a call to Scott. After several rings, his victim answered. Putting on his most earnest voice, Skid said, "I saw your sign about the truck for sale. I know it's close to supper time, but I just got off work. Would it be too much of an imposition if I came over now to look at the vehicle? I've been looking for a '69 K20 for a while now and am prepared to pay cash tonight if I like what I see."

Eager for the money, Scott took the bait like a bass swallowing a frog topwater fishing lure. "Of course. It's no imposition at all. Come on over. I'll turn the porch light on for you."

Smiling like a Cheshire cat, Skid said. "Excellent. I'll be there in a half hour."

He grabbed a handful of zip ties, a bottle of bleach and a can of lighter fluid and placed them in his backpack. He slid his Thompson 22 LR pistol in his shoulder holster, put on his hooded parka, and placed a book of matches and his new toy, his stun gun flashlight, in his coat pocket. With his backpack in hand, he headed out the door and got in his truck. Setting his backpack next to him on the bench seat, he started his vehicle.

It was only 4:15 p.m., but, since it was after the winter solstice, daylight was in short supply and darkness was closing in fast. The night was cold but clear. As he waited for his vehicle to warm up, he took his CD case out of his glove box and leafed through the discs, finally settling on one from the British extreme metal band, Cradle of Filth. Placing the disc in his player, he backed out of his driveway and headed up the road.

After traveling east for twelve miles on Highway 34, Skid turned right onto Five Rivers Road. Just then, the track, "An Enemy Led the Tempest," began to play. *How prophetic*, he thought. He listened to the lyrics, and when the part he liked best surfaced, he turned up the volume and barked out the lyrics in unison:

"Thou art no more
An Angel filled with light,
But a leech to be abhorred
And thou shalt suffer
My burning will…"

Skid turned off the music as he drove up the driveway, leading to Scott's place, to focus on the task at hand. There were two flood-lights on over the barn, and as Scott had promised, there was also a yellow, globe-shaped, outdoor porch light on, welcoming him to the entrance to the house.

Leaving his truck, Skid placed his right hand in his coat pocket to reassure himself that his stun gun flashlight was still there. As he mounted the steps to the front door, he could hear the sound of a TV blaring inside. *The guy's either asleep or hard of hearing.* He rang the doorbell. Through the small window on the front door, he could see his fat quarry getting up off his recliner in the living room and lumbering to the entrance.

Scott was dressed in a discolored, white Pabst Blue Ribbon T-shirt and jeans. The shirt had a big stain down the front. Skid giggled as he tried to figure out whether the stain was from mo-tor oil or some food which had failed to make it into Porky's mouth.

When Scott opened the door, Skid immediately understood why the TV's volume was cranked up so high. It was because the fan on Scott's fireplace insert, which was blowing hot air into his living room, was rattling so loud that it made it difficult to hear the program he was watching.

Scott extended his hand and smiled broadly. Several of his front teeth were missing in both the upper and lower jaws. Speaking loudly, so he could be heard over the cacophonous racket produced by the clattering fireplace fan and blaring TV, he asked, "Are you the guy who is interested in the GMC?"

Skid bit his tongue to keep from laughing. *With his miss-ing teeth and pumpkin-shaped head, this guy looks like a flesh-colored*

Jack-O'-Lantern, he thought. He shook Scott's hand and returned a smile. "That would be me," he said.

Scott raised his right arm and pointed to the barn. "The truck's in there. It's a beauty." Despite the cold weather, he didn't bother to grab a jacket. He moved past Skid and walked down the steps with Skid close behind.

As they made their way to the barn, Skid asked, "So why does your truck have so little mileage?"

"I only use it on the farm and to go to town occasionally. I love that truck and wouldn't be selling it if I didn't need the money to make alimony payments to my ex-wife and cover lawyer's fees."

Skid saw an opportunity to ingratiate himself with Scott. "I hate lawyers. They're all fucking scumbags!"

"Damn straight! On the phone, you said you were willing to make a deal today. That's right, isn't it?"

Skid pursed his lips and smiled smugly. The fact that Scott was starting negotiations meant that he had swallowed his story hook, line and sinker. "Yes. If the truck is in the shape it should be in with such low mileage."

Scott grinned with confidence. "Oh, there's no question about that. Did I tell you that the truck has a power take-off winch?"

Skid was genuinely impressed. "Are you kidding me? That was a special order option!"

Scott was excited that his potential buyer appreciated the rarity of the find. *This guy's going to buy the GMC,* he thought. "I'm glad you can appreciate what a steal this truck is at $10K."

Skid went back into negotiating mode. "Or best offer. I haven't seen it yet. That still remains to be seen."

Scott opened the gate to the horse corral, which led to the barn. As the two men made their way through the wood post-and-rail enclosure to the barn entrance, Skid was pleased to see that the overturned, 300-gallon, galvanized stock trough, which he had seen on his earlier reconnaissance missions, was still there, outside the barn, on the right side of the door.

Scott took a key out of his front pocket, unlocked the barn door and slid it open. Walking inside, he flipped a light switch on the wall inside the barn, which turned on the pendant lights overhead. Skid followed him in and was immediately repulsed by the fetid odor of decaying horse manure and urine-soaked bedding material which permeated the air. Scott seemed to not notice the malodorous scent or find it offensive, and Skid found this to be even more disgusting than the smell itself.

Scott's prize truck was washed, waxed and sitting in the open section of the barn, front and center. Skid walked around the truck, pretending to inspect it in every detail. In reality, he wanted to get behind the truck so he could observe the horse stalls, which were obscured from view.

When he got there, he was sickened by what he saw. The stalls were filled with manure, just like the newspaper article had described, but for some reason, seeing it himself had a greater impact on him and increased his sense of rage. He was struck by the dichotomy between the way Scott had babied his truck, an inanimate object, and the way he had neglected and mistreated living creatures in his care. He knew his decision to kill this piece of crap was justified.

He clenched his fists and gritted his teeth, struggling to control his anger. *Get a hold of yourself,* he thought. *You can't let this scumbag know you hate his guts. You'll lose the element of surprise. Calm down.*

While Skid stood behind the truck, trying to regain his composure, Scott opened the hood and called to him, "Hey, come here. I want you to see this."

With a painful grin plastered firmly in place, Skid walked around the truck and saw Scott pointing to the engine. Looking under the hood, Skid said, "It's a small block Chevy."

With his back to him, still admiring the engine, Scott said proudly, "Yeah, but it's a four-bolt main with factory four-barrel."

Skid saw his opportunity. He seized the stun gun flashlight out of his coat pocket, turned it on and placed the prongs of the device squarely on Scott's lower back, holding it there until his victim dropped face down on the ground. Skid zapped him again. Laughing giddily, he said, "I love technology. This stun gun flashlight is awesome."

With the sensation of millions of pins and needles coursing through his body, Scott lay helpless at his feet. Skid quickly removed the zip ties from his backpack, fashioned a pair of homemade handcuffs out of three of them and bound Scott's arms behind his back. He used additional zip ties to bind Scott's legs together. He then took a rag out of his coat pocket and stuffed it in his victim's mouth.

With his quarry trussed up and incapacitated, Skid left the barn and headed for the overturned stock trough. Righting it, he dragged the tank to the center of the barn door, positioning it under the trolley/chain fall system, which was used to lift hay bales to the storage loft above.

Finding a stack of cement blocks nearby, he placed four of them under the water trough. He then used a wheelbarrow, which was leaning against the side of the barn, to retrieve firewood from a stack, which was protected from the rain by a silver hay tarp.

After placing the logs under the trough, Skid grabbed the can of lighter fluid from his pack, squirted it on the wood and reached into his coat pocket for the matchbook. Lighting one of the sulfur sticks, he tossed it on the pile and watched as the fire came to life.

Satisfied that the flames would continue unabated, he took the wheelbarrow inside the barn and stopped briefly to check on the status of his victim. The effects of the stun gun had worn off, and Scott was fighting feverishly but futilely against his restraints.

Skid looked down at his prey and stared at him with a sinister smirk on his face. He thought briefly about zapping him yet again with the stun gun but decided Scott's vain, frenetic attempts to free himself were more psychologically debilitating. Patting his victim on the head, he said, "I'll get back to you later."

Skid then wheeled the push cart around the truck to the horse stalls. Grabbing a spade, he filled the wheelbarrow with manure and transported it with the shovel to the water trough outside the barn. Removing the bleach he had in his pack, he poured the contents of the bottle into the empty trough. He then shoveled the horse dung on top of the bleach. After several more trips to the barn, he had the water trough half-full with excrement.

Returning to the barn, Skid grabbed the remote control for the electric hoist and maneuvered it across the motorized trolley until it was directly over his victim. He then lowered the hoist's hook, secured it to the zip ties that bound Scott's arms and lifted his struggling prey up to the rafters above. Advancing the hoist forward on the trolley, he transported his victim outside the barn to the end of the steel I-beam and then lowered him down to within two feet of the stock trough before stopping the hoist. Grabbing Scott's bound legs with one hand, he pulled them forward, righting his victim in the process. He then started the hoist again and lowered Scott slowly into the trough so that he was positioned face up in the steaming pile of shit. He then disconnected the hook, used the remote to raise the hoist and run it back into the hay loft.

When Scott was securely ensconced in the heated manure hot tub, Skid placed his face directly over his victim, looked him squarely in the eyes and said, "So, do you know why I'm doing this to you?"

Twisting back and forth in the trough as he struggled in vain to escape his worst nightmare, Scott shook his head violently.

"It's because of what you did to your horses. I'm not going to lie. I'm probably going to kill you for what you did to those defenseless animals. But if you can explain why you did what you did, it might change my mind. I want to give you a fair chance to defend yourself, but that means we have to communicate. We can't do that with a gag in your mouth. If you promise not to scream bloody murder, I'll take the rag out of your trap and give you a chance to explain your actions.

As soon as you break your promise, the gag will go back in, we'll be done talking and your script will be written. What do you say?"

Looking up at his captor, Scott shook his head vigorously in the affirmative.

Obviously pleased with the response, Skid smiled broadly and removed the gag from his victim's mouth. "Here's your chance to defend your actions. The Court is in session."

Talking frantically, Scott retorted, "The horses weren't mine. They belonged to my ex-wife. She cheated on me and then filed for divorce, claiming I had abused her. I never lifted a hand to that bitch. It was all a lie, but that didn't make any difference in court. She hired a high-priced lawyer from the valley and took me to the cleaners. If anyone should be guilty about the treatment the horses received, it's her. They were her animals. She abandoned them."

"But they were in your care," Skid countered.

"Only because she didn't have any place to board them after our divorce. She wanted me to pay for their care. That's bullshit! It was just one more way she came up with to bleed me of any money I still had after she and her slimebag lawyer took everything else I owned."

"So your ex-wife's a bitch, I get that. But that doesn't excuse you from the horrible way you treated the horses under your care. The poor animals were not pawns in some perverted, legal chess match between you and your wife. They were living beings for Christ's sake!"

"They're not dead. They're still alive."

"Yeah, thanks to the concerned neighbor who turned you in to the Sheriff's Office. I saw the article in the newspaper. How do you think I found out about you? Do you even know why I've got you in a tub of horse shit?"

"To humiliate me?"

Laughing and shaking his head, Skid said, "No, to kill you! The same way you were slowly killing the animals under your care. Urea in horse's piss and shit is converted to ammonia when it is left to accumulate. There's still piss and several feet of shit in your horses' stalls even now. You forced your animals to stand in this shit and breathe it in constantly. This can lead to a host of health problems, like heaves, thrush, abscesses and hoof damage. According to the *News Times*, the veterinarian who examined your animals confirmed that your horses are suffering from some of these very symptoms."

"So you're going to cook me in this pot like a cannibal?"

Shaking his head slowly from side to side, Skid laughed heartily. "No, I'm not going to cook you. You're too fat to eat. You'd clog my arteries. I started the fire just to warm up the manure so it would react more quickly with the chlorine bleach I put in the bottom of the water trough. Let me give you a chemistry lesson so you know how I expect you to die. The ammonia from the horse shit will mix with the bleach to form toxic gases called chloramines. Inhaling this shit will eventually render you unconscious and kill you."

Scott started coughing, and his eyes began to water profusely.

Skid looked down at him and laughed. "The process is beginning. The gas is starting to attack your eyes and mucous membranes, and that's my cue to leave."

With his victim fighting him feverishly, Skid stuffed the rag back in Scott's mouth and used a pair of zip ties to secure the gag in place. Patting him on the head, he said, "I wish I had an apple to put in your mouth instead. It would have been so perfect. Oh well, I guess I can't think of everything."

Skid returned to the wood pile, removed the hay tarp that was protecting the wood and used it to cover the water trough. He used rope to secure the tarp to the cinder blocks at the corners of the tank. He then returned to the barn, turned off the interior lights and the floodlights out front and slid the barn door closed. Retrieving his stun gun flashlight from his coat pocket, he turned on the light. As he walked back to his truck, he had a satisfied grin on his face. *Damn, I'm getting good at this*, he thought.

EIGHTEEN

I awoke to the sound of my front doorbell chiming. I glanced at the clock on the nightstand next to my bed and saw it was ten. I hopped out of bed, pulled on a pair of sweatpants and ran down the stairs to answer the door.

Dave was on my doorstep with a shovel in his hand and a broad smile on his face. "Hey, Cramps, you just getting up? I thought old people got up at the crack of dawn?"

I pursed my lips. "It's the weekend."

"What difference does that make? You're retired. All days are the same for you."

"I'm glad you think you know so much about my daily routine. What do you want?"

"We've got to go up to the water system. Chloe just tried to take a shower, and the water pressure's low. With all the rain and wind we've had over the last few days, I'm sure there's a bunch of sand and leaves, plugging up the intake. Get dressed, bring a shovel and meet me at my truck in five minutes." Without waiting for an answer, he bounded down the steps.

I ran upstairs, went to the bathroom to relieve myself, traded my sweatpants for a pair of jeans, threw on a sweatshirt and wool jacket and headed to the kitchen to get some beers for the trip.

As I passed by Spencer's bedroom, I saw his door was closed, so I assumed he was still sleeping. Not wanting to wake him, I left him a note on the kitchen counter, telling him that the water pressure was low and that Dave and I were on our way to the water system to fix it. Grabbing some beers out of the fridge, I placed them in a plastic bag and headed out the door. I put on my rubber boots, which were on the front porch, and retrieved a spade from the garden shed on the side of the garage.

Dave was already in his truck, revving the engine. I threw the shovel in the bed, put my Coors Light in the cooler next to Dave's Hamm's and opened the passenger door to get in, but Roscoe was sprawled out on the bench seat. I grabbed his butt and tried to move him, but he pushed back stubbornly and refused to move.

Dave gently grabbed his dog and pulled him closer to the center of the seat. "Come on, Roscoe, give Cramps a little room." Roscoe reluctantly acquiesced, and I was able to get in and fasten my seatbelt.

Detecting a foul smell, I scrunched up my nose and said in disgust, "Roscoe, you stink. You need a bath."

Dave chuckled. "So do you, Cramps, but Roscoe and I have enough social graces to not say anything."

"Ha-ha, very funny. You're a laugh a minute."

Our water source is a natural spring which flows year-round out of the side of the hill about two hundred feet above the Alsea on the opposite side of the river from where our homes are located. Seven homes are on our water system, and since Dave is the youngest homeowner, he was the unanimous choice to assume responsibility for maintaining the system. As his friend and neighbor, I was the logical choice to be his assistant.

For safety reasons, we have a rule that no one goes up to the water system alone and for good reason. It's a thirteen-mile trip one way, the slippery, moss-covered rocks leading up to the holding pond are always a treacherous traverse, and it's so remote that if you were by yourself and got injured, there'd be no one to help. It might be days or weeks before someone came by and found you.

We usually go up to the water system about once a month to clear brush and to clean out any leaves, twigs and stones which have collected around the screen box protecting the opening of our intake pipe. We like to think we're being proactive in keeping the water system free of problems, but, in truth, it gives Dave and me an excuse to drive in the woods and drink beer for a couple of hours.

Three miles up the highway, Dave took a right, crossed the bridge over the river and navigated the winding Forest Service roads for several miles before coming to a cattle guard and locked gate, which marks the boundary between the national forest and the private land where our water system is located.

Hopping out of the truck, I grabbed a Coors Light out of the cooler, opened it and took a healthy swig. I handed Dave a Hamm's and grabbed the key ring off the dash to unlock the gate. Dave sipped his beer as he watched me, fumbling with the large set of keys, trying to find the one that would open the gate.

"Do you need your glasses, Cramps? It's the small brass key. Bring the keys here, and I'll find it for you."

I placed my beer down on the ground on the side of the dirt road near the cattle guard and looked back at Dave. "I don't need your help. You've just got so many keys on this ring that it's hard to find the right one."

"I have a lot of cars."

"Yeah, but most of them are junk, like the rust buckets that have been between our houses for years. They have weeds growing out of them, and a skunk was even living in one of them last year!"

"Only for about a month or so," Dave protested. "Those vehicles are priceless."

"Yeah, I guess. Maybe if the price of scrap metal skyrockets, you'll make a fortune. OK, I found the key."

As I unlocked the gate and swung it open, Dave purposely drove toward the edge of the road and ran over the beer I had placed on the ground before crossing the cattle guard.

"You asshole, that beer was nearly full."

Dave laughed heartily. "Well, then you shouldn't have left it on the road. I guess you won't make that mistake again. Oh wait, that's right. You probably will. You know what they say. You can't teach an old dog new tricks."

Picking up the crushed can, I threw it in the bed of the truck and grabbed another beer out of the cooler before getting back in the vehicle. Shaking my head, I asked, "Why do you have to be such an asshole?"

"Because I'm good at it."

"Just drive. Let's get this over with."

As we approached the water system, the sound of rushing water increased in volume, and even before Dave stopped the truck, I knew we had reached our destination. Dave looked out his window and said, "There's not as much water running into the sediment tank at this time of the year as there should be. We've definitely got something partially plugging the intake."

Opening his door, Dave looked at Roscoe and said, "Stay here, old man." He then looked at me with a smirk on his face and said, "Not you, Cramps. I was talking to Roscoe."

"You're about as funny as Henny Youngman."

"Who?"

"You know, the comedian. The master of the one-liner: Take my wife, please."

Dave looked confused. "I don't get it."

"It's before your time. You're like the kids today. You think the history of the world started when you were born."

"It did for me. I wasn't born in 1955 B.C. like you."

I exited the truck, grabbed my shovel and walked to the fence, which kept elk and cattle from defecating in our water. As I undid the wires that held the gate in place, I looked at my surroundings and appreciated the beauty of the scene.

Water cascaded down the steep, rocky slope amid a stand of bigleaf maples and western hemlock before collecting in a small holding pond behind a manmade dam. The understory was dominated by salmonberry, and there was a blanket of moss-covered logs and large rocks with oxalis, maidenhair, sword and bracken ferns, competing for the muted light that made it to the forest floor.

At the bottom of the holding pond was an eight-inch PVC pipe. A steel screen box covered the opening, but leaves, sticks and rocks, over time, had collected in the pool around the perimeter of the protective screen, reducing the volume of water entering the pipe.

The large volume of water flooding over the dam flowed into a culvert, which passed under the road and eventually plummeted down the steep bank to the river below.

The water that entered our water system traveled for thirty feet in the pipe before being deposited into a sediment tank covered by a triangular, quarter-inch mesh screen. About half way up the tank, a four-inch pipe carried the partially-filtered water under the road where it eventually connected to a three and a half-inch seamless pipe that carried the water across the river to the main line feeding our homes.

Dave and I gingerly scaled the slippery rocks to the holding pond and cleaned out the leaves, sticks and stones that had settled in the pond and were blocking our intake pipe. When these were removed, we used our shovels to dig out the larger rocks that had worked their way down the hill and were filling up the pond.

Once we had the pond clear and the water flowing as fast as possible, we made our way back to the truck. While Dave put our shovels in the bed of his vehicle and got us two beers from the cooler, I secured the gate. Once we were both in the truck, Dave grabbed his phone off the dash and said, "There's a text from Chloe."

"How can you get a text up here?" I asked. "My cell doesn't work up here."

"Who's your provider?"

"Verizon," I answered.

"Well, that's why. AT&T owns the nearest cell tower to our house. Verizon can't use it. Get either AT&T or Consumer Cellular, which has access to their network." Dave turned his attention back to his phone. As he read the message, his face darkened suddenly. "Did you see yesterday's *News-Times?*"

"No. Why?"

"The lead story is that the Sheriff's Office is asking for the public's help in solving a string of homicides, including Harlan's and Ryder's murders."

"So we're looking at a serial killer?"

"Looks like it."

Thrusting my arms forward and then pulling them back toward my sides, I did my best Al Pacino impression and said, "Just when I thought I was out, they pull me back in!"

Dave looked at me quizzically. "Who was that supposed to be?"

"You know, Al Pacino as Michael Corleone in *The Godfather, Part III.*"

Dave burst out laughing. "You sounded more like Tony Montana in *Scarface.*" Doing his own impression of Pacino, he said, "Say hello to my little friend."

Shaking my head in disdain, I said, "My Al Pacino was better."

Dave shrugged his shoulders. "Whatever. We both sucked. Just drink your beer. Let's get home and find out what else the Sheriff's Office had to say about these unsolved murders."

NINETEEN

When Dave and I got back to his house, we unloaded his truck and headed for the garage. Chloe was in Dave's recliner, smoking a Marlboro red. Dave took two Hamm's out of his fridge and offered me one.

Before accepting it, I asked, "Are you sure I don't have a Coors Light in there? I think I left a couple in there a few days ago."

Chloe piped up. "I drank them last night. I ran out of Modelo."

Dave chuckled. "Thanks to Chloe, it looks like you have to have a real beer."

I grudgingly grabbed the beer out of his hand. "I guess it's better than nothing."

Laughing, Chloe grabbed the newspaper off her lap. "You guys are like little kids. Do you want to hear the news or not?"

Shaking our heads affirmatively, Dave and I opened our beers and sat down on the sofa next to the wood stove while Chloe held the newspaper in front of her and read aloud. "The Lincoln County Sheriff's Office held a news conference today, asking for the public's help in finding a serial killer who murdered four people in South Lincoln County over the last two years. Despite multiple investigations, detectives have been unable to find the suspect responsible for the killings.

The following cases were identified as being related:

Victim 1: Tommy De Silva, a 27-year-old white male, who was shot to death on July 26, 2014.

Victim 2: Harlan Gannet, a 64-year-old white male, who had his throat severed on May 15, 2015.

Victim 3: Ryder Driscoll, a 63-year-old white male, who was poisoned in his home on October 18, 2015.

Victim 4: Lenny Scott, a 45-year-old white male, who died of chloramine gas poisoning and hypothermia, on December 23, 2015."

Chloe became excited and stopped reading. She took the last drag off her cigarette and threw the butt in the wood stove. "I recognize that last name. He's the guy who was arrested for abusing horses up on Five Rivers. When he didn't show up for his court case in January, the cops went to his house and found him dead in a water trough filled with horse shit."

"Is that all that the newspaper article says?" I asked.

"No, there's more." Continuing to read aloud, she said, "A spokesperson for the Sheriff's Office has confirmed that all of the slayings occurred within a twenty-five-mile radius along the Alsea River. When asked whether the four cases were forensically linked, the spokesman for the Sheriff's Office declined to comment. Anyone with information on any of these cases is encouraged to call the Lincoln County Sheriff's Office at (541) 867-blah-blah-blah-blah. A reward of $5,000 is offered for information leading to the arrest and prosecution of the person responsible for these murders. Callers may remain anonymous."

Dave's eyes got big. "Wow, so the killer has stepped up his frequency of attacks. He killed one victim in 2014 and then three in the last seven months of the past year. His success has emboldened him. He thinks he can't be caught."

"Or the sick mother fucker is really getting off on killing and can't wait that long to get his jollies," I responded. "Either way, he's got to be stopped."

Chloe said, "There's another possibility to explain the increased frequency of his attacks. The first two murders all occurred in the late spring and summer. The last two occurred in October and December. What if the killer had originally been just a seasonal visitor to the coast, and then, this last year, finally moved here and became a full-time resident? It would explain the seasonal discrepancy between the early and most recent attacks and why the frequency of killings has increased."

"It makes sense," I said, "but we really don't know enough about the individual murders to make an informed decision on which of these scenarios, if any, is correct or if it's some weird combination of all of these." I jumped off the sofa and said, "I'm going home to get on my computer and research the two murders I don't know anything about. The original newspaper accounts will tell me a lot more about each case than what was provided in that article Chloe read."

"Oh good, you're leaving," Dave said. Holding up his empty beer can, he added, "Since you're getting up, can you get me another beer before you go?"

Shaking my head, I opened the fridge, grabbed a can of Hamm's out of the box and threw it to him. "Hopefully, I shook it up enough that you'll get a beer shower when you open it up."

"You're a dick!"

As I went out the door laughing, I retorted, "That's what I like, recognition!"

TWENTY

When I got home, I ran upstairs and got on my computer. I obviously didn't need to research Harlan's and Ryder's deaths since I was unfortunate enough to have firsthand knowledge of their murders. I googled the one killing which had occurred after theirs, and found out what Chloe had said was accurate. Lenny Scott had been arrested for animal abuse and was scheduled to go to court in January of 2016. When he didn't show up, the police went to his house and found him tied up and dead in a stock trough outside his barn. Chemical analysis determined that the trough had been filled with bleach and horse manure, and the Oregon State Medical Examiner's Office ruled that the cause of death was chloramine gas poisoning and hypothermia.

I then researched the first slaying which had occurred before my two neighbors were killed. I learned that Tommy De Silva was a level three sex offender, who had been found guilty of first degree rape and kidnapping of a minor. He had served his time and was no longer on supervision when he moved to the Central Oregon Coast. As required by law, the Sheriff's Office notified the public through newspaper articles and their website that this predatory sex offender had moved into the area. Within a month of the community notification, I found this article in the Newport *News-Times* dated July 30, 2014:

Man Found Dead on Tidewater Road

Tommy De Silva, a 27-year-old convicted level three sex offender, who had only recently moved to Lincoln County from Idaho, was found dead at the gravel rock quarry, which is located approximately ten miles up Tidewater Road. A local resident, who went to the quarry to sight in his rifle, found the victim and called 911. According to this witness, the victim's body was propped up against the quarry wall and his hands were tied behind his back. There was a bullseye paper target taped to his chest with three bullet holes near the center of the shooting target.

Just then, Spencer ran up the steps. "Hey, Uncle G, I was listening to music with my headphones on and didn't hear you get home. Did you guys fix the water problem? Can I take a shower now?"

"Yes, it's fixed. Do you want me to make you something to eat?"

"No, I already ate lunch. I'm gonna take a quick shower. My buddy Joe will be here in a half hour to pick me up. We're going to the skate park in Waldport and then to his house to play some video games. Is it OK if I stay over his place tonight?"

"Yes, as long as his parents are fine with that." I opened my wallet and handed him a twenty. "Get something for you and Joe to eat after you're done boarding."

Bounding down the stairs, he yelled. "Thanks, Uncle G."

I remember when I had that much energy. When you're young, you take your vitality for granted and really don't appreciate what you have until you're old and it's gone. Rubbing my sore back, I thought wistfully, *I wish I could have bottled up that pep I used to have in my step and uncork it like a fine wine and savor it today.*

Turning my attention back to my laptop, I looked at the screen and considered what I had learned through my research. One of the victims was a convicted sex offender and another was charged with animal abuse. Harlan was universally hated for his penchant for sticking his nose in other people's business and trying to californicate the Alsea. What was Ryder's crime?

I thought back to the Halloween party and realized that the locals' animosity was clearly directed at Harlan alone. No one even mentioned Ryder by name. His only offense was guilt by association: he was Harlan's buddy.

It made no sense…unless the killer viewed his victims as throwaways, people who nobody cared about and whose murders would soon be forgotten. If this was the case, then it would explain why the killer targeted Ryder for death.

Since no one liked Harlan, it was only natural to assume that no one would lose any sleep over his demise. But Ryder started asking questions. He was a devoted and loyal friend. To him, Harlan wasn't a throwaway. He wasn't going to rest until Harlan's killer had been brought to justice. He was like a bad rash that wouldn't go away. If Ryder was eliminated, there would be no one to keep stirring the pot, and Harlan's death would soon become a distant memory.

While this, I thought, was the most likely explanation to account for Ryder's murder, I realized that there was another explanation that could also account for the slayings of the other victims. It was conceivable that the murderer saw himself as an avenging angel, a vigilante who took the law into his own hands to ensure that his victims received the punishment he believed they deserved. The prospect that this deranged killer saw himself as both judge and jury scared the hell out of me, and I shuddered at the thought.

TWENTY-ONE

I was on my hands and knees on my front lawn, teaching Spencer how to set mole traps when a beat up, bone-colored VW bus sputtered into my driveway. As I got up and started to approach the van, a tall, thinly built man with bristly, jet black hair got out of the vehicle. The lenses of his thick rim glasses magnified his large amber eyes, giving him an owl-like appearance. He wore a grey, herringbone striped topcoat over a tie-dyed T-shirt and blue jeans. I pegged him as a Deadhead and guessed he was in his early-to-mid-thirties.

"Can I help you?"

Handing me his business card, the man said, "Good morning, Mr. Riker. I'm Mason Fowler, a reporter with the *News-Times*. As you probably know, the Sheriff's Office is asking for the public's help in finding what they believe is a serial killer. I know you found two of the victims, and I'd like to ask you some questions if you've got the time."

"You're a little late, aren't you? That was months ago. I'm not interested in talking to the press. I've already told the police everything I know."

I turned away, intent on returning to my task at hand, but Mason followed me across the lawn. Raising his voice and speaking rapidly, he begged, "Please, just give me a few minutes. I have reason to believe the same serial killer is responsible for another murder the Sheriff's Office did not include in the list they released to the press. I promise I won't take up much of your time."

Turning back to face him, I asked, "You think there's another cold case they haven't reported?"

"Yes...well, no. The Sheriff's Office doesn't consider it a cold case. They nailed someone for this murder, but I've always thought that the guy who was convicted was framed." Becoming animated, he said, "Look, if you give me some time, I'll explain."

Spencer looked up at me and said, "I think I've got this, Uncle G."

Patting my nephew on the back, I said, "I know you do. I'll be back to help you as soon as I can."

I let out a heavy sigh and gestured to the reporter to follow me to the front door. "Let's go inside. I'll make a pot of coffee."

Mason followed me into the house, and I motioned for him to take a seat at the breakfast nook. Once I had the coffee brewing, I joined him.

"So tell me about the case you think should be included in the string of homicides the cops think are the work of a serial killer."

"The victim was a lowlife named Shane Hartlett, who, after he was murdered, was allegedly found to be a drug dealer. He had his skull bashed in with a tire iron."

"You said somebody was arrested and convicted of the crime."

"Yes, a kid named Dane Hutchinson. He had been Waldport High's star quarterback and had just graduated."

"I don't follow high school sports, but that name sounds familiar."

"It should. He took us to the state championship his senior year. He was a hell of an athlete."

"So why do you know so much about this case?"

"I was a cub reporter for the paper when Hartlett was killed in 2010. After his body was found, the cops searched his home and found evidence that he was making meth and selling it and other illegal drugs to high school kids. I'm sure the murder of a drug dealer looked like a nonstory to my boss, so he assigned the case to me. Then the cops arrested Waldport's 'Golden Boy' for the murder, and it became big news overnight. It was my chance to make a name for myself."

"Now that you mention it, I do remember reading about the trial in the paper, but that was a while ago. Tell me more about the case."

"A cyclist found Hartlett's body in the marsh off North May Road in Drift Creek and called it in. The guy who found the body said the victim was lying face down in the marsh about ten feet off the road and that he had a big gash in the back of his head.

I did a short article on the murder, and after it appeared in the paper, the Sheriff's Office got an anonymous call from someone who supposedly saw the victim's Subaru Outback and an older model, red Toyota pickup parked at the scene of the crime at roughly the same time that the murder was committed.

The caller said the Toyota was pretty beat up and that the right rear quarter panel was badly pitted with coast cancer. He also reported that there was a purple W sticker affixed to the middle of the rear window of the cab. Long story short, Hutchinson drove a rusty, red '91 Toyota pickup. He had received a scholarship to play football for the University of Washington Huskies starting in the fall and had a purple W sticker on his back window."

"That sounds pretty incriminating. So did the cops find anything when they searched his vehicle?"

"The cops found nothing inside the truck, but when they looked under the bed, they noticed a piece of clothing hanging down from where the spare tire is located. When they lowered the spare and pulled it out, they found a bloody tire iron wrapped in a U Dub sweatshirt in the center of the wheel. The blood on the tool was subsequently determined to be Hartlett's."

"Sounds like an open and shut case to me."

"Initially, you'd think that, but there's more to the story."

Just then, the coffee maker sputtered. I got up, grabbed two mugs out of the cupboard and filled them with joe. "How do you like your coffee?"

"Just black, thanks."

Handing Mason his cup, I returned to my seat. "So why do you think Hutchinson was framed?"

"There are several reasons. First among them is the questionable veracity of the person from the Sheriff's Office who was the first one to arrive at the crime scene and the first to search Hutchinson's vehicle. It was Deputy Sheriff Darby."

"He was the officer who investigated both murder scenes I was involved in, and we butted heads on our second go round. He was only too eager to assume I was the killer."

"And I think it was the same way here. He was new to the force, and he wanted to impress his superiors."

"So you think he planted the evidence?"

"I have no proof, but it's certainly a possibility. I've known him since elementary school, and he's been a bully for as long as I've known him. I'm sure becoming a cop was the realization of his biggest wet dream."

"I'll admit I don't like the guy. He walks around like he has a stick up his ass. But I have a hard time believing he'd send an innocent kid to prison just to advance his career. You said you had a few reasons for believing Hutchinson was framed. What else do you have?"

"The tire iron they found in Hutchinson's vehicle had the drug dealer's blood on it, but it didn't have Hutchison's fingerprints or DNA on it and neither did the U Dub sweatshirt it was wrapped in. The sweatshirt looked like it was brand new and never worn. Doesn't it seem strange that the kid would take such pains to make sure he left no forensic evidence behind at the crime scene that could incriminate him and then be so careless as to leave the murder weapon with his victim's blood in his truck?"

Taking a swig of coffee, I agreed, "Yeah, that does seem odd, but there's also the witness's testimony that identifies the vehicle at the crime scene as being Hutchinson's."

"No, there was no testimony under oath. Remember, I said the cops got an anonymous tip. The identity of the caller was never established. Without a credible witness, the cops knew they didn't have enough probable cause to get a warrant. Instead they went to Hutchinson and told him a crime had been committed and asked for his consent to search his vehicle. The cops got lucky, and he agreed."

"If Hutchinson knew he had the murder weapon stashed in his spare tire why would he do that?"

"That's my point exactly. A guilty person would have refused and told the cops to get lost. Once they had the murder weapon, they had probable cause and got a warrant to search his home. The cops found nothing in the house that was incriminating."

"So, other than the anonymous tip, there was no other evidence linking Hutchinson to the murder besides the bloody tire iron?"

Mason grimaced. "There was one other bit of incriminating evidence. When Darby searched Hartlett's body, he found a burner phone in his pocket. It included the names and numbers of middle and high school students from Waldport. Hutchinson's name was among them. At the trial, Hutchinson admitted that he had bought cocaine from Hartlett on occasion but denied meeting him on the day he was murdered."

"What did the cops find when they checked the phone log on Hartlett's cell?"

"Hartlett made no calls on the day he was murdered. The only entry in his phone log that day was a call he received just one hour before he was murdered. The call lasted only about a minute. The cops traced the number to a pay phone outside the convenience store near Eckman Lake. They think this was the call that set up the meeting at the marsh."

I was incredulous. "A call from a phone booth, are you kidding me?"

Mason laughed. "I know. I had the same reaction. Trust me. I checked. There was still a phone booth there at the time."

"So the cops are portraying this as a drug deal that went bad."

Mason nodded. "Yep, that's it exactly."

"Did Hutchinson have an alibi for the afternoon the murder was committed?"

"He said he was up Boundary Road in the Siuslaw National Forest doing hill training. He claimed it was part of his normal workout routine."

"And, of course, no one happened to see him up there," I added.

"No, he said he didn't see anyone the whole time he was out there."

Shaking my head, I argued, "It's not much of an alibi if it can't be corroborated by someone else."

"I know, but it doesn't prove he's not telling the truth either. I think there were enough unanswered questions in the prosecutor's argument that a good defense lawyer could have convinced a jury that there was enough reasonable doubt to get him acquitted. Hutchinson was dirt poor. His mom was a single parent who worked as a waitress in a greasy spoon in Newport and could barely pay the rent and keep her three kids fed. She was a loving mother, but there was no way she could afford to pay for a good criminal lawyer to represent her oldest son."

"So, who did the court appoint to defend him?"

"Quentin Tenpenny."

"Tenpenny is a hack."

"Exactly, he was way over his head with this case. There was no way he was going to take the time or had the expertise needed to give the kid a credible defense. He actually tried to convince Hutchinson to take a plea deal, but the kid refused. Hutchinson always maintained his innocence and still does to this day."

"OK, so now I know the murder you think should be included in the string of homicides the cops say are the work of a serial killer, but I don't know why."

"I've answered a lot of your questions. Before I respond, can I ask you a few questions first?"

After taking a gulp of my coffee, I said, "That's fair. Shoot."

"What condition was Harlan Gannet in when you first found him?"

Trying to be provocative, I said, "His throat was slit from ear to ear, and his body was being torn apart by a group of turkey vultures."

Mason was unfazed by my answer. After jotting down something in his notepad, he looked up at me and said, "I knew what your answer was going to be, but I wanted to hear it from you to confirm it. Shane Hartlett was being fed upon by vultures when the cops arrived. The same is true of Tommy De Silva, the first victim the Sheriff's Office cites as being the work of the serial killer. And now, as you've just confirmed, Harlan Gannet was number three. Don't you find that strange?"

"I do, but I'm not in the habit of finding dead bodies, so I wouldn't know," I countered.

"Come on, take your blinders off! You're a zoologist, for Christ's sake! You think that this is what the authorities find every time a dead body is found in the woods?"

"Look, it makes sense that turkey vultures would be the first scavengers to arrive on the scene," I argued. "They soar high above the ground, so they would be the first to locate a dead organism in the open, and they have keen eyesight and an amazing sense of smell."

"Thank you, Captain Obvious. And do most killers leave their victims in the open or do most try to hide them or bury them so they'll never be found?"

"Obviously, the latter." Getting my back up, I said, "Hell! I don't know! I'm not a cop or a serial killer! How do I know if what you're saying is true? I haven't seen anything about this in the newspaper."

"Was there anything in the paper about the vultures feeding on Gannet when you found him?"

"No."

"No, of course not. It's not the kind of information that authorities typically share with the public. I've lived in Newport all my life, have been a reporter for eight years, and have reliable sources in the Sheriff's Office. Trust me. I know what I'm talking about."

"OK, you made your point. You said you had several questions for me. What else do you want to know?"

"When you found Ryder's body, where was he?"

"In his living room."

"So, obviously, no vultures were involved in this case."

"No. Of course not," I snapped.

Mason could see that I was losing patience with this line of questioning. "Bear with me. I'm just trying to make a point. And no vultures were involved in the last murder either. Can you think of any reason why the murderer changed his MO?"

"Refresh my memory," I said. "Give me the dates the murders occurred and how the victims were killed."

Mason leafed back through his notebook. Reading aloud, he said, "Shane Hartlett – blunt force trauma, June 3, 2010; Tommy De Silva – hanged, July 26, 2014; Harlan Gannet – throat severed, May 15, 2015; Ryder Driscoll – poisoned, October 18, 2015; and Lenny Scott – chloramine gas poisoning and hypothermia, December 23, 2015."

After taking a long time to mull over the information, I replied, "I don't think you can say the killer had an MO. There's a four-year gap between the murder you think is connected and the first one the cops say is the work of the serial killer they're looking for. If my math is right, the murders the cops think are connected all occurred within about a year and a half. All of the people murdered were eliminated in different ways. But I can tell you why only the first three victims were being fed upon by vultures when they were found. Turkey vultures are migratory birds. They typically arrive here in late February or early March and leave in late September. The birds weren't here when the last two victims were killed."

"I didn't know that, but it makes sense. Anything else you can think of off the top of your head?"

"Yes. I believe Ryder Driscoll died of tetrodotoxin poisoning."

"How do you know this?" Mason asked. "The cops reported that he was poisoned, but they never stated publicly what the poison was."

"After I found Ryder's body, the sheriff asked me what I knew about rough-skinned newts. I've done research on them and know they are extremely poisonous. Their skin secretes a powerful neurotoxin called tetrodotoxin. I figured the only reason Whittaker would bring this up is if Ryder was killed by being fed these newts. So I assumed the cause of death was tetrodotoxin poisoning."

Mason smiled. "You don't disappoint. You've already made my trip here worthwhile."

"OK, so now I've answered your questions, and it's time for you to tell me why you think Shane Hartlett was murdered by the serial killer the cops are looking for."

Mason smiled broadly. "I only have one compelling reason."

"And what would that be?"

"I believe Harlan Gannet was killed because he shared my view that Hutchinson was framed and that he was getting close to finding out who the real killer was."

"You knew Harlan?"

"Yes. He was the one who initially contacted me. He said he was a retired investigative reporter, who had learned about Hartlett's murder and wanted to write a book about the case. He saw it as a local version of the O.J. Simpson trial, a football hero who falls from grace and becomes a killer. He said he had read my articles covering the trial and asked if I'd meet with him to share what I knew about the case. I agreed, and we hit it off."

I couldn't hide my excitement. "His housemate, Ryder, told me before he died that Harlan had found a local murder case he wanted to write a book about. But Ryder had given me the impression that Harlan thought the subject of his book was guilty of the crime."

"Yes, at first he did. But after he and I had talked a while, he came around to my way of thinking. He eventually believed the kid was framed, and he started doing his own research."

"Wow! That's the kind of story a tabloid journalist like Harlan would die for. It's starting to make perfect sense now."

I could see by the look on his face that Mason was irritated by my comment.

"You can think what you like about Harlan's style of journalism," he said. "I admit it's not my cup of tea. It's intrusive and salacious. But give Harlan his due. He was good at what he did. At his urging, I used my contacts in the Sheriff's Office to get additional information on the evidence used in the case against Hutchinson. Remember, I was still wet behind the ears when I initially covered the case and didn't have those contacts at the time. It was Harlan, who saw something in the evidence that everyone else, including myself, had initially overlooked and that could have possibly been used to raise reasonable doubt and ultimately vindicate Hutchinson at trial."

"And what was that?"

"Remember the tire iron which was supposedly found in Hutchinson's truck with the victim's blood on it?"

"Of course."

"Well, that tire iron was for a vehicle with 7/8" lug nuts, which would have been a one ton truck. The lug nuts on Hutchinson's '91 Toyota pickup were 13/16ths, so the tire iron found in the spare would have been too big for his truck."

"I admit that's interesting, but it doesn't prove anything. Maybe Hutchinson was more devious than you think. Maybe he thought using a tire iron that didn't fit his truck would lead the jury to question his guilt and lend credence to the theory that he was being framed."

"Yeah, right, the same criminal mastermind who gave the cops permission to search his vehicle when they didn't have probable cause to get a search warrant."

"Did his lawyer bring this information up at trial?"

"No, nobody caught it! At least Tenpenny didn't. If the prosecutor did, he sure as hell wasn't going to bring it up."

"Wow!" Not knowing what else to say, I sat in silence and drank my coffee. I didn't know what to believe. I wasn't ready to admit it just yet, but Mason's arguments were beginning to win me over. I was beginning to consider seriously the premise that Hutchinson may, indeed, have been set up.

I think Mason may have sensed this because he just sipped his coffee and didn't say anything for a while. He let me marinate in my indecision. When he finally spoke, he said, "I believe with all my heart the kid was framed."

"So you think the anonymous caller set him up?"

"I think it makes the most sense. Don't you? Everyone in Waldport knew what Hutchinson drove. The description of the truck the caller provided was very detailed. To me, it was like a neon sign, blinking on and off: HERE'S YOUR KILLER. If it wasn't for the call, the cops would never have zeroed in on Hutchinson."

"Did you and Harlan bring this information to the sheriff's attention?"

"Of course, but as you can imagine, Whittaker was not willing to consider the possibility that his office might have screwed up and inadvertently sent an innocent kid to prison for a murder he didn't commit. You know the sheriff is retiring soon, don't you?"

"Yes, I'm well aware of that."

"Well, Whittaker obviously doesn't want to leave office with his reputation besmirched. The sheriff called my boss at the paper and pressured him to muzzle me. My boss wasn't convinced there was enough evidence to pursue the case and told me to back off. Harlan, however, had no inclination to fall in line. It only made him more dogged in his determination to pursue the case. He started asking teachers and former students what they remembered about Hutchinson and whether they thought he had any enemies who might have had a motive to do him in. It was shortly after this that he was murdered."

"That's very interesting," I said. "In the news conference, asking for the public's help in finding the serial killer, the sheriff's spokesman refused to say whether there was a forensic connection between the murders. After I found Harlan's and Ryder's bodies, Whittaker started looking seriously at me as being his prime suspect. He asked me to give him a DNA sample, which only makes sense if they have the killer's DNA to compare it to. Do you know which crime scene they found the sample at?"

Mason shook his head. "I don't. Look, do you want to work with me on this?"

"I thought you said your boss didn't think there was enough evidence for you to pursue the case."

"Yes. That was before the cops came out asking for the public's help. Now, he's totally on board. There's a $5K reward out for anyone who provides information leading to the arrest of the serial killer."

I laughed. "Yeah, I read that. When Ryder started asking questions, everyone he spoke to clammed up, like they had lock jaw. It will be interesting to see if the reward suddenly loosens some lips."

"So you'll help me?"

"I'll do what I can. I know some of the teachers at the high school because my nephew is a student there. I'll see if I can find out who Harlan talked to about the Hutchinson case. Do you think you can find out from your contacts at which crime scene the cops recovered the killer's DNA?"

"I'll give it a shot." Mason extended his hand. "So we're a team? We're working this story together?"

Grabbing his hand firmly and shaking my head back and forth, I said, "I can't believe I'm saying this. You've convinced me that there's something more here than meets the eye. I'm in, at least for now."

TWENTY-TWO

After Mason left, I went up to my study, fired up my laptop and got on the internet. I googled Shane Hartlett and immediately found the news articles related to his murder. I really didn't learn much that I didn't already know. The only article which provided me with a lot more detail was the one where the authorities searched Hartlett's home after his death and found evidence that he was a drug dealer. It was from the *News-Times'* Friday edition, dated June 11, 2010:

Murder Victim Suspected of Making and Selling Meth

A spokesman for the Lincoln County Sheriff's Office has confirmed that 36-year-old Shane Hartlett, the Waldport man found dead in the marsh off North May Road on June 3rd, was allegedly manufacturing and selling methamphetamine as well as selling other illegal drugs, including heroin and cocaine. When detectives searched his residence at the Bayview Mobile Home Park, they found large amounts of methamphetamine, heroin and cocaine, packaging materials and numerous items associated with an on-going meth manufacturing lab, including cold and asthma medications, Coleman fuel cans, lighter fluid, drain cleaner and a digital scale. Several firearms and over $10,000 in cash were also recovered at the scene.

An autopsy performed by The Oregon State Medical Examiner's Office has confirmed that the cause of death was blunt force trauma. An investigation is currently underway to find Hartlett's killer.

I then brought up the articles from the local paper which dealt with Hutchinson's subsequent arrest and trial. Everything Mason had told me proved to be accurate. It was the anonymous call which led the cops to search Hutchinson's vehicle where they found the tire iron with Hartlett's blood on it, wrapped in a U of W sweatshirt.

At trial, Hutchinson's attorney presented a weak defense which consisted of little more than arguing that his client had been set up and that the evidence found in his vehicle was planted there.

The jury deliberated for five days before arriving at a verdict. In the end, the jury ultimately failed to accept the defense's version of events, and Hutchinson was sentenced to 30 years in jail for the murder of Shane Hartlett.

I sat in front of my computer and stared at the screen. If Mason and Harlan were correct and Hutchinson was innocent, who would have hated him enough to want to frame him for murder? He was only eighteen. He was still a kid. The only thing that made any sense to me was that it had to be a cohort, someone roughly of his same age group, if not a fellow student from Waldport, then maybe someone from a rival school.

I knew my next step was to visit the high school and talk to some of the teachers who were there when Hutchinson was a student. I wanted to find out which of them, if any, had talked to Harlan about the Hutchinson case before he was murdered.

TWENTY-THREE

I contacted the principal of the high school to explain my interest in the Hutchinson murder case and to get her permission to seek interviews with some of her educators. She gave me her blessing with the stipulation that the meetings would have to be arranged with the teachers in advance and could only be conducted after the school day had ended.

I had met a few of my nephew's teachers at a parent-teacher conference earlier in the school year. While I thought our previous meeting would help get me a few minutes of phone time, I knew I'd have to gain their buy-in before they'd agree to actually meet with me. When I called them to set up interviews, I, therefore, explained in detail to each of them why I was revisiting the Hutchinson case now, so many years later, and what my personal connection was to the case.

A few of the educators I contacted said they hadn't been teaching at the high school when Hutchinson was a student there, so I crossed them off my list. Two teachers, however, who had known Hutchinson and had been approached by my neighbor Harlan Gannet, agreed to meet with me.

Spencer's English teacher, Emily Crick, was the first one I interviewed. I knew she had grown up in Waldport and had started teaching at the high school when she was fresh out of college. I chose to meet with her first because my nephew and his friends all thought Miss Crick was cool. If any teacher would have her pulse on what was going on with the student population, I knew it would be her. I thought it was a good place to start.

She was a pistol. In her early thirties, she was tall and very thin with a wiry thatch of fiery red, spiked hair. She looked like a lit match head. Her forearms were heavily tattooed, and she had a small, almost imperceptible, Black Flag tattoo above her right eyebrow. The first time I met her, I had initially thought it was just a beauty mark, but then I realized what it was.

When I walked into her classroom, she had a big stack of papers on her desk and was feverishly marking up the paper that was in front of her.

"Looks like that student is going down in flames," I joked.

"Oh no, not at all! He's one of my best students. I was just writing how much I loved his paper. The project I assigned my students was to take the Oedipus story and to modernize it. They were to write a short play with that theme in a present day setting. The next stage is for my students to act out their creations in class." Laughing, she said, "I can't wait to see what they come up with."

"You're an incredible teacher. My nephew and his friends have told me how much they love your class."

"That's very kind of you to say, but I'm sure you didn't come here to lavish praise on me. How can I help you, Mr. Riker?"

"Please call me Grady. As I explained on the phone, I want to learn more about Dane Hutchinson. Who were his friends? Did he have any enemies? You know, that sort of thing. You've already told me you were teaching here when he was a student. Was he one of your pupils?"

"He was. I had him as a student his senior year."

"Was he a good student?"

"I'd say he was average. He certainly wasn't a shining light scholastically."

"So, a C student basically?"

"Exactly."

"What did you think of him? Did you like him?"

As she considered these questions she bowed her head, and a doleful look came over her face.

"It saddens me when I think of what happened to him. His story is reminiscent of a classical Greek tragedy. He was the hero who falls from grace because of his hubris."

"What do you mean?"

"Hutch had a lot of gifts. He was an incredible athlete and had such promise for a successful career in the NFL. He was also a very handsome young man, who, if he chose to, could charm the socks off you. I don't think there was a girl in school who didn't have a crush on him."

"I would have liked to have had those kinds of problems when I was in school," I joked.

Ignoring my lame attempt at humor, Emily continued. "The problem was that Hutch was all too aware of his assets and loved himself a bit too much. It was his self-obsession which ultimately proved to be his fatal flaw. Hutch liked to brag about his sexual conquests. While I'm sure there were some male students who envied him and liked hearing about his exploits, I know for a fact there were others who took offense to it. He seemed to take particular delight in taunting those students who were obviously smarter than him but were socially challenged. He seemed to get some perverted pleasure in demeaning them for some reason. He called them eggheads and said the fact that they weren't sexually active was a clear sign that they were gay. I had to reprimand him several times for verbally bullying them. His treatment of the female students was equally appalling. He treated them like they were his own personal Baskin and Robbins. He'd court a girl until he got in her pants, and then move on. I spent more than a few afternoons after school, consoling some of the girls in my classes who had dated Hutch, who felt humiliated when he unceremoniously dumped them for his new flavor of the week."

"So it's safe to say there were a lot of students who didn't like him very much."

"Yes. I think that's accurate."

"He must have had some friends."

"As you'd expect, he hung around with the other jocks on the football team. How close they were, I can't say."

"When we spoke on the phone, I explained that my neighbor, Harlan Gannet, believed Hutchinson was framed and was actively trying to prove his innocence when he was murdered. You indicated that he had contacted you."

"Yes, we met. To be honest, I thought he was too aggressive in his questioning. He made it crystal clear he thought Hutch was innocent and was obviously irritated when I wouldn't tell him which of my former students I thought hated Hutch enough to want to frame him."

"Did Harlan explain why he thought Hutchinson was innocent?"

"Yes. He told me everything. He told me the murder weapon was a tire iron that didn't fit Hutch's truck, and he explained how incompetent the defense had been at trial. I told him I thought the evidence he uncovered might be grounds for an appeal, but that I was not going to unjustly accuse any of my former students as being likely suspects in having had a hand in framing Hutch."

"The newspaper reported that when the cops searched the murder victim's residence, they found evidence that he was a drug dealer and was selling meth and other drugs to students at the high school here. At the time, did you think any of your students were taking meth?"

"I thought about that when I first read it in the paper. At the time, I didn't see any physical signs that would have set off any alarm signals."

"No severe weight loss, excessive sweating or hyperactivity?" I asked.

"No, nothing like that. In retrospect, I did see some behavioral changes in a few of my students, but that's normal for this age group."

"What do you mean?"

"At the beginning of the school year, some of my best students were shy and too obsessed with getting good grades."

"I don't understand."

"They had no social life. All they did was study. However, midway through the year, they came out of their academic chrysalis stage and became social butterflies."

"And that's normal?"

"Absolutely! They starting dating, and that's when their priorities changed dramatically. They were still my best students, but they blossomed and were now multi-dimensional. It's what I love best about teaching seniors."

I appreciated her enthusiasm, but I knew I wasn't going to be any more successful than Harlan in getting her to offer up names of likely suspects. I started to plan my exit. "I should let you get back to grading your papers."

"If you haven't done so already," she offered, "you should talk to Brett Benson, the football coach. He can probably provide you with a lot more insight than I can. Have you met Brett?"

"Yes. We met last fall at the parent-teacher conference. He's my next interview. I told him I was meeting you here today after school, and he told me to stop be his office when you and I were through."

"You want me to walk you down to the gym?"

"No need," I responded. "I know where it is. But, I'd like to ask you one more question before I leave, if I may?"

"Certainly."

"You knew Hutch. Do you think he was capable of murder?"

"It's not my position to say. I didn't hear the testimony the jury did, and I'm not a trained psychologist."

"I appreciate that, but you surely followed the trial in the newspaper. I'm just asking for your gut feeling. Knowing him, do you think he was guilty?"

She closed her eyes and contemplated the question. When she opened them, she looked me directly in the eyes and said,

"No, I don't. Given the number of people he had alienated, I think there's a good chance that someone set him up. I just refuse to speculate on who that might have been. Hutch had some growing up to do, but I don't think he was an evil person, certainly not someone who could take another person's life."

TWENTY-FOUR

When I got to the gym, Coach Benson was there to greet me. After shaking his hand, I said, "I hope you haven't been standing here long, waiting for me."

"No, not at all. After you left her office, Miss Crick called me and said that you were on your way over here. I know my office is a little hard to find, so I figured I'd meet you here and eliminate any chance of confusion."

Although he was in his early sixties, Brett Benson was still in relatively good shape for his age. He had a big beer gut, but he was heavily built, and the muscles in his arms and legs were well developed. It was obvious that he still worked out with weights on a regular basis. His head was shaved, and I guessed that this was a calculated move. He was probably going bald and decided shaving off what little hair he still had was better than going for the comb-over option.

He led me to his glass-enclosed office, which was adjacent to the boys' locker room and shower facilities. Gesturing for me to take a seat across the desk from him, he said, "So what do you want to know about Hutch?"

"As his coach, you probably spent more time with him than any other teacher here. What's your take on him?"

"As a football player, he was the best I've ever had the privilege to coach."

"No, I'm sorry. I should have been more specific. What's your take on him as a human being? He was the quarterback who took Waldport to the state championship his senior year, so I'd expect that he'd be universally loved by your student body, but I've heard that's not the case."

"It's true, on the field, he was a hero, but off the field, he had his share of detractors."

"Why do you think that was?"

"On the field, his greatest asset was his confidence. If the opposing team was a couple of touchdowns ahead and we were at a third down and ten-yard situation, he didn't get rattled. He believed so completely in his ability that he made plays happen. He made his teammates believers as well. It worked more than once. We went undefeated that year. Off the field, his confidence translated into cockiness. He had no humility. He seemed to revel in reminding just about everyone how great he was."

"I heard he was a notorious womanizer. Is that true?"

"From what I've heard, he was tapping a new girl every weekend. The problem with that was that some of those girls had boyfriends at the time."

"I imagine that led to a lot of fights."

"Yes. If that was all, I would have overlooked it, but some of those boyfriends were his teammates. It started to cause problems on the field. I started to see a lot of dropped passes that should have been caught. I saw offensive linemen who inexplicably let smaller defensive players get around them to sack Hutch. It became clear to me that some of his teammates were deliberately trying to sabotage him and, in the process, jeopardizing our chance of winning. That's when I stepped in and put a stop to it. I called Hutch into my office and told him in no uncertain terms that I was not going to let his dick get in the way of us winning a football game. I told him if he continued shitting in his own backyard, I'd drop him from the team.

I called a team meeting and basically told all the players the same thing. I said, 'I don't give a rat's ass what your personal feeling is for another player. If you don't back up each other on the field and give a hundred and ten percent, you're gone.' It worked. Hutch stopped hitting on his teammates' girlfriends, and everyone gradually started working together as a team again."

"On the phone, you indicated that you had spoken to my neighbor, Harlan Gannet, shortly before he was murdered."

Nodding his head, he said, "Yes. We talked. I basically told him the same thing I've told you."

"I'm sure you know that the person Hutchinson was convicted of killing was a drug dealer and that the cell phone the cops recovered from the victim included the names and phone numbers of middle and high school students from Waldport. Hutchinson's name was among them. At the time, did you suspect any of your players were taking drugs?"

"Certainly not. I would have recognized the signs if any of my players were taking meth."

"What about other illicit drugs? At trial, Hutchinson admitted to occasionally buying cocaine from the murder victim."

"I read that in the paper. I don't condone drug use, mind you, but I can't say I was shocked by the news. Did you ever experiment with drugs when you were in school, Mr. Riker?"

"In college, I smoked pot and tried some other drugs as well."

"Did you ever snort coke?"

"Yes."

"Did you like it?"

"I liked it too much. It made me feel like Superman."

"Why did you stop using it, if you don't mind me asking?"

"I was lying in bed late one night, after snorting a bunch of lines, and my heart started fibrillating. It scared the hell out of me."

The coach laughed. "I appreciate your candor. I experimented with drugs when I was in college too. I'm guessing you are a few years younger than me, but that we're close to the same age. Do you remember what it was like being eighteen?"

"Yeah, I was in excellent shape physically and had an over-abundance of energy."

"You look like you still work out."

"Yes, but it's a constant battle. I do it to maintain my muscle mass, but each year, I notice myself losing ground."

"Exactly, when you were eighteen, you could just look at a set of weights and bulk up. It's no wonder kids think they are invincible. The sad fact is that kids grow up a lot faster today. Some start experimenting with drugs when they're still in grade school. So, was I disappointed to learn Hutch was using cocaine on a recreational basis? Of course. He was an incredible athlete, and I held him to a higher standard, probably unfairly so. Was I surprised? No, not at all."

"I know this is a difficult question for you to answer, but I have to ask it. Do you think the jury got it right? Do you think Hutch was guilty?"

Without batting an eye, Benson said unequivocally, "No. No way in hell! I knew the kid probably better than anyone else on the staff here. Yeah, he was an arrogant prick at times, but he wasn't a killer."

"I know you said Hutch had his share of detractors, but can you think of someone in particular who might have hated him enough to want to frame him for murder?"

Benson shrugged his shoulders. "Who can say? Like I said, Hutch was an equal opportunity offender. It could have been anybody."

"On the afternoon the murder was committed, Hutchinson claimed he was up Boundary Road doing hill training. He said it was part of his normal workout routine. As his coach, does that ring true to you?"

"Absolutely. Hutch had a strict five-day workout regimen that he followed religiously. Hill running was part of his routine, and he did it on Tuesdays and Thursdays every week, rain or shine."

"So his workout schedule was common knowledge. If some-one wanted to frame him they'd know when he'd be in the woods alone on one of his hill workouts and less likely to have an alibi that could be verified by someone else."

"Yes, I suppose so."

"I've been told that Harlan Gannet, in addition to talking to a few teachers, also interviewed some former students who were Hutch's classmates. Did he happen to mention anyone to you who he had talked to or was interested in questioning?"

"No. Not that I can recall."

I started to get up when he added, "No, wait. He did ask me about Vic Dyer. He said he wanted to talk to him."

Sitting back down, I asked, "Who's Vic Dyer?"

"Vic was our standout wide receiver. He was Hutch's best friend before they had a falling out."

"What caused the rift between them?"

"Vic found out Hutch was screwing his girlfriend, Sydney Westlake, and that was the end of their relationship. Even after Hutch dropped Sydney, he and Vic were never the same again."

"But you said you had a come-to-Jesus meeting with the team and that Hutch stopped hitting on his teammates' girlfriends."

"Yeah, during football season. Once football was over, Hutch went back to his old ways. That's when he started hitting on Sydney."

"So you think Harlan was looking at Dyer as a likely suspect?"

"He never came out and said so specifically, but that's the only thing that makes any sense to me. Love and hate are both extreme emotions. When you go from love to hate, that's a powerful motivator."

"Do you know if Dyer still lives in this area?"

"Yes, he went to Notre Dame but got injured and couldn't play football anymore. He lost his scholarship and dropped out of school. He works for his dad now, who owns Dyer Builders, a construction company specializing in custom homes and remodels here in Waldport."

I pulled out the notepad and pen I had in my back pocket and jotted down the information.

"Do you know if Sydney still lives in the area or if she got married?"

"I don't have a clue."

I struggled to hide my excitement. I didn't know how good it was, but I finally had my first lead.

"I'd like to look at a copy of the 2010 yearbook, the year Hutch graduated from high school, so I can put names to faces. I don't know the school librarian. Would you be willing to introduce me to her?"

"I could certainly do that, but there's really no need if the only reason you want to meet her is to see a copy of the yearbook. I've got copies for every year I've been teaching at the school. I'll let you borrow mine as long as you promise to return it."

Coach Benson went to his bookshelf and pulled out the yearbook. Handing it to me, he said, "You're welcome to keep this as long as you like, but please return it when you're through. I'd hate to have my set broken up."

"I understand totally. Books are important to me. One of my pet peeves is loaning books to friends and never getting them back. I promise I'll return it."

We shook hands, and I left the school. I couldn't wait to get home and peruse the yearbook.

TWENTY-FIVE

When I got home, I poured myself a glass of merlot and took it and the yearbook up to my study. Sitting down at my desk, I sipped my wine and started to examine the yearbook. I went to the index at the back of the book first to find out where I could find pictures of the varsity football team.

Pages 122-126 were devoted to the 2009 football season. A team photo of the twenty-seven players, seated in three rows, stretched across the first two pages. The caption below the picture identified each player. I scanned the names, looking for Dane Hutchinson and Vic Dyer. I had no way of knowing whether their placement in the photo was just happenstance or deliberate, but they were seated on opposite ends of the first row of players.

On the last two pages, there were a couple of shots of the coaches, but the rest of the photos were of players in action on the field. One showed offensive linemen opening a hole so Hutch could run down the middle for a first down. Another was of Hutch releasing a forward pass. There were several pictures of defensive players making tackles, one of the placekicker kicking a field goal and one of Vic Dyer running into the end zone for a touchdown.

I then located the couple of pages which featured the school's cheerleaders. The first page was devoted solely to the eight varsity cheerleaders, the last page to the J.V. squad. Since Sydney Westlake had dated both Hutch and Dyer, I thought it likely she might be a cheerleader. My hunch was correct. Her name was among those listed under the varsity team's photo. She was the team's captain.

Sydney was a knockout. Of average height, she was athletically slim, but with just the right amount of muscle mass to give her a sexy physique. Her silky black hair fell easily down to her shoulders, and her skin was flawless. I wondered if she was still as attractive today as when this photo was taken.

Next, I shifted my focus to the main body of the yearbook, which featured the individual photos of each member of the senior class presented in alphabetical order by last name. Below each person's name were the sports or extracurricular activities they had engaged in as well as their interests/hobbies and future career goals.

I was interested in learning who Hutch's contemporaries were. Having lived in the area for some time, I hoped I'd recognize a few people I knew at least casually. I thought they'd be the most likely to agree to meet with me to talk about Hutch.

As I leafed through the first few pages, I didn't recognize anyone and was starting to think this exercise was a waste of time. All that changed when I got to the D's. I looked at the photo in front of me and knew immediately who it was even before I read the name. I'd recognize that nose anywhere. It was Jacob Dietrich, the young mechanic who works for my neighbor Dave. Below his picture, was the caption: Girls...Muscle Cars...Fishing.

I assumed that Jacob and Darwin, my neighbor's other mechanic, were roughly the same age, but I didn't know whether they had been in the same graduating class. I knew Darwin's last name was Nettles. I jumped ahead to the N's and found his picture. Under the photo it read: Good times... Toyotas rule... Future Auto Mechanic.

Since both these guys spent a lot of their free time, working on their cars in my neighbor's garage, I thought they'd answer my questions candidly, and I couldn't wait to see what they had to say about Hutch and his relationship with Dyer.

TWENTY-SIX

The next day, I drove to Dave's shop to talk to Jacob and Darwin. Not wanting to disrupt their work, I arrived at closing time with the yearbook under my arm and a six-pack of Hamm's beer in hand. Dave was just locking up the place when I walked in.

"What are you doing here, Cramps?"

A few days earlier, I had told Dave I was planning on going to the high school to interview teachers about the Hutchinson case, so little explanation was necessary.

"I met with a few teachers at the high school yesterday and got a copy of the yearbook for the year Hutch graduated. I found out that Jacob and Darwin were classmates of his. I want to talk to them to see if they can shed any new light on the case."

Dave looked at the six-pack I was carrying. "And the beer is an inducement for them to stick around after work to talk to you?"

"Pretty much."

"Well, they are both in the last bay installing a new exhaust system on a customer's rig. I think they'll be more than happy to quit for the day and have a beer. Having to deal with you, however, is another matter. I don't know if you've brought enough beer for that."

"Why do you always have to be such an ass?"

"I don't know. I guess you just bring out the best in me."

120

Ignoring his comment, I said, "Can I go in the back to talk to them?"

Dave laughed. "Yeah, let's go, old man."

When we got to where they were working, Jacob and Darwin had just finished for the day and were lowering the garage door.

"If you can stick around for a few minutes," Dave said, "Sherlock Homeless over here would like to ask you a few questions. Before you run for the door, you should know he has beer."

I pulled four cans from the plastic six-pack ring and placed the remaining two in the mini-fridge under the work counter.

Passing out the beers, I said, "I'm sure you know that the Sheriff's Office has asked for the public's help in catching a serial killer. There's reason to believe that another homicide may have been the work of the same killer but that the cops may have arrested the wrong person in this case. I'm talking about Dane Hutchinson, who was convicted and is currently serving time for the murder of a drug dealer named Shane Hartlett." Holding up the yearbook, I said, "I just discovered you guys went to high school with Hutchinson. How well did you know him?"

Jacob was the first to answer. "I knew him, but we weren't close. I thought he was an ass."

Darwin agreed. "He was a prick. I had a few classes with him. He mostly hung with the other muscle monkeys from the football team."

"I heard Vic Dyer was his best friend," I said.

Jacob snickered. "For a while, but that didn't last long. Vic found out Hutch was screwing his girlfriend, and that was the end of their bromance."

"You're talking about Sydney Westlake?" I asked.

Jacob nodded. "Yeah, that's right. She was a fox. I can't say I blame Hutch for wanting to tap that."

"So Dyer had a reason to hate Hutch," I said.

"Yeah, so did a lot of people. So what's your point?"

"Maybe Vic set him up."

"That's crazy. How do you come up with this shit?" Jacob

retorted. "Hutch was buying drugs from that creep. The guy probably shorted him, and Hutch got pissed and killed him. He never could control his temper." Looking at his watch, Jacob pounded his beer and stood up. "Look, I gotta go. My girlfriend gets off work in ten minutes, and I have to pick her up. She'll be pissed at me if I'm late."

As Jacob headed out the door, I looked at Darwin to see what he would say.

"Jacob's right," he said. "You're barking up the wrong tree. Hutch wasn't framed. He did the deed. There's no doubt about it." Darwin downed the rest of his beer and tossed the can in the recycle bin in the corner. Standing up, he said, "I've got to go too. There's an '85 Toyota MR2 race car for sale that I've had my eye on. It needs some body work, but I think it's worth the price the owner's asking. I'm going over to talk to him now." As Darwin left, he said, "Thanks for the beer."

I went to the fridge and got the two remaining beers for Dave and I. "Well, that was a waste of time," I observed.

Dave giggled. "What did you expect? They care about themselves. They don't give a shit whether Hutchinson is guilty or not."

"Well, that's a sad commentary on the kids today."

"Oh, I know. Back in your day, everything was hunky-dory."

"Hunky-dory?"

"Yeah, isn't that what they said back in 1955 B.C.?"

"No," I said sarcastically. "We hadn't yet mastered verbal language by then. We were still using physical signs to communicate. Some are still in usage today." Giving him the middle finger, I said, "I think you know what this means."

TWENTY-SEVEN

The following day, I called Dyer Builders and left a message for Vic. Within an hour, he returned my call and said he was on a job site but that he'd be willing to meet with me at his home after work.

I brought the yearbook with me and arrived at his house at six. It was a beautiful home, overlooking the ocean on Highway 101, about midway between Waldport and Newport. Vic's wife greeted me at the door with a toddler in tow. She was an attractive woman with curly blond hair, powder blue eyes and a winning smile, and she was very pregnant. Based on the size of her baby bump, I guessed she was in her third trimester.

"You must be Mr. Riker. I'm Sally, and this is Courtney."

I bent down and smiled at the little girl. "Hello, Courtney, nice to meet you."

The tot turned away from me and hid her face in her mother's leg.

The mother picked up her child, kissed her and laughed. "She's shy. Come in. Vic is expecting you. He's out working on the deck."

I followed her through the living room and out through the sliding glass door that opened on to the deck. Vic was installing wooden benches along the perimeter. He was a tall, good-looking man with short, chestnut colored hair and hazel eyes. You could tell from his physique that he had been in great shape just a few years earlier but was now starting to enjoy his wife's cooking a bit too much. His arms and chest were still well developed, but he was more than a few pounds overweight.

When he saw us, he jumped up and ran to his wife. "I'm sorry, honey. I didn't hear the doorbell. Why don't you lie down and take a load off your feet. I'll make dinner soon and let you know when it's ready."

Looking at me, Sally explained, "The extra weight's been killing my back."

"I understand completely. I'm sorry. I didn't mean to impose."

"Don't be silly. You're fine." Turning away, she said, "I'll leave you men alone so you can talk."

Vic smiled and shook my hand. "It's Grady, right? Would you like a beer?"

"I don't want to take you away from what you're doing. I can come back at a later date if that's more convenient."

"No need. I was getting ready to take a break anyway. I want a beer. How about you?"

"I'd love one."

Vic went into the kitchen and retrieved two beers. Handing one to me, he gestured for me to take a seat next to him and asked, "So how can I help you?"

"On the phone, you said Harlan Gannet had talked to you about the Hutchinson murder case. As you know, he believed Dane Hutchinson was innocent and wrongly convicted. He was contacting teachers and former students shortly before he was killed. I'm trying to find out whether there's any connection between the Hutchinson case and Harlan's murder."

"What's your interest in the case? Are you a detective or a reporter?"

"No. Harlan was my neighbor, and I was the one who found his body. I was also the one who found his housemate, Ryder Driscoll, when he was murdered a few months later. The cops are asking for the public's help in finding the serial killer who murdered them, and I'm just trying to help. I'd really appreciate anything you can tell me about your conversation with Harlan."

"Harlan knew that Hutch and I had been best friends at one time but then had a falling out." Vic took a swig of beer and smirked. "I think he thought I was the one who had framed Hutch."

I tried my best to show no reaction. "I heard your fight was over a girl."

"Sydney Westlake. She was my girlfriend before Hutch started screwing her."

"So your best friend betrayed you. You had every right to hate him."

Vic sipped his beer and snickered. "Oh, trust me, I did, but he ended up getting a taste of his own medicine."

"What do you mean?"

"Sydney started cheating on him and ended up breaking up with him."

"I heard Hutch dumped her."

"Oh, I'm sure that's what he was telling everybody, but I know for a fact it was the other way around. And the best thing about it was that she dumped him just a week before the Senior Prom. He had to scramble to find another date. By then every good-looking babe was already committed to going with someone else. He had no problem fucking a bat-faced chick, but he sure as hell wasn't going to be seen at the big dance with one on his arm."

"So what happened?"

Shaking his head, he said, "I don't know how he did it, but, like a cat, he landed on his feet. Somehow or other he found a pretty girl to be his date."

"Who was she?"

"Hell, that was a long time ago...I don't remember. She wasn't somebody I hung with."

I handed him the yearbook. "If you saw her picture, would it jog your memory?"

"I don't know...maybe." Vic started to leaf through the photos of the senior class. It didn't take long. "Yeah, that's her, Stacey Atwood. Look at that peach! There's no way she didn't have a date for the Prom when Hutch hit her up. I think she ditched whoever she was supposed to go with when she got a better offer."

"Do you know if she still lives in the area?"

Shaking his head, Vic replied, "No, she's deceased. She died in a car accident a few months after we graduated. It happened when she was home from college for Thanksgiving. The paper said she was on her way to the outlet stores in Lincoln City to do some Christmas shopping when she went off the road near Cape Foulweather. You know the spot I'm talking about, right?"

"It's on the way to Depoe Bay," I answered. "It's like a 500-foot drop into the Pacific Ocean at Foulweather."

"Yeah, there's no way she could have survived a fall like that. The paper said she died instantly."

"Was the weather bad?" I asked. "Was the road slick?"

"I don't think so, but I really don't remember. That was years ago."

Changing the subject, I asked, "So you and Hutch never reconciled?"

"No, I hated him, and to be totally honest, I was secretly pleased when I heard he was arrested for murdering that drug dealer. But things change, and life goes on. I'm happily married now and have a good life. I didn't think so at the time, but Hutch actually did me a favor by hitting on Sydney."

"I don't understand."

"Sydney was a gold digger. When I got hurt playing football in college, if we were still together, she would have dropped me like a hot potato when my chances of making big bucks in the NFL fizzled out. I dodged a bullet by not marrying her, and I have Hutch to thank for that."

"Does she still live around here?"

"The last I heard, she married a rich lawyer and moved to Portland." Chuckling, he said, "The guy's like thirty years older than her and looks like Darth Sidious."

"Who?"

"You know, the Emperor from *Star Wars*."

"Well, they say beauty is in the eye of the beholder."

Vic giggled. "Yeah, right, in Sydney's case, it's more like the size of that fossil's bank account."

I finished my beer and got up to leave. "I should let you get back to building your benches."

Vic stood up to show me out. When we got to the door, he shook my hand and said, "Good luck to you, Grady. If Hutch really is innocent, I hope you find the guy who set him up. I mean that."

I wanted to think he was lying, but I believed him. As I walked down the front steps, a song by Queen came to mind, and all I could hear in my head was Freddie Mercury's voice, singing to me with a subtle change of lyrics: *And another one gone, and another one gone. Another lead bites the dust.*

TWENTY-EIGHT

A few weeks later, Mason Fowler called and asked if we could meet to compare notes. Since I was going into Newport that afternoon to work out at the gym, I suggested we meet at his office at three.

When the receptionist at the front desk contacted him to let him know I had arrived, he came out immediately to greet me. I was struck by how different he was dressed from the first time we met. Mason looked like he just stepped out of an ad for GQ magazine. He wore a tan corduroy blazer over a blue gingham dress shirt. He sported a red power tie, his dark brown pants were neatly pressed and his burgundy wingtips were newly polished.

In my faded blue jeans, University of Oregon sweatshirt and beat up Chuck Taylor low tops, I felt underdressed and a bit self-conscious.

"Wow, you clean up well," I joked.

Mason grinned. "Didn't you ever hear the saying, dress for the job you want, not the job you have?"

"Yeah, I always thought that was bullshit."

"Well, that's probably why you're unemployed today," Mason said sarcastically.

"It's called retirement."

Mason laughed. "Follow me. I've reserved a conference room in the back where we can talk in private."

The room had a long, oak table with twelve chairs around it. I took a seat at the middle of the table. Mason took a seat across from me.

"So how's it going?" Mason asked. "What have you learned so far?"

"I interviewed the football coach and one other teacher who had been contacted by Harlan. They both agreed that there were a lot of students who had good reason to hate Hutchinson. He slept around a lot and didn't care if the girls he was screwing had boyfriends or not. He even hit on his best friend's girl."

"Did you find out who that was?"

"Yeah, his name's Vic Dyer. The football coach told me Harlan asked him specifically about Dyer and indicated he wanted to talk to him. The coach thought he was Harlan's prime suspect."

Mason sat up in his chair.

"Before you get too excited," I said, "I met with Dyer. I don't think he's the guy we're looking for."

"How can you be so sure?"

"I'm not. I'm just giving you my gut feeling. I liked him, and he seemed really honest to me."

"That doesn't mean anything. Maybe he's just a good actor."

His quick dismissal of my assessment angered me. "I talked to him, you didn't. If you don't trust my judgment, then go talk to him yourself."

Mason raised his hands. "I'm sorry. I value your opinion. I do. I just don't understand how you can so quickly dismiss him as a suspect from just one meeting. What was it he said that made you believe him?"

"Dyer admitted that he hated Hutch for betraying him and was initially happy when he heard Hutch was arrested for killing the drug dealer. But, he also said his girlfriend was a gold digging tramp and that he later realized she would have left him anyway for someone with a bigger bank account. She ended up marrying a rich lawyer in Portland who's old enough to be her grandfather. I also met Dyer's wife. They seem happy and have a second child on the way."

"Anything else?"

"Yes. I did get some information from Dyer that could be significant. He told me his former girlfriend dumped Hutch a week before the Senior Prom and that Hutch had to scramble to find himself a date for the dance. He found a good-looking girl named Stacey Atwood to go with him. Vic argued that a hottie like her would already have had a date for the dance. He thinks Stacey probably dropped that guy when Hutch asked her to go with him."

"It's an interesting theory. If correct, the guy she dumped would certainly have it out for Hutch and have a reason to want to get back at him."

"He'd also have a reason to hate Stacey. It may be just a co-incidence, but Stacey died in a car accident just a few months after high school graduation. She went off the road at Cape Foulweather. I checked the paper's archives online and found the article about the accident. It said the cause of the accident was mechanical failure, but it didn't go in to any detail. I'd like to know what the police report actually said."

Mason's eyes opened wide, and I could see that he was ex-cited. "Wow, that's certainly something worth looking into. I'll see what I can find out."

"I also have one other bit of information I think is interest-ing. The football coach confirmed that Hutch adhered to a strict workout schedule and that it was common knowledge that he did hill workouts up Boundary Road the same two days every week. If someone wanted to frame Hutch, it would be the perfect time to do it, when he was alone and had no one to corroborate his whereabouts at the time of the murder."

Mason was obviously enthused. "You did good, Grady. This is all useful information."

"So now it's your turn," I said. "Tell me what you've learned from your contacts in the Sheriff's Office."

"You were right. The cops do have the killer's DNA."

Pounding my fist on the table, I said, "I knew it! Did you find out which crime scene they got the DNA from?"

"Yes, all four of them."

I was gobsmacked. "It's obvious that the killer isn't stupid, so the fact that he's left his DNA at each crime scene has to be a deliberate move on his part. Either it's a cry for help and he wants to get caught or he thinks he's smarter than the cops and is thumbing his nose at them."

"The cops think it's the latter," Mason said. "They don't think the killer is just being careless. They think he's intentionally leaving his DNA at each crime scene because he's proud of what he's done and wants everyone to know that this string of homicides is his handiwork. They think the fact that he's been successful so far in eluding capture has emboldened him and that he's now killing his victims in ever increasingly bizarre ways to gain even more publicity."

"What about the Sheriff's Office's outreach effort asking for the public's help in identifying the killer? Do you know if they've gotten any good leads?"

Mason shook his head. "Not that I'm aware of. There have been a few crackpots, tweakers and homeless individuals who have come forward with implausible stories, hoping to cash in on the reward money, but I don't know of anyone who's come forward with credible information the cops think is worth pursuing. I know that since the Sheriff's Office came out asking for the public's help in catching the killer, they've been barraged with requests for interviews by the media. Whittaker is in the spotlight right now and under intense pressure to make an arrest."

"So where do we go from here?" I asked.

"I don't know. I was hoping you did."

"I think we're at an impasse until some new information comes to light. Look, Mason, I believe Hutchinson may indeed be innocent, and I think looking for the real killer is something that should be pursued. But I'm beginning to doubt that the person who killed Shane Hartlett is the same person the cops are looking for today. There are just too many differences between the drug dealer's murder and the murders the cops are currently investigating. There is no DNA evidence linking the drug dealer's murder to any of these other cases, and it happened so many years before the recent spate of homicides, that it's hard to see a connection."

I stood up and got ready to leave. "I'm happy to help in any way I can, but right now, I don't think I have anything else to contribute. I'm retired, but I still have to make money as a freelance writer to pay my bills. I've got a few deadlines coming up, and I haven't even begun to start work on these projects yet. I have to bow out, at least for the time being."

Mason patted me on the shoulder. "I understand completely. I still think the cases are connected, and I'm not giving up. But I respect your opinion. You do what you have to do, and I'll continue to snoop around. If I get something I think is important, I'll give you a call."

TWENTY-NINE

I was happy to take a backseat and let Mason do the detective work. As a reporter, he had a better skill set for the work than I did. And, more importantly, I had bills to pay and writing deadlines to meet. I spent the next several weeks writing articles for a variety of nature magazines. When I was caught up with my work, I was ready for a welcome break, and gardening was the perfect distraction.

It was April, and the weather was gorgeous and unusually warm for this time of the year. I was tempted to go to the local nursery and buy plants to start my vegetable garden, but I've lived here long enough to know that you don't plant vegetables until mid-May at the very earliest since a late cold snap is still more than just a remote possibility.

I decided I'd satisfy my urge to get outside and work in the yard by purchasing a variety of early spring annuals that I could plant in window boxes, in pots on my deck and around my fish pond. As I left my driveway and drove down the road to the highway, I considered my choices: verbena, WAVE petunias (my favorite), pansies, violas and geraniums. I knew I'd end up buying more than I needed because that's what I always do when the rain lets up and our long, gray winter finally comes to an end.

As I drove past Edwina Risley's place, I saw her lying on her side, spread out on the lawn in front of the flower bed to the right of her front steps, with her right hand extended and her fingers moving vigorously. A white bucket was sitting upright beside her.

I pulled over to the side of the road, stopped the car and ran to her, screaming, "Mrs. Risley, are you OK?"

When I grabbed her shoulder, she turned to me with a scowl on her face. "Jesus, you scared the crap out of me. What's wrong with you?"

"What's wrong with me? I saw you lying on the ground and your hand twitching. I thought you had had a stroke or a heart attack. Are you OK?"

"Yes! I'm just pulling weeds."

"Lying on your side, like that?"

"That's the only way I can do it. My arthritis is debilitating. I can't bend over for any length of time. It hurts too much."

I looked into the white bucket and saw it was filled halfway with weeds. "So, you're OK?"

"Yes, I'm fine."

Edwina slowly got up on her hands and knees and then gingerly made it to her feet. She looked like an arthritic praying mantis, moving in slow motion, and then she started to cackle uncontrollably, which eventually devolved into a wracking cough.

"What's so funny?" I asked.

"You, you're the real deal."

"Real deal, what's that supposed to mean?"

Edwina leaned down and looked me straight in the eyes. "You *are* a Good Samaritan, after all. It's not an act."

"I was just worried about you."

"You don't even know me."

"You're my neighbor."

Laughing, she patted me on the shoulder and said, "I bet you helped old ladies across the street when you were a Boy Scout growing up in New Jersey. Did they give you a merit badge for that?"

"How did you know I was from New Jersey?"

Clucking like a hen, she said, "I make it my business to know everything about everyone on my stretch of the river."

"But I was never a Boy Scout."

Wrapping her scrawny arm around me, she laughed, "You're a goody two-shoes. That was just an educated guess. Come on. You seem a bit frazzled. I can't let you leave like this. I won't hear of it. You have to come inside and have a cup of tea."

I followed Edwina up the front steps with trepidation. *She's an old lady. What am I scared of?*

As I crossed the threshold, I saw that there was a Winchester 30-06 propped up inside the door, ready to greet any unwanted intruder. It was sweltering and stuffy inside the house, and the air smelled stale and musty.

Having worked in a nursing home as a college student, I knew only too well the typical, grassy odor of an old person's smell, but this was different. What I encountered was an olfactory stew of unpleasant odors. In addition to the characteristic old person smell, there was also the unmistakable, indelible stink of cigarette smoke, which I guessed was forever imbedded in the cushions of the furniture and the fabric of the curtains. There was also the lingering smell of burnt food, which I thought was likely the result of Edwina falling asleep and failing to hear the stove's timer when it went off to let her know that the cooking process was done.

There were no lights on inside the house. All of the curtains facing the road were drawn, but the drapes on the windows on the river side were all open. As I walked across the burnt orange shag carpet in the living room, I noticed that there was a 12-gauge shotgun leaning against a wing chair that was facing one of the large windows that overlooked the river. There was a small oak side table next to the chair, and on the table, there was a glass ash tray, a pair of binoculars, a pair of reading glasses and an Audubon bird field guide. I guessed that this was where Edwina spent much of her day, smoking and watching the diverse array of birds that frequent the river.

I looked out the window and from this vantage point I could plainly see the spot where I had found Harlan's body. *Was Edwina sitting here when the murderer dragged the body to that location? Does she know who the killer is?*

There was a large card table just before the kitchen. A pile of white tiles were scattered across the surface, and each tile had a large number painted on it in one of four bright colors: black, orange, blue and red. A large ash tray with a mole-size mound of spent cigarette butts sat in the middle of the table. There were also four tile racks positioned strategically near each of the padded chairs that circled the table.

Chloe had told me that Edwina hosted a tile rummy game for her lady friends every Thursday, and I assumed that this was where she held court. Chloe had explained to me that this was the way the old biddies shared news of what was going on along the river. I remember me asking her if it was just local gossip, and I remember her laughing at my question and responding, "All I can say is that I'd trust the accuracy of their news over what the local newspaper reports any day."

As I entered the kitchen, Edwina placed a small pot of water on the stove and turned on one of the burners. I looked around the room. An inch of dust covered the shelves over the sink, and large cobwebs clung stubbornly to the rafters on the ceiling. I had been around old people long enough to know this wasn't an indictment of Edwina's housekeeping skills but a sign of her advanced age. She simply couldn't see what I saw.

Edwina opened a cupboard over the sink, and there was a .44 Magnum revolver sitting on the shelf next to a box of green tea. She grabbed the tea, closed the cupboard and placed the box on the countertop. Removing two teabags, she placed them in the boiling water and then opened the fridge and took out a saucer with some lemon slices on it.

After placing a slice in each of the two empty cups, she opened the drawer below the countertop and grabbed a spoon. There was a small .38 caliber Derringer pistol, resting on its side and ready for action. At this stage, I had no doubt where Edwina stood on her Second Amendment right.

She gestured for me to take a seat at the tile-covered counter that separated the kitchen from the dining area. I took a seat at the counter on the opposite side from where she was working. Edwina grabbed the tag on one of the tea bags and lifted it out of the boiling water. Placing the steaming bag in the spoon, she wrapped the string around the shallow bowl, and squeezed the paper sack, draining any liquid that was still in it into the pot. She did the same with the second tea bag.

Edwina then poured the piping hot tea in the two mugs and handed one to me. She grabbed a bottle of rye whiskey off the counter next to the microwave, filled a shot glass with its contents and poured it into her tea. Stirring it slowly with her spoon, she looked at me and asked, "Do you want a hot toddy too?"

"No, thank you. I'm going into town."

Ignoring my answer, she filled the jigger again with whiskey, emptied it into my cup and stirred it into my tea with her spoon. "Don't be a wuss. It's only a shot."

I didn't argue. I took my cup and sipped my drink.

Edwina grabbed the pack of Marlboro Reds, which was on the kitchen counter, took a cigarette out and lit it. Taking a long drag from the cancer stick, she held the smoke in her lungs while she stared across the counter at me with a sly grin on her face. I had the uncomfortable feeling that she was sizing me up.

Eager to break the silence, I resorted to small talk. "Mrs. Risley, do you have any pets?"

Turning her head to the right and blowing the smoke away from me, she placed her cigarette in an ashtray on the countertop, grabbed her tea and took a sip. "We did when the kids were young," she said, "but that was years ago. Pets are all freeloaders as far as I'm concerned. I don't take care of anything that I can't eat or that can't lay eggs that I can eat."

"What about companionship? I know a lot of senior citizens who have dogs and cats just for that reason."

Without hesitation, she responded, "Weak individuals! That's what they are. Have you ever been to Walmart and seen all those screwed up people who bring their pets inside the store?"

"You mean the people with therapy animals?"

Raising her hands in air quotes and cackling, Edwina said, "Yeah, therapy animals, what a joke. Last week I was in Wally World, and there was this woman who had three dachshunds in her cart. I thought to myself, oh my God, how fucked up do you have to be to need three therapy dogs?"

Trying hard not to laugh, I replied, "I have to agree that seems a little excessive even to me, but I worked in a retirement home when I was in college, and I can attest to the physical, mental and emotional benefits therapy animals can provide."

"People have just gotten soft. That's what it is."

Perhaps it was the shot of whiskey taking effect, but I was beginning to feel a little more comfortable around the crusty, old woman and couldn't resist the opportunity to be provocative. "Did you know that it's not only dogs and cats that can be therapy animals? They can also be a whole host of other critters like birds, guinea pigs, rabbits, pot-bellied pigs and even rats."

Edwina exploded. "Rats! Are you kidding me? If I saw someone hauling a rat into the grocery store, I'd bludgeon the rodent to death right there on the spot in front of the weak social misfit who brought it in." Chuckling, she said, "Let's see how emotionally therapeutic that would be for that sick son-of-a-bitch."

I burst out laughing. "Don't candy-coat it, Edwina. Just tell me what you really think."

She started laughing as well. "You're a smart ass. I like that."

I took a swig of my spiked tea. "Let's talk about something else. From my own experience, I know how frustrating it can be as we get older and can't do everything we used to do when we were younger. Have you ever thought about hiring someone to do your yard work for you?"

"I used to have a kid who did a good job for me, but he moved away. There aren't any kids around here anymore. Almost everyone now on our road is just waiting to die, and if they're not senior citizens, they're damn close. Any kids they had are now middle-aged."

"What about your grown sons? They live nearby. Why can't they do it for you?"

"Are you kidding me? They haven't come by to see me in years. They're as worthless as tits on a boar hog."

"I know a teenager who's looking to make money so he can fix up his car. He'd do a good job for you. It's my nephew, Spencer. He's living with me for the next year or so."

Edwina shook her head. "I know, and from what I've heard, the kid has done a good job around your property. My lady friends tell me your yard looks a lot better now than when you were taking care of it."

I knew she was right, but it rubbed me the wrong way. "Thanks for the compliment," I said sarcastically. "So should I send my nephew over so you can meet him?"

Taking some time to think it over, she finally said, "Hell, why not? Send him over. Tell him that if I like him, I'll pay him ten bucks an hour, and if he does a good job, he can work as many hours as he wants."

"That's most generous. I'll let Spencer know."

As I finished my tea and got up to leave, I thanked Edwina for her hospitality. She started to get up but stopped and sank back down in her chair. I could tell from the contorted look on her face that she was in pain.

"Please don't get up," I begged. "I can show myself out."

"That's good because my back is killing me. I probably over-did it outdoors today."

"Do you want me to help you to a more comfortable chair in the living room?"

Shaking her head, Edwina grabbed the bottle of whiskey and poured an ample helping in her tea. "No, I'll just sit here a while and self-medicate."

"Is there anything I can get you before I leave?"

She responded to my question with a scowl, but I knew her anger was directed at her failing health and not my offer of assistance. "No. Just go," she said.

As I left the house and walked back to my car, I wondered whether I could sell Spencer on the idea of taking Edwina up on her job offer. Ten bucks an hour was good money for a kid his age, but Edwina would be a hard task master. When I told him who he'd be working for, I knew he'd be reluctant to take her up on her offer, and I couldn't blame him if he didn't just say no, but hell, no.

THIRTY

I returned from my trip to the nursery with the bed of my truck filled with flats of flowers. As I pulled into my driveway, I noticed that the door to my neighbor's garage was open and there was a Camaro inside. I knew the vehicle belonged to Dave's young mechanic, Jacob, and that Dave was helping him install a 383 stroker small block Chevy engine in the car. Spencer was there too, handing them tools and helping out in any way he could. I went next door to see what progress they'd made and also to see if I could get my nephew to tear himself away long enough to help me unload the plants in the back of my truck.

Dave was the first one to notice my presence. "Hey, Cramps. What's up?"

"Not much. I'm just getting back from town. I bought a bunch of flowers at the nursery. How's the engine install going?"

Jacob heard my voice and raised his head from under the hood. "Oh, hello old man. I didn't smell you coming."

"That's surprising. With a beak that big, I would have thought your olfactory sense would best that of a bloodhound."

Dave piped up, "Now girls, don't fight. Let's take a break." Walking over to the fridge, he opened the door and grabbed a Hamm's for himself and a Rolling Rock for Jacob. "You want a Hamm's, Cramps?"

"You don't have a Coors Light?"

"No. But if you want water, there's a garden hose outside."

"I'll take a Rolling Rock," I said.

Dave handed me the beer. "You can thank Jacob for the Rolling Rock. They're his."

I popped the top and took a swig. "I know. That's why I picked it." Looking at Jacob, I said, "He's drank enough of my beer. I'm sure he won't mind."

Jacob laughed. "Help yourself, old man. Maybe you'll learn what a real beer tastes like. Can you still learn at your advanced age?"

"I don't know," I said with a straight face. "I can't remember."

Dave shook his head and laughed. "Spencer, you want a pop or something?"

My nephew responded, "No. I'm good."

Turning to my nephew, I said, "Hey, Spence, after you're through here, helping these guys, I was hoping you could help me unload the plants I bought at the nursery."

"Sure thing, Uncle G. You want to do it now?"

"In a few minutes, after we finish our beers." Turning to Dave, I said, "Spence tells me you and he have done all the work you said was needed to get the Honda in good shape."

"We have. Spence did most of the work. He's a natural mechanic."

Spencer stood up straight and puffed up his chest, clearly savoring the praise.

Looking at my nephew, Dave continued, "But we're not done working on the car just yet. When the car becomes his—assuming he gets good grades his last semester, and I have no doubt that he will—Spencer wants me to help him customize the car with ground effects."

I saw an opportunity to broach the subject of the part time job. "You're talking about an aftermarket kit?"

"Yeah, to give the car a race-inspired, lower-appearance look."

"So it looks bad ass," Spencer interjected.

"What will that cost?"

"That depends on the style Spencer wants to achieve and the kit he selects," Dave said. "But a good ball park figure would be in the $650 to $1,000 range for the kit. Since the parts come unpainted, they'd need to be painted, which would obviously add to the cost."

Turning to my nephew, I said, "Well, I was going to wait until later tonight to bring up the subject, but I think I've found a great part-time job for you within walking distance. It would give you the money you need to pay for all this. There's an old lady on our road, who's arthritic and can't do her own yard work. She's willing to pay you $10 an hour, and she said that if she likes you, you can work as many hours as you want."

Dave and Jacob were both eager to spur Spencer to take the job.

"Ten bucks an hour? That's great money for someone your age," Dave offered.

"Hell, if you don't want the job, buddy, I'll take it," Jacob said. Winking at Dave, he added, "My boss pays me slave wages, so I could use the extra money."

My nephew's eyes grew big, and he was obviously excited. "That's awesome, Uncle G. Who's the old lady?"

"Edwina Risley."

At the mention of her name, Dave and Jacob clammed up and stood there motionless, staring at me with their eyebrows raised and their lips puckered, like they had just tasted the worst lemon in their lives.

Spencer hung his head and was crestfallen. "That crazy old lady? Everybody knows she's a bitch!"

"Watch your language," I rebuked.

Jacob came to my nephew's defense. "He's right. She is a —"

Cutting him off, I retorted, "She's ninety years old!"

"I don't care," Spencer said defiantly. "She's still a bitch, and she'd make my life a living hell."

"I'm not going to make you take this job. All I'm asking is that you go talk to Mrs. Risley. If after talking to her, you don't want to do it, it's your decision. And if you decide to give it a try, you can always quit anytime you want."

Wanting to be supportive, Dave said, "And you'd be helping out an old lady who doesn't have much longer to live. It would be good karma, Spence. At least go talk to her as your uncle asks."

Jacob also tried to lend his support for the idea. "A fart can muffler and ground effects would be bad ass on your car, little buddy. You'd be the man. At least go talk to the hag."

I shot a dagger from my eyes to Jacob.

"I mean old lady," Jacob added.

"It's your decision, Spence," I said. "What do you say?"

Spencer furrowed his brow, pursed his lips and looked me straight in the eyes. "I have a bad feeling about this, but I guess it wouldn't hurt to at least go talk to her. She's not going to try to throw me in her oven like the witch in the Hansel and Gretel fairy tale, is she?"

Dave and Jacob looked at each other and were noticeably silent.

"No. Of course not," I reassured him. "If you give her a chance, I think you'll actually get to like her. I had tea with her today. I admit that it takes some time for her to grow on you, but she's just a harmless old lady who needs help. Just give her a chance, and after you meet her, you can always politely refuse the job. Oh, and by the way, I have no doubt you're going to get good grades this last semester. I don't have to wait to see your report card. The Honda's yours."

THIRTY-ONE

I was in the living room in my recliner, trying to read a book, but I couldn't concentrate. All I could think about was my nephew. I knew he had gone over to Edwina's place to introduce himself, and I wondered how their meeting was going. I looked at my watch. Spencer had been gone over an hour.

I put the book down on the coffee table and grabbed the remote and turned on the CD player. Within seconds, "I Am the Highway" by Audioslave weaved its way through the speakers. I turned up the volume and kicked out the footrest on my chair, eager to relieve my anxiety and immerse myself in the music.

Just then, Spencer burst through the front door and ran to the kitchen.

I grabbed the remote and turned off the music. "So how was your meeting with Mrs. Risley?"

Grabbing an energy drink out of the fridge, Spencer opened the can, took a sip and said, "I'm not sure."

I stood up from my chair and looked at him. "Did she offer you the job?"

Spencer looked confused. "I think so," he said.

"What do you mean? Either she did or she didn't."

"It's not that simple, Uncle G. She seemed like she was on something."

"On something? What does that mean?"

"Like she was on drugs or something."

"What made you think that?"

"She kept fading in and out. At first, she didn't know who I was or why I was there."

"Did you introduce yourself?"

"Of course. I told her I was your nephew. She didn't know who you were at first either. I had to tell her where we live on the road."

"And then what?"

"It took a while, but then she eventually remembered who you were. She asked me why I was there. I told her you said she was looking for someone to do yard work for her and that she told you to send me over so she could meet me and decide whether she wanted to hire me or not."

"And what was her response?"

"She said, 'I don't remember saying that, but it makes sense. I do need someone to do my yard work. How did you find out I needed someone?' I told her, like I said before, from my Uncle Grady. And then she said, 'Oh, that's right, you said that before. I'm sorry, I forget a lot.'"

I finally understood what was going on. "Spence, the old lady is up there in age. She probably has dementia. Your grandmother was the same way. One day she'd be lucid, and then the next, she'd be disoriented and not know what day it was. So did you take the job?"

Taking a swig off his drink, Spencer said, "Yeah, I texted Jacob when I was at Mrs. Risley's place and asked him what I should do. He told me to take it. So I did. I start work tomorrow after school. I gotta go, Uncle G. I'm going over to Dave's to help him and Jacob finish work on the Camaro. Why don't you come over?"

I knew Spencer looked up to Jacob, but I was admittedly a little hurt that my nephew went to him for advice rather than coming to me. "Maybe later," I said as I watched Spencer dart out of the room.

THIRTY-TWO

My nephew's first day working for Edwina went better than I had hoped. I knew Spencer was concerned that Edwina would be a real slave driver and be breathing down his neck the whole time he was working, but his fear proved unfounded. Edwina told him what she wanted him to do and then left him alone to do it. Whether this was by design or because she was in failing health, I didn't know, but either way, the outcome was the same. Spencer appreciated the freedom he was afforded and worked harder as a result. Edwina was pleased with his work and asked him to come back. Spencer soon settled into a routine working three days a week at her place.

Edwina's cognitive impairment concerned me for I knew she was estranged from her sons and had no one looking out for her welfare. Since my nephew was the only person who saw her several times a week, he was the best source of information on how this nonagenarian was doing.

At dinner, on those days he worked for Edwina, I'd question Spencer about his interaction with her. From what he told me, it was evident that Edwina's short term memory loss was getting worse. On more than one occasion, she'd give my nephew a job to do one day, and when he came back the next time to work, she'd direct him to do the same thing. He'd have to show her that he had already completed the task, and then she's assign him something else to do.

At the time, there was no way I could have imagined that my concern for Edwina's welfare would eventually provide new information which would spur me to resume my quest to find the serial killer, but that's exactly what happened.

One night, after working for Edwina, Spencer was wolfing down his food.

"Spence," I said. "Chew your food. What's the big hurry?"

"Darwin's bringing his MR2 up to Dave's. Jacob's coming too. We're going to start working on it tonight."

"I didn't hear a car pull up," I argued. "I don't think Darwin's even here yet. Trust me, you've got time. Tell me how your day went working for Edwina."

"I spent the whole day killing rats."

"Rats?"

"Yeah. Edwina feeds the Steller's jays and chipmunks each day near the garden shed behind her house. There's a wood pile next to the shed, and there's a bunch of rats living in it. She said they come out every day and eat the seeds and nuts she puts out for the birds and chipmunks. She told me she wanted them gone and gave me a .22 air rifle to shoot them. I asked her if she had anything I could use as bait to coax them out. She gave me a package of hotdogs. I cut the franks up into small pieces and spread them out on the grass near the wood pile. I then found a good spot behind a bush and waited for the rats to come out for the food. It didn't take long. Within a couple of hours, I killed about a half dozen. I waited a while longer, and when no more came out, I went up to the house and asked Edwina what she wanted me to do with the dead rats. She said, 'Throw them on the bank down by the river and feed them to your pets like you always do.' I didn't know what she meant. I said I don't have any pets. She said, 'Yeah, you do, silly. I'm talking about the buzzards. What's wrong with you, Skid?'"

"Who's Skid?" I asked.

"Damned if I know."

"I think she may have been confusing you with the boy who

worked for her years ago. It's not uncommon for people with dementia to exhibit short term memory loss one day and then to suddenly recall an event which occurred years earlier."

I sat at the table stroking my chin. "So, Edwina referred to the vultures as Skid's pets. That's really interesting. Skid has to be a nickname. I'd like to find out what the kid's real name is. Spence, are you just about done eating?"

"I was done a half hour ago. You were the one who made me settle down and eat slower, remember?"

"Yeah, you're right. You said you were going over to Dave's to help him and Darwin work on the MR2. I think I'll go over with you."

When we got to the garage, Darwin and Jacob were already hard at work on the race car.

Spencer immediately went over to help Jacob, who was removing the right front quarter panel. I went over to talk to Darwin, who was in the process of taking off the badly dented passenger's side door.

"Darwin, I know you said the car needed some body work, but I didn't know the damage was this extensive."

"The guy I bought it from sideswiped a guard rail, so the whole right side is fucked up."

"Where's Dave?" I asked.

"He's upstairs taking a dump. He'll be down in a minute." Pointing to the door he was removing, Darwin said, "This is going in the scrap heap. I found a used one at the salvage yard that's in perfect shape."

Just then, the door opened, and Dave walked in. "Hey, Cramps, did you come here to see what real work is like?"

"I know what real work is. I worked my whole life."

"Yeah, I bet you have some war stories to tell about your years as a desk jockey, pushing papers."

"I actually have several stories that would keep you enthralled," I said sarcastically. "My favorite is the one where I get an especially nasty paper cut."

Laughing, Dave went to the fridge and opened the door. "Do you want a beer?"

I pulled a Coors Light out of my coat pocket. "No thanks. I came prepared."

Grabbing a Hamm's for himself, Dave said, "So if you didn't come here to work, why did you come at all?"

"To ask you a few questions. Edwina had a kid working for her a while back who went by the nickname, Skid. Do you remember who that was?"

"Hell, that was years ago," Dave answered. "It's not something I would have paid attention to. What's all this about anyway?"

"Today, when Spencer was working for Edwina, she had him shoot rats that were living in her wood pile. When he asked her what she wanted him to do with the dead rodents, she called him 'Skid' and told him to throw them on the bank and feed them to 'his pets' like he always does. She was talking about the turkey vultures. I think she confused Spencer with the boy who did yard work for her years ago and that his childhood nickname was Skid."

"So you think this kid is the serial killer?"

"I know it sounds crazy, but it's something worth pursuing. I don't think it is just a coincidence that when I found Harlan's body on Edwina's property, he was being fed upon by vultures. Maybe the sick son-of-a-bitch has gone from killing nuisance animals to murdering people he thinks are despicable. Maybe in his mind he sees them both as vermin that need to be eradicated."

Dave scratched his head. "Wow, that's quite a theory."

"Well, somebody around here has got to know who Skid is," I argued. "I know that the old ladies meet at Edwina's every Thursday to play tile rummy. Chloe told me that if anyone knows what's going on around here, it's these old ladies. Your grandma is part of the group, isn't she? Maybe she knows something."

"I can introduce you to my Grams if you want. I haven't seen her in a while, and I owe her a visit. We can ask her if she knows who worked for Edwina in the past, but it's not likely she'll remember. She's not as old as Edwina, but she's getting up there in age. She's already pretty forgetful."

"Maybe she could ask the other old ladies at the tile rummy game. Maybe one of them would remember."

"It's worth a shot, I guess," Dave said grudgingly. "I'll give her a call tomorrow. Right now I've got to get back to work, helping these guys with the car."

THIRTY-THREE

The next day, Dave and I went to visit his grandmother. When we got to the house, a diminutive woman in her mid-eighties greeted us at the door. She had ghost white hair, which was pulled back severely and rolled in a tight bun. She looked like the quintessential librarian or schoolmarm. It didn't take long before I realized the straight-laced image I had of her was far different from the person she really was.

Dave bent down and kissed her on the cheek. "Grams, I'd like you to meet my neighbor."

Extending my hand, I smiled and said, "It's a pleasure to meet you. My name's Grady."

"Forget the handshake," she said as she opened her arms. "Give me a hug. I'm Martha."

I bent down and embraced her warmly. The smell of alcohol was heavy on her breath.

Releasing me from her grasp, she said, "I need a cigarette. Let's go to the kitchen to talk."

Grandma sat down at the table and gestured for us to take seats around her. I got the impression that she thought she was holding court. She grabbed a pack of Camel unfiltered cigarettes out of her housecoat, took one out, stuffed it in her mouth and lit it. Taking a deep drag off the stud, she then grabbed the rocks glass that was on the table in front of her, held it high above her head and shook it vigorously. The half-melted ice cubes in the bottom rattled against the glass. "Davey," she said, "I need a refill."

I looked at the clock on the wall. It was 11 a.m. Dave grabbed the glass dutifully from his grandmother and went to the freezer to get some new ice cubes for her drink. "You want your usual, Grams?"

She cackled. "Do bears shit in the woods?"

Dave opened the bottle of Old Crow, which was on the counter next to the sink, and poured a few jiggers of bourbon over the ice cubes. He gave his grandmother her drink.

"Make one for you and your friend too, honey."

Turning to me, Dave said, "You want one, Grady?"

I'm never in the mood for cheap bourbon and especially not at that time of the morning, but I knew it wouldn't be wise to cross the old woman, especially when I was about to ask her for a favor, so I shook my head in the affirmative.

Dave grabbed two tumblers out of the cupboard and made us drinks. He handed me mine.

Grandma took a long swig of whiskey and then a long drag off her Camel stud. "Are you boys hungry? There is TV dinners in the freezer. My dogs are barking, so I'm not getting up to wait on you. You can help yourselves."

Dave sipped his drink and grimaced at the taste. "I'm fine, Grams. I'm not hungry."

"Well, what about your friend, Brody? Maybe he's hungry."

Dave looked at me and his upper lip curled into a satisfied smirk. "You hungry, Brody?"

I bit my lower lip to keep from laughing. "No, I'm fine."

"Well, now that we've got that established," Dave said, "let's get down to business. When I called grandma, I told her why you wanted to meet, so you don't have to bore her with a long-winded explanation."

"Great. As I'm sure Dave told you, we're trying to learn more about the young boy who worked for Edwina some years ago. His childhood nickname was Skid."

Grandma nodded. "Dave said you think this kid may be connected in some way to the murders the sheriff is currently investigating."

"He'd be a man in his mid-twenties now. We don't know if he's involved, but we think it's a possibility, and it's the reason we're trying to learn his identity. Do you remember a boy who lived around here who went by the nickname Skid?"

"Yes, he was Winifred Longbough's grandson. She and her husband, Alfred, had a small farm a few miles upriver."

"Do you happen to remember what the boy's given name was?"

"No, I only saw him a few times. He spent summers at his grandparents' place until they moved to Portland to be closer to their doctors. I felt sorry for the kid. He loved it on the river and was heartbroken when he found out they were selling their farm."

"How well did you know the Longboughs?" I asked.

"Winnie was a member of our tile rummy group. She and I were casual friends but not close."

"Do you know if the Longboughs still live in Portland?"

"No, they're both deceased. They were both in poor health when they moved away. Alfred had cancer and died shortly after they moved up to Portland, and Winnie only lived another year or so after that. I think she had a stroke or a heart attack. I'm not sure which."

"So Longbough is Skid's surname?"

"It's hard to say," grandma answered. "The Longboughs were the boy's maternal grandparents. Their daughter Felicia got pregnant out of wedlock when she was seventeen. Winnie had old-fashioned values and shipped her daughter off to stay with a family friend in Raymond, Washington until she gave birth. Winnie's plan was for her daughter to give the child up for adoption and come home like nothing had ever happened, but Felicia refused. She kept the kid and stayed in Raymond. I heard she eventually met a man, and they got married.

Whether he actually adopted the kid or not I don't know, so your guess is as good as mine what family name is on the kid's birth certificate."

"You wouldn't happen to know if they still live in Raymond would you?"

Shaking her head, she said, "No, I've told you everything I know."

"Do you think any of your lady friends, who you play tile rummy with, might know more about this kid?"

"I don't know. Some of them were closer to Winnie than I was, so it's possible, but like me, they're all up there in age and getting a little forgetful, so it's hard to say. But I'd be happy to ask them at the game this Thursday. Dave tells me you want me to wear a wire."

Dave snickered. "My grandma watches a lot of cop shows on TV."

I pictured Dave and me taping a microphone wire to this frail old lady's sagging chest. I wanted to erase this image from my mind immediately, but I knew it was so sick that it would linger in my brain long past its shelf life. I immediately started laughing. "No, nothing that intrusive."

I took a small digital voice recorder out of my pocket and handed it to her. "You'd just take this with you in your purse and turn it on just before you got to Edwina's." Showing her how it works, I said, "You just slide this button up to start recording. It is voice activated, so it will automatically stop recording if no one is talking and start up again when someone starts to speak. The recorder is just to make it easy for you so you don't have to take notes. Also, the ladies will obviously be more forthcoming if you're not jotting down everything they say."

Grandma chuckled. "They'd be even more pissed if they found out I was recording them."

"They don't have to know," I argued. "We're just trying to find out as much as we can about this kid. We don't care who provides the information."

"Hell, I don't care what those old biddies think. Let them try to run me out of town. Let's see who would win that fight."

I smiled broadly. "My money's on you, Martha."

"It would be easy, Grams," Dave interjected. "You could mention that you noticed that Edwina has a new kid doing yard work for her and ask your lady friends if any of them know what ever happened to Skid, the boy who worked for Edwina before. We'd review the recording when you got home to see if we learned anything about Skid we don't already know."

"I hope that little machine can record for a long time," Grandma said, "because these women like to talk. They go on incessantly about what's new in their kids' lives, brag about their grandkids and complain about their own ailments. And when they get sauced, which happens every week, they ramble on even more."

"That's not a problem," I answered. "You can record nonstop for twelve hours or more."

"You could be our secret agent, Grams," Dave exclaimed.

"What do you say," I asked, "will you do it?"

Grandma set the recorder down on the table, downed her whiskey and thought for a minute. "Hell, why not? I guess it's harmless enough, and it sounds like fun. Count me in, boys."

"That's great, Grams," Dave said. "I'll come by on Thursday before you leave for Edwina's to review the plan with you one last time, and I'll take you to her house and pick you up after the game. You can tell your friends that you left your car at my shop so I could change your oil."

The old lady chuckled. "Who do you think you're kidding? I know you think I'm getting a bit loopy, and you just want to make sure I don't screw up. But that's OK." She kissed Dave on the cheek. "It gives me another chance to see my favorite grandson."

"I'm your only grandson."

She patted Dave on the shoulder. "That's why you're my favorite, honey." Shaking her empty rocks glass with nothing in it but a few melted ice cubes in his face, she smiled and said, "How about filling me up one last time before you leave?"

THIRTY-FOUR

It was Thursday, and I was trying futilely to eradicate the tangle of Himalayan blackberries that were choking out the rhododendrons in my front yard. I knew that Dave had taken his grandmother to the tile rummy game at Edwina's and was going to come over after he brought her home so we could listen to the recording on my laptop. I was anxious to learn whether Dave's grandmother had garnered any information which would help us identify who Skid was.

I heard the front door slam and saw my nephew bounding down the steps. "Can I borrow your truck, Uncle G?" Spencer asked, as he ran up to meet me.

"What's wrong with your car?"

"Nothing. I'm going to trim a bunch of bushes and trees at Edwina's today and need the truck to take the yard waste to the dump."

I dug into my front pocket and handed him my keys. "Sure thing, buddy, I'm not planning on going anywhere, but I'll take my car if I need to go into town for any reason. I haven't used the truck in a couple of days, and it might be low on gas." I reached for my wallet. "Do you need some cash?"

"No, I'm good." As he ran to my truck, Spencer yelled, "See you later, Uncle G."

I continued what I knew was a losing battle with the

blackberries for several more hours before Dave pulled into his driveway. Thankful for an excuse to quit working, I left my loppers on top of the large mound of cut blackberry canes in my wheelbarrow and hobbled over to see him. "How did it go?"

Holding up the recorder, Dave said, "I made sure Grams turned it on before we entered Edwina's house. For some reason, she decided to make a big pot of stuffed peppers as her contribution to the potluck. It was heavy, and I was worried that she might fall going up the steps, so I carried it to the house. I can't tell you what happened after I left."

"Well, get your ass over here, and let's see."

Handing me the recorder, he said, "Get it set up, and I'll be over in a few minutes. I left Roscoe in the garage this whole time. He's an old dog, and I'm sure he probably needs to take a piss or a dump if he hasn't done so already. I'm sure you can relate."

Ignoring the dig, I said, "OK. Just hurry up."

When Dave came over, I turned on the recorder. There was a long, mournful creak as Edwina opened the front door.

By her gasp, it was obvious that she was surprised to see Dave with his grandmother. "Oh, my stars, I didn't expect to see you, Davey."

"I'm just carrying Gram's contribution to the potluck. I didn't want her to fall down, coming up the steps with this heavy pot."

"Oh, that's sweet," Edwina said. "Martha, you're so lucky to have such a good grandson."

"He could be better," Martha said.

I could hear Dave on the recording, laughing. "Oh, Grams, I don't know if I can handle such lavish praise. I might just get a big head."

Grandma countered, "Oh, hush. You don't come by that often to see me."

Edwina came to Dave's defense. "At least he comes by. My sons have disowned me, and my grandkids haven't visited me in years."

"Are we going to have to stand in your doorway the whole time or are you going to invite us in?" It was obvious from the tone of her voice that Dave's grandma didn't like being lectured to.

Edwina tittered. "I'm sorry. Where are my manners? Come in."

"Wow," I said. "I didn't expect that response from Edwina. I thought she'd rip your grandma a new asshole."

Dave laughed. "The old ladies are like a pack of dogs. If you show weakness, they'll go for your jugular. But, if you raise your hackles and bare your teeth, they respect that."

On the recording, we could hear the muffled sound of Edwina, Grandma and Dave walking across the carpet in the living room. It didn't take long before the two other elderly women who were in the room saw Dave.

A woman with a deep, hoarse voice asked, "Who's that good-looking young man with Martha?"

I turned to Dave. "Who's that? She sounds like Gilbert Gottfried."

Dave snickered. "That's Mildred. She's a heavy smoker. Probably goes through four packs of Pall Malls a day."

Another woman with a squeaky voice piped up, "That's Davey, Martha's grandson."

Mildred croaked, "I know that, you twit. You're the one who's getting senile. I was just trying to be cute."

Anticipating that I would ask him who the other woman on the recording was, Dave beat me to it and answered, "That's Emma. Her mousy voice fits her to a T. She's a tiny thing. She can't be over four and a half feet tall. She's a widower and lives in Little Albany."

On the recorder, I heard Dave place the pot of stuffed peppers on the stove, so I knew the trio had made it to the kitchen. A few seconds later, I heard the clink of ice cubes being dumped into a glass. I guessed Edwina was making a drink for someone, presumably Dave's grandma.

"I know what Martha drinks," Edwina said. "What's your pleasure, Davey?"

"Thank you, but none for me. I've got to take off. But before

I leave, I wanted to tell you how good your yard looks. I saw Spencer working in the yard as we came in. He's my neighbor's nephew. He's a good kid. I hope you're happy with the job he's doing."

"So far, so good," Edwina responded. "I spy on him through the window to make sure he's working. I haven't caught him goofing off yet, but give him time. He's at that age where he's going to start looking at girls, and then he'll be useless."

Just then, Grandma's voice came on the recorder. "Davey, honey, shouldn't you be leaving? You still have to change my oil, remember?"

Dave chuckled as he heard her comment. "I was trying to tee it up for Grams, but she thought I was stealing her thunder."

On the recording, Dave said his goodbyes to the ladies and made his exit.

"Is anyone else coming?" Grandma asked.

"No. This is it," Edwina replied. Raising her voice, she said, "Mildred and Emma, you need to come up here and try Martha's stuffed peppers. They're delightful."

There was the sound of chairs being scraped slowly against the wood floor in the dining room as the ladies got up and walked to the kitchen.

"Where are Grace and Alice?" Grandma asked.

"Grace's arthritis is acting up again," Mildred said gratingly, "and Alice has a doctor's appointment in Corvallis."

We heard a loud slurping sound, and then Emma squeaked enthusiastically, "Oh, Martha, your peppers are scrumptious. You must tell me what the secret is."

"The secret is always the sauce," Mildred barked. "Try the sweet-n-sour meatballs I brought."

The women sampled the meatballs and agreed they were very good.

Mildred laughed. "The meatballs are no big deal. They're store bought. It's the sweet-n-sour sauce that makes them special. It's my own personal concoction."

Engaging in a round of one-upmanship, the women exchanged recipes for what was in reality only about fifteen minutes but seemed like an eternity. I was beginning to worry that Grandma had lost her focus. "Do you think she's forgotten what we asked her to do?"

Dave tried to put up a good front, but I could see by the look on his face that he also had his doubts. "Just give her time," he said. "She'll do it."

With each passing minute, I knew the chances of Dave's grandma broaching the subject of Skid became increasing less likely. Then Edwina said, "Let's take our plates over to the table so we can start the game."

It wasn't long before we heard the shuffling of plastic tiles, so we knew the game had begun. As the old ladies were choosing their tiles and setting them on their racks, they carried on several conversations at the same time. I couldn't keep track of who was saying what, and I don't think Dave could either. The incessant chatter was disconcerting, and I lashed out at Dave. "Your grandma's forgotten what we asked her to do!"

Dave got his back up and screamed, "Jesus Christ, you're the one who thought up this cockamamie scheme in the first place. I told you Grams forgets a lot."

Just then, we heard the sound of Edwina's front door being opened and recognized Spencer's voice on the recording. "Sorry to interrupt, Mrs. Risley. I just wanted you to know I'm taking the yard waste to the dump now, and then I'm going home."

"Thank you, Spencer. When will I see you again?"

"I'll be back on Saturday afternoon." We heard the creak of the front door closing.

The sight of my nephew must have jogged Martha's memory. "Oh, what a nice young man he is," she said. "He reminds me of the boy who used to work for Edwina years ago. You know who I'm talking about. He was Winnie's grandson. He had an unusual nickname." Pretending to have trouble recalling the sobriquet, Dave's grandma said, "His name's on the tip of my tongue. Let me see, what was it? Oh, I remember now. It was Skid."

"He did work for me as well," Mildred added. "If I remember correctly, his given name was Alan, but he liked being called Skid for some reason. He used to ride his bike over to my place. He didn't have a driver's license yet, so I think he was a few years younger than Spencer is now."

"Does anyone know what happened to him after the Longboughs sold their place?"

"I don't know," Mildred replied, "but I don't imagine it was good. The kid told me his stepdad used to beat him. He hated the man. That's one of the reasons he loved coming down here. It gave him a chance to escape the abuse for a few months in the summer."

"I know," Edwina added. "I kick myself for not reporting that man to Child Protective Services. I wanted to, but Winnie begged me not to. She swore she'd take care of it, but she never did. She just turned a blind eye to the abuse."

"That sounds like Winnie," Emma interjected. "You know how she was. She didn't want anything to get out that would disparage the family name."

"It's the same reason she sent the daughter away when she got pregnant," Mildred barked. "If she hadn't done it, Felicia would never have gotten mixed up with that worthless piece of shit."

"Well, it's too late now," Edwina scolded. "There's nothing we can do about it, anyway. Enough of this endless palaver, let's talk about something else."

Dave pumped his fist in the air triumphantly. "Grandma came through after all!"

"Yeah, your grandma did good. I wish we could have learned more, but there's no way Edwina was going to let the conversation continue."

Dave and I listened to the rest of the recording, but, as we expected, the subject of Skid never came up again.

My cell phone rang, and I grabbed it out of my pocket. I saw a number I didn't recognize, but, thankfully, I answered the call. It was Sheriff Whittaker.

"Hello, is this Mr. Riker?"

"Yes, Sheriff, what can I do for you?"

Whittaker cleared his throat. "Your nephew's been in an accident."

My heart stopped. "Oh my God," I yelled. "Is he OK?"

The sheriff did his best to reassure me. "He's a little shaken up, but I think he'll be OK. He's being transported to the hospital to be checked out right now."

"What happened?"

"It's still too early to tell. We're still investigating the accident," the sheriff said.

"Where did it occur?"

"On Highway 34, about six and a half miles east of Waldport. Your nephew went off the road and hit a tree. It probably saved his life. It stopped him from plunging into the river, which would have been a twenty-foot drop at least. The vehicle is being recovered right now. It will be at Will's Chevron, so you can go there to get your personal items out of the truck and pay the towing bill."

Shaking, I said, "Thank you for the call, Sheriff."

Dave had a concerned look on his face. "What's wrong?"

"Spencer's been in an accident! The sheriff says he thinks he'll be OK. He's being taken to the hospital now to be checked out. I gotta go."

"Is there anything I can do to help?"

"The sheriff says they're having the truck towed to the Chevron station in Waldport. Can you go there and check it out?"

"Of course," Dave responded.

We both jumped out of our chairs and ran for the door.

THIRTY-FIVE

When I got to the emergency room, I went to the nurse who was at the admittance desk. "I'm Grady Riker. I'm here to see my nephew, Spencer Edwards. He was in a car accident."

"Yes. He's here. Come with me, Mr. Riker. I'll take you back to see him."

When I got to the examination room, Spence was lying on the bed with his eyes closed. He had a nasty shiner around his right eye and a gauze bandage taped on the right side of his forehead. Hearing us walk in, he opened his eyes. "Uncle G, I'm so sorry. I wrecked the truck, but it wasn't my fault. I swear."

Giving him a hug, I said, "Don't be silly. I'm just thankful you're OK."

The nurse turned to leave. "I'll let the doctor know you're here."

I squeezed Spencer's shoulder and tried to lighten the mood. "With that black eye, you look tough as nails. You remind me of Rocky Balboa." Putting on my best Rocky impression, I bellowed, "Adrian! Adrian!"

Spencer started laughing. "You're sick, Uncle G."

Getting serious, I asked, "How are you feeling?"

"I'm a little sore, but I'm OK."

The doctor entered the room, and we shook hands. "I'm Doctor Cassidy," he said. "We took some X-rays, and there are no broken bones. Your nephew had a laceration on his forehead, which required eight stitches. You'll have to bring him back in four days so we can remove the sutures. The swelling around his right eye should decrease in a few days, and his black eye should be totally gone in a week or two. Other than that, he's fine." Turning to exit, he said, "The nurse will be in shortly with some paperwork for you."

Within minutes the nurse returned. "Here's a prescription for some pain medication and Spencer's After Visit Summary." She lowered the railing on the side of the bed and pointed to the chair next to the door. Talking to Spencer, she said, "Your clothes are right there. Get dressed and then your uncle can take you home."

As we left Newport and headed south on Highway 101, I asked my nephew about the accident.

"I was on my way to the dump, and all of a sudden, the truck started making a howling and whining sound."

"Could you tell where the sound was coming from?" I asked.

"I think it was coming from the back of the truck."

"And then what happened?"

"About a mile later, the rear end started hopping which sent Edwina's yard waste scattering all over the highway. That's when I got sideways, went off the road and crashed into the tree."

"Thank God that tree was there," I said solemnly. "The sheriff said it stopped you from falling into the river."

Spencer shuddered at the thought. "It freaks me out just thinking about it."

When we got home, I started to prepare dinner, but Spence said he wasn't hungry.

"You should eat something, buddy," I protested.

"Maybe later. It's been a long day, and I have a splitting headache. Right now I just want to go in my room and lie down." Spence gave me a hug and retired to his room.

There was a knock on the door, and Dave walked in. "I just came over to see how Spencer's doing."

"He's a little beat up, but he's going to be fine. He's in his room taking a nap."

"I saw the bigleaf maple he hit on my way into Waldport," Dave said. "Kind of hard to miss it with all of the bark taken clean off the tree and Edwina's yard shit strewn all over the place."

"I know. I saw it too when I was on my way to the hospital. It scares the hell out of me to think what could have happened if he went into the river."

"It's a ways down there. If the impact didn't kill him, he would probably have been knocked out and drowned."

I closed my eyes and sighed wearily. "I don't want to think about it. I need a drink." I grabbed a rocks glass out of the cupboard and filled it halfway with Jack Daniels. "You want one?"

"Yeah, but don't make mine as stiff as yours. I'll take half the Jack and a few ice cubes."

Handing Dave his drink, I asked, "Did you check out the truck?"

"Yeah, it's totaled. Did Spencer tell you what happened?"

I recounted what my nephew had told me about the accident.

"The rear tires on the truck were flat spotted," Dave said. "By Spencer's description, I'd say the rear end locked up. When I got under the truck, the drain plug in the differential was in but only finger tight. I'd say somebody must have drained the gear oil because the only holes in the differential cover were from the inside out where the bearings ceased up and sent pieces of the ring and pinion through the cover."

"I'm not a mechanic. I don't know what that means."

"It means the crash wasn't an accident. Somebody intentionally sabotaged your vehicle, and you were the intended target. Spencer just happened to be collateral damage. You've been nosing around a lot, asking questions that somebody doesn't want answered. I think you should drop this detective shit before you become the killer's next victim."

THIRTY-SIX

The next morning, I called the Sheriff's Office and asked to speak to Whittaker. The receptionist put me on hold, and I expected that she'd forward me to his voicemail. I was surprised when Whittaker answered.

"Hello, Mr. Riker. How's your nephew doing?"

"He's going to be fine. Thank you for your concern. I'm curious if you were able to determine the cause of the accident."

"We think the cause of the accident was mechanical failure. It looks like the rear end locked up. Your truck has a lot of miles on it, so I'd guess it's a maintenance issue."

"I know it's an old truck, but I'm meticulous in my maintenance. My neighbor is a mechanic. I have him check the vehicle out thoroughly every time I take it in for an oil change."

"I'm not casting aspersions on your friend. I'm sure he's a fine mechanic, but nobody's perfect. If he was very busy the last time you took your truck in, he might have cut corners to save time and not checked everything he normally would. It's certainly possible he overlooked this."

"I don't buy that at all. I had my neighbor look at the truck yesterday after the accident. He said someone drained the gear oil out of the differential and that's what caused the rear end to lock up. He said he thought somebody deliberately tried to

167

sabotage my vehicle. I think the person who did it is the same person who killed my neighbors. I think he's after me now."

"Hold on. Don't get carried away."

"I'm not imagining this. If you don't believe me, then go talk to my neighbor. His name's Dave McConnell. He owns Mac's Auto Repair on Mill Street. He can do a better job of describing what he found than I can."

"I intend to contact him, but right now I have a few questions for you. Let's say you're right and someone did indeed tamper with your vehicle. How can you be so sure it's the same person who murdered your neighbors, and why would he be targeting you?"

"Because I started asking questions, just like my neighbors did. I know that's why he killed them and that's why he sabotaged my vehicle."

"So you've been playing detective again, is that what you're saying?"

Playing detective? I bit my tongue to keep from telling the pompous ass what I really thought, which was: *Fuck you, and the horse you rode in on.* After a few seconds, I responded to his question and said calmly, "I've been trying to find information which might be helpful in identifying the serial killer. I thought you wanted the public's help in finding the bastard."

"We do. We welcome any information that will help us catch the killer, but we're not asking the public to do our jobs for us. You're not a detective. Let us handle this and stop interfering in our investigation."

"How am I interfering?"

"We've had reports that you've been talking to teachers and former classmates of Dane Hutchinson who was convicted of murdering that drug dealer, Shane Hartlett. From what we've heard, you're telling people you think Hutchinson was framed and that the real murderer may, in fact, be the serial killer we're currently looking for."

"Has somebody lodged a complaint?"

"Not formally, no, but people have called us to question your involvement."

"I haven't broken the law," I argued, "and I haven't misrepresented myself in any way. I've always been straight forward with the people I contacted and told them why I was interested in the case. If someone didn't want to talk to me all they had to do was say so."

"You're asking questions about a murder case that's already been solved. Hutchinson had his day in court. A jury of his peers found him guilty."

"Well, I believe Hutchinson was set up. I think there were a lot of holes in the case and that a good defense lawyer could have gotten him acquitted. I know my neighbor Harlan Gannett believed Hutchinson was innocent and that he was interviewing people who had knowledge about the case when he was murdered. If Harlan was right and Hutchinson was framed, it would be a good reason for the real killer to go after Harlan, to shut him up so he couldn't dredge this case back up."

"That's a fanciful theory and one I've heard before. There's only one thing wrong with it. It's complete horse shit. I think you've been talking to that reporter from the paper, Mason Fowler. He's full of crackpot ideas. If you hang around him long enough, he'll have you believing in Bigfoot and the Loch Ness Monster."

"You mean they're not real?"

My sarcastic remark was met with deafening silence, and I instantly regretted saying it. I knew Whittaker was struggling to control his temper. When he finally spoke, he talked slowly in a carefully measured voice to make sure I understood in no uncertain terms what his message was. "I'm telling you to drop this crazy notion right now. You're telling people we put an innocent man in prison and that the real murderer is still at large. You're maligning my department and eroding the public's confidence in us. I won't have it."

I wasn't about to stop looking for my neighbors' killer, but I knew I had to be less conspicuous about how I went about it in the future. It was obvious to me the sheriff didn't believe that someone had sabotaged my truck. If he wasn't going to take my concern seriously, there was no point in continuing this conversation. To placate him I lied. "Well, you don't have to worry about me interfering any longer. I've exhausted all the leads I had, and there's no way I'm going to put my nephew in harm's way again. I'm done with this."

"I'm relieved to hear that," the sheriff said. "As I said earlier, we'll contact your mechanic friend, and if we determine this wasn't just an accident but a crime, we'll pursue it further. If you're right and someone did tamper with your vehicle to scare you off so you'd stop nosing around, you shouldn't have anything to worry about now that you've stopped asking questions."

I didn't find that very reassuring. It's basically what I told Ryder when he thought he had a target on his back. *Trust me,* I remember telling him, *you'll be fine.* And look what happened to him.

THIRTY-SEVEN

The little I had learned about Skid from Dave's grandma and her lady friends was not enough to sate my curiosity. I knew I needed to find out more about the boy and his family history before I'd be able to say with any certainty whether he was a viable suspect or not. What was Skid's, or more accurately, Alan's full legal name? Did his mother, Felicia, ever marry her abusive boyfriend? Did he adopt her illegitimate son? Did Skid move to the Central Oregon Coast and, if so, when?

If anyone could help me find the answers to these questions, I knew it would be Liz Stoddard, a retired librarian who had worked at the New York Public Library and had over forty years' experience in genealogical research.

I met Liz a few years ago at our local gym shortly after she moved to Newport from the East Coast. She had recently lost her husband and was still coping with his death at the time. She told me she volunteered at the Toledo Public Library where she donated her time, showing people how to use the library's resources to research their family histories. I told her I was a semi-retired, nature writer who had grown up in New Jersey just a few miles from New York City. We discovered we had a lot in common. We both loved gardening, bird watching, reading and enjoying an occasional glass of wine. We soon became fast friends.

When I called to ask her to help me find out more about

the boy nicknamed Skid, she was only too happy to oblige. I explained at length how I became involved in looking for my neighbors' killer, told her why I thought Skid might be involved and gave her what little information I had about the boy and his family. She told me she'd start working on it right away and get back to me when she had something to report.

I expected to hear from her in a few weeks, but she called me back just three days later to tell me she had some information she thought would interest me. She tried to hide it, but I could tell from her voice she was excited. She invited me to come by at five to have a drink and discuss what she had found.

I was a little too eager and arrived at her place a half hour early, so I just sat in my car outside her house, watching the clock on my dashboard count down the minutes. At the appointed time, I walked briskly up the sidewalk, ascended the front steps and rang the doorbell.

Liz was a handsome woman in her early seventies. She wore her years proudly and didn't try to hide her age with make-up. Her silver hair, which was cut in a pixie style, complemented her oval face and made her look a little like the English actress, Judi Dench. Her most noticeable feature was her beautiful green eyes, which sparkled when she smiled.

"Hello, my friend," she said, as she embraced me warmly. "It's so good to see you. Come in, come in."

Walking into her elegantly furnished living room, I was struck by how much it reminded me of a library or museum. Fine art prints and impressionistic landscape photographs graced the walls, and glass sculptures by Dale Chihuly, Harry Pollett and Rick Satava were on display in vitrines on antique side tables placed strategically around the room. There was a large glass display cabinet against the far wall, which contained a collection of rare books and first editions.

Liz motioned for me to take a seat on the blue camelback sofa, which was on the right side of the room across from a large stone fireplace. "Make yourself comfortable while I get my laptop," Liz said. She disappeared in another room and returned with the computer.

She placed the PC on the rectangular glass coffee table in front of the sofa and pushed the power button. "While we're waiting for it to boot up, I'll get us something to drink." She went into the kitchen and came back with two glasses of pinot noir. Handing me mine, she took a seat next to me on the sofa.

I raised my glass and toasted, "Salud."

"Salud," she repeated, as we clinked glasses.

As we sipped our wine, Liz said, "So I've kept you in suspense long enough. Let me tell you what I've found out about Felicia Wilkes."

"Wilkes?"

Shaking her head, Liz said, "I'm sorry. Wilkes was Felicia's married name. Her maiden name was Longbough. She was the only child of Alfred and Winifred Longbough. She married a man named Carter Wilkes, who, I assume, adopted her son."

"I'm confused. If he adopted the kid, wouldn't his name be on the kid's birth certificate?"

"I wasn't able to find a birth certificate for her son."

"Why not?"

Liz smiled. "It's complicated. I'll get to that a little later. Right now let me tell you what I do know for sure. Felicia's dead. She was only thirty when she died, and she and her husband Carter both died on the same day. I found photos of their gravestones on one of the genealogical websites on the internet."

She grabbed the wireless mouse and opened a folder labeled cemetery markers. Two documents popped up, and she clicked on the first one. "This is Felicia's headstone. You can see she died on June 26, 2005," Liz said. The caption under the picture provided the inscription on the grave marker and gave the name and location of the cemetery and the GPS coordinates for the cemetery and the grave's location.

Liz then pulled up the visual image of Carter's cemetery marker.

I read the date. "Yes, you're right. They both died on the same day."

Like a teacher, guiding a student through the discovery process, Liz handed me the mouse and asked, "Is there anything else in these two documents that you find curious?"

I scanned both files again. "OK...yes. Felicia's headstone has her maiden name, Longbough, not her married name, Wilkes."

"Very good," Liz said encouragingly, "but there's something else you're missing. Don't be in such a hurry. Take your time."

Frustrated, I accessed both files again and studied them closely. Suddenly it dawned on me. "Felicia is buried in the Longbough family plot in the Waldport cemetery. Carter is buried in a cemetery in Raymond, Washington."

"Exactly! They were married, both died on the same day, but they were not buried next to each other in the same cemetery."

"Why was that?"

"That's what I wanted to know. I found Felicia's obituary in the *News-Times*, but it didn't give a cause of death. I then accessed the local paper in Raymond, Washington, the *Willapa Harbor Herald*, to see if I could find Carter's obituary. There wasn't one. I then went back to the *News-Times* and reviewed the news stories in several issues that came out after June 26th to see if there was a car crash or something else involving the Wilkes. There was nothing, so I turned my attention back to the *Willapa Harbor Herald*. This time I had my answer."

Liz told me to open the Herald file, and I accessed the file as she directed. The date of the newspaper article was June 27, 2005, and the headline read:

Pacific County Couple Found Dead

A Pacific County dispatcher received a 911 call just after 4:00 p.m. on June 26th from a frantic thirteen-year-old boy who said "his dad was beating his mom and was going to kill her." A woman could be heard in the background screaming and pleading for

174

her attacker to stop. The call was then dropped, and the dispatcher wasn't able to get the boy back on the line.

About an hour later, the boy made a subsequent 911 call and, crying uncontrollably, screamed, "My mom's dead! My stepdad killed her. I knew he was going to kill me too, so I shot him. He's dead...I killed him. I didn't have a choice. I had to do it."

When the detectives who responded to the domestic violence call arrived on the scene, they found both the husband and wife dead and the son, who made the 911 call, beaten severely. The couple has been identified as Felicia May Wilkes and Carter James Wilkes. Because of his age, the son's name is being withheld.

A spokesman for the Raymond Police Department noted that the husband had a history of spousal abuse and that officers had previously visited the Wilkes home on seven separate occasions to investigate domestic violence.

Carter Wilkes also had a history of substance abuse, and police suspect that he was under the influence of methamphetamine at the time of the attack.

The Department spokesman confirmed that initial evidence supports the boy's version of events but stressed that the investigation is ongoing and a final determination has not yet been made in the case.

"So what happened to the kid?" I asked.

"A grand jury looked at the evidence and decided the son was acting in self-defense. He was never charged. Felicia's obit says she was preceded in death by her parents, Alfred and Winifred Longbough. If there was no other close relative who was willing to take him in, then the kid would have gone into foster care. If he got adopted, his name would have been changed, and his original birth record and adoption documents would have been sealed. Without a court order, it would be impossible to find out his new identity. This would explain why I couldn't find the kid's birth certificate."

Placing her right hand in the pocket of her white lace cardigan, Liz pulled out a flash drive and handed it to me. "I've copied all the vital documents and relevant newspaper clippings on this thumb drive for you. I hope it helps."

"Are you kidding me? You've been a big help."

Liz smiled sweetly, picked up her glass and finished off her wine. "So where do you go from here?"

"Tomorrow I'm going to contact Raymond's Chief of Police to see if I can convince him to tell me more about the case and give me the kid's name."

Liz giggled. "That's what I thought you'd do. I've done some digging to save you some time. The man who was the sheriff when this crime occurred is now retired. His name is Virgil Sackes. He and his wife still live in Raymond." Liz dipped her hand back into the pocket of her sweater, retrieved a piece of paper and handed it to me. "Here's his address and phone number."

THIRTY-EIGHT

I turned off the highway and drove down the long, gravel road, which was lined on each side by a row of poplar trees. At the end of the road was an old, two-story, red brick farmhouse. After my four-hour drive, it felt good to get out of the car and stretch my legs. I walked slowly up the long sidewalk, scaled the front steps and rapped the black iron door knocker several times.

A tiny woman with white hair, who was in her late sixties or early seventies, answered the door. Her eyes were the same shade of blue as the full rim plastic frames she wore. Although she had crow's feet at the corners of her eyes, her skin was remarkably smooth for her age. She was an attractive woman even now, and I guessed that she was probably quite a knockout when she was young.

"Hello, I'm Grady Riker. You must be Mrs. Sackes. I spoke with you on the phone a few days ago when I called to set up a meeting with your husband."

Extending her hand, she said, "Yes, of course. We're not formal here. Please call me Betty. Can I call you Grady?"

"Of course."

"Please come in. Virgil's inside watching TV."

She led me through the entryway into the living room. A 110-inch flat screen television was the dominant feature in the room. Across from the TV were two recliners. Virgil was rooted in the one on the right, watching a golf tournament.

Virgil was a big man, both in stature and in weight. He was over six feet tall and weighed about 270 pounds. He wore his silver gray hair in a military burr cut either out of habit or, more likely, as a way to hide his patchy bald spots. He had a prominent hawk nose, and below it rested a neatly trimmed lampshade moustache.

As Betty led me into the room, Virgil shut off the television and stood up to greet me. Towering over me, he said, "You must be Grady Riker. It's a long drive from the Oregon Coast. Betty, can you get us some iced tea?"

"Of course, honey," Betty said, as she went to the kitchen.

Sitting back down, Virgil motioned for me to take the recliner next to him. "On the phone, you said you had some questions about the Wilkes murders and wanted to learn more about the son who made the 911 call. You said you thought it might have something to do with the murder of two of your neighbors."

"That's right, Harlan Gannet and Ryder Driscoll."

"You know," Virgil said, "there are basically two reasons why I agreed to meet with you. When I was the police chief, if I got a call from someone like you, who was not in law enforcement, I would have just hung up the phone. But now that I'm retired, nobody cares about anything I have to say, and I'll talk to anybody who'll listen to me. So you caught me at the right time."

I tried to show no reaction, but I was deflated by his comment. My shoulders slumped involuntarily. *I've come a long way to talk to you*, I thought. *I hope you didn't just agree to meet with me so you could have someone other than your wife listen to your verbal meanderings.*

Just then, Betty entered the room, carrying a tray with a pitcher of iced tea and two glasses. She placed the tray on the coffee table and went back to the kitchen. Virgil and I each grabbed a glass and poured ourselves tea.

Sipping his beverage, Virgil continued his train of thought. "But my vanity wasn't the main reason I agreed to meet with you.

When you mentioned Harlan Gannet's name, it caught my attention and raised my curiosity."

I nearly jumped out of my chair. "So you knew Harlan?"

Shaking his head slowly from side to side, Virgil said, "No, we talked on the phone, but I never met him. He contacted me in early May before Betty and I went on our trip to Arches National Park. Like you, he was interested in talking to me about the Wilkes murders."

"Did he tell you why he was interested in them?"

"Not specifically. He just told me he was doing research for a true crime novel he was working on."

"Did he lead you to believe the book he was writing was going to be about the Wilkes murders?"

"No, he made it clear that it wasn't," Virgil said emphatically. "He said his book was going to be about the murder of a drug dealer on the Oregon Coast. He said he thought the guy who had been arrested and convicted of the crime was innocent."

"So then why was he interested in learning more about the cases here? Did Harlan explain what the connection might be between the Wilkes murders and the one he was working on?"

"No, he said it was a long story, and he'd fill me in when we met face to face. We were scheduled to meet in June after Betty and I got back from our vacation. When we got home, I called Gannet to confirm our meeting but just got a recording that the number was disconnected or was no longer in service. I never gave it another thought until you called. So now it's my turn to ask questions. What is this all about?"

"As I said on the phone, I'm a nature writer and don't know the first thing about looking for a killer. The only reason I'm pursuing this is because two of my neighbors, Harlan Gannet and his roommate, Ryder Driscoll, were murdered, and I was the unlucky one who happened to find their bodies. The authorities don't seem to have any leads or the motivation to look deeper to find some. To be quite frank, nobody liked the two guys who were killed. In fact, most of the locals are secretly happy they're gone."

Sipping his tea, Virgil said, "So you still haven't told me what the Wilkes murders have to do with any of this."

"Before his grandparents sold their home, Felicia Wilkes' son used to spend his summers at their place on the Oregon Coast. He did yard work for an elderly woman who lived near me, and it was on her property that I found Harlan's body. I think it's possible the kid came back to Oregon after his mother died and is involved in some way in my neighbors' murders. To be totally honest, I know it's a long shot, and I'm probably just grasping at straws. I'm hoping your input will either tell me I'm onto something or that this is a dead end."

Betty reappeared with a platter of smoked salmon dip and crackers. Placing it on the table next to the pitcher of iced tea, she said, "I thought you guys would like something to munch on."

As Betty retired once again to the kitchen, Virgil made himself a couple of appetizers and stuffed them in his mouth. With crumbs clinging to his moustache and some falling from his lips, he mumbled, "Help yourself. The dip is really good. Betty makes it from scratch."

"Your wife's great," I said. "You're a lucky man."

Virgil grabbed another cracker and topped it with a healthy helping of dip. Shoving it in his mouth, he said, "Yeah, I know. She's a keeper. Are you married, Grady?"

"No, I'm divorced."

"Sorry to hear that."

"Don't be. We weren't a good fit. We spent five years making each other miserable. We're both happier now."

"So ask your questions," Virgil said.

Setting my drink on the table, I leaned toward Virgil. "The newspaper article I read said that Carter Wilkes beat his wife to death and physically abused his stepson as well. It said the kid killed his stepfather in self-defense. Can you give me more specifics about what happened that day?"

Virgil sipped his drink and laughed. "That was eleven years

ago. At my age, I would have a hard time telling you what I ate for breakfast this morning. Lucky for you, you gave me a heads up. Knowing you were coming, I went to the station this morning and dug out the file on this case, so it's fresh in my mind. It's basically like the newspaper said. The old man came home hopped up on meth. He thought his wife was cheating on him and beat her to death. When the kid tried to intervene, the stepdad took his wrath out on the boy. The kid was pretty beat up when we got there."

I was crestfallen. "So that's it. There's nothing else?"

"I didn't say that. When we got there, the kid was on his front porch waiting for us. After what he had been through, I thought he'd be a basket case, but he displayed no obvious signs of stress or remorse. He seemed remarkably calm, almost relieved, which was especially surprising given how distraught he sounded when he made the 911 call. I asked him where the victims were located. He said his mother's body was in the living room and his stepdad's was in the backyard. Two of my men went in the house to inspect the woman's body, while the boy took me and another officer around back. The stepfather's body was lying face down in the field, and there were a couple of dead buzzards and several half-eaten raccoon carcasses on the ground about twenty yards further out from him."

Scratching my head, I said, "I guess I don't understand."

"Don't feel bad. Until I questioned the kid in detail, I didn't either."

I struggled to hide my frustration. I knew the old man loved the attention he was getting and was milking it for all it was worth. I bit my tongue. *Just tell me what you know!* "So what did the kid tell you?" I asked.

"The kid said his stepdad had already beaten his mother up pretty good by the time he called 911 for help. When his old man saw him talking to the dispatcher, he knocked the phone out of his hand and then started kicking the shit out of him as well. But apparently, that SOB hated the boy so much that beating him up wasn't enough. He wanted to abuse the kid emotionally as well as physically so he grabbed his 12-gauge shotgun and went outside and shot two of the buzzards that were feeding on the dead raccoons the kid had shot the night before."

I shook my head. "Back up, you've lost me."

Virgil laughed. "That's not surprising. The explanation is pretty convoluted. OK, here it is. The kid liked to shoot the varmints that came into his yard and feed them to the vultures. It could be raccoons, possums, rats…it didn't matter. Each night, he'd leave the animals he shot in the open field behind his house for the vultures to eat the next day. After some time, the buzzards got used to having this predictable food source, and they'd be there each morning, feeding on what he had killed. He fed them the same way you and I would feed songbirds."

"Yes! The kid did the same thing when he worked for my neighbor in the summer. He had an obsessive attachment to those birds for some reason."

Shaking his head vigorously, Virgil said, "That's what I'm saying."

"So what happened then?"

"The kid ran into his bedroom, got his 10-22 long rifle, went outside and shot his stepdad in the neck at close range, severing his spine. He then went inside and called 911 to report the murders. He said his stepdad had beaten his mother to death and then attacked him. He said he feared for his life and had no choice but to kill his stepfather to protect himself."

"And you believed his story?"

"Yes. It all checked out. The dead vultures had 12-gauge pellets in them, and the old man's fingerprints were the only ones on the shotgun. The kid's prints were on the 22 LR, and the autopsy confirmed that the stepfather had a .22 slug in his neck. The kid passed a psychological evaluation, and the grand jury determined that he acted in self-defense in killing his stepfather. No charges were ever filed against the boy."

"Do you know what happened to the kid?" I asked.

"No. After the grand jury proceedings, the boy was placed in the care and custody of Washington State's Department of Social and Health Services. If he didn't have any immediate family, he would have been placed in foster care until DSHS could find a family to adopt him. At his age, that might have been difficult. It's possible he wasn't adopted at all and that he was just passed around to different foster families until he reached legal age. I really don't know."

"I know that the kid's given name is Alan," I said. "Can you tell me what his last name was at the time you had contact with him?"

"Yeah, it was Wilkes," Virgil answered.

"So the scumbag who killed his mother did adopt the boy." Shaking my head slowly from side to side, I said, "That poor kid couldn't catch a break. I guess I'm no closer to finding out the kid's identity now than I was before I got here."

"I'm sorry I couldn't be of more help," Virgil said.

As I stood up to leave, I said, "No, you gave me a lot to think about. Thank you for your time. You and Betty have been more than gracious."

As Virgil was showing me out, he suddenly stopped dead in his tracks and said, "You know, it's probably nothing, but the Wilkes' boy's first name was spelled A-L-L-Y-N, which is a much less common variant than either A-L-A-N or A-L-L-E-N. If the kid was adopted by a relative or a friend of the family and moved to your area, you might be able to find him that way. That's assuming, of course, that the adoptive parents didn't change his first name. There can't be a lot of kids transferring to your School District from Raymond with their first names spelled like that. There's no way the School District would divulge that information to you, of course, but you might have your sheriff check it out. It might not be of much help, but it's something to consider."

THIRTY-NINE

As I inched slowly along behind a conga line of camper trailers and large motorhomes, I cursed my decision to take Highway 101 rather than the faster but more monotonous Interstate 5. I knew the scenic route would add at least an hour or more to my trip, but it was a beautiful summer day, and I wasn't in a hurry. Virgil Sackes had given me a lot to think about, and I thought a more leisurely pace southward with spectacular views of the coast would be preferable to the endless string of strip malls I knew I would encounter if I took the interstate.

If the bumper to bumper traffic I was stuck in was due to an accident I wouldn't have minded so much, but I knew the tie-up was caused by tourists slowing down to rubberneck. *That's what the scenic overlooks are for you assholes!* I had a king-size headache coming on. I couldn't tell if it was caused by stress or from inhaling the nasty diesel exhaust, which was belching out of the tailpipe of the mammoth land boat in front of me.

My cell phone started ringing, and I plucked it out of the center console. It was Mason Fowler. "Hey stranger, what's up?"

"That's what I was going to ask you," Mason replied. "Where are you?"

"Stuck in traffic on 101."

"It's that time of year. I hate the tourists, but the businesses on the coast couldn't survive without them."

"Too bad we couldn't get them to stay home and just send their money to us."

"Wouldn't that be nice?" Clearing his throat, he said, "I'm calling cause I told you I'd let you know when I had something to report. I got the police report on the Stacey Atwood accident. She was driving a 2003 Honda Civic with a five-speed manual transmission. There was no gear oil in the transaxle, so the cops think either the transmission or the differential failed, causing the accident."

"Holy shit! That means somebody probably messed with her vehicle too."

"What do you mean *too?*"

"Somebody sabotaged my truck a couple of weeks ago," I answered. "Whoever it was, drained the gear oil out of the differential, which caused the rear end to lock up. I wasn't in the truck. My nephew was driving. He skidded off the road and hit a tree. The vehicle's totaled."

"Oh my God, is he OK?"

"Yeah, he was lucky. He just needed a few stitches. Whoever tampered with the truck was out to get me. It happened after I started asking questions again. I think whoever did it was trying to send me a message to lay off."

"Did you report this to the Sheriff?"

"Of course, but as you might expect, he blew me off. He tried to blame the accident on shoddy maintenance, which is bullshit. He said I was just imagining things. He told me to stop playing detective and to stay away from you."

"You mentioned me? You told him we're working together?"

"I didn't have to," I retorted. "He figured that out for himself. He said you had crackpot ideas, and if I hung around you long enough, you'd have me believing in Bigfoot and the Loch Ness Monster."

"Fuck him. He's an asshole."

"Tell me something I don't know. Did you find out anything else you think is important?"

"No, I wish I had more, but that's it so far. How about you? You said somebody sabotaged your truck after you started asking questions again. You must have uncovered something somebody didn't want you to find out. What was it?"

I told Mason about Skid and his affinity for vultures and what I had learned from the old ladies at their tile rummy game and from my meetings with Liz Stoddard and Virgil Sackes.

Mason was obviously blown away by the news. "Wow, that's huge! So we were right. It wasn't just a coincidence that three of the murder victims were being fed upon by vultures when they were found. The killer is obsessed with these birds for some reason."

"Yeah, and listen to this. Sackes told me Harlan had contacted him in early May last year and wanted to ask him about the Wilkes murders."

"That was just before Harlan was killed!"

"I know. The two were supposed to meet in June, but obviously that meeting never happened. So I think we're on to something here."

"Did the police chief tell you what happened to the kid?" Mason asked.

"He didn't know. He said the boy was turned over to DSHS, and if he didn't have an immediate family member who wanted to take him in, he would have been placed in foster care until they could find a family to adopt him."

"Do you know if the kid had any close relatives living in our area?"

"None that I know of," I said. "His mother was an only child, and her obit said she was preceded in death by her parents."

"So where do we go from here?" Mason asked.

"That depends on whether you know anyone in the Lincoln County School District that has access to student records," I responded.

"As a matter of fact, I do. My ex-girlfriend is a secretary in the superintendent's office. Why do you ask?"

"Because when I was leaving Sackes' place, he pointed out that the Wilkes boy's first name was spelled A-L-L-Y-N, which is not that common. The Raymond School District is fairly small. It can't be much more than five hundred students, including the elementary grades, so there probably aren't a lot of kids, if any, of high school age, transferring to our School District from there in a given year. If we find a kid named Allyn, transferring from Raymond to one of our high schools in 2006, 7, 8, or 9, there's a good chance it's our boy. It could be a way for us to find out if he was adopted and, if so, what his new surname is."

"How do you know the kid's new parents didn't give him a new first name?" Mason asked. "Given his past, they might have renamed him just to protect the kid's privacy."

"That's certainly a possibility, but I still think it's something we need to pursue."

Mason's response was circumspect. "The District has strict rules about not giving out student information, so I don't want to get your hopes up. But I'll call my ex-girlfriend and ask her if she'll check the records. I mean we're not asking for much, and no one needs to know she was involved. I'll let you know what she tells me."

"It's worth a try. Hey, the traffic's starting to move again. I gotta go." I hung up and threw the phone back in the console.

FORTY

The long drive home had taken its toll on me. When I got out of my vehicle, I had a stiff neck and hunchback posture. As I stood there, squeezing my shoulder blades together in an attempt to straighten my back, my neighbor came out of his garage to greet me. I noticed there was an older model, blue Toyota pickup in his driveway.

"I thought I heard an old beater pull in," Dave said.

"My KIA's not a beater. It only has 176,000 miles on it."

"I wasn't talking about your car," Dave replied. "I was talking about you. You look like you've been through the mill."

I exhaled laboriously. "It's been a long day. I need a stiff drink. Come over. I can use the company."

I hobbled up the front steps with Dave in tow. We entered the house and walked through the living room. When we got to the kitchen, I opened the cabinet where I keep my hard liquor and turned to Dave. "What's your poison?"

"Nothing fancy, just something on the rocks."

After taking a minute to survey the bottles in front of me, I selected a fifth of Johnnie Walker Black Label and placed it on the kitchen counter. I then grabbed two rocks glasses out of the cupboard and retrieved an ice cube tray out of the freezer. I used a large metal spoon to crack the cubes into the tumblers and then filled both glasses with the twelve-year-old

Scotch. Handing Dave his drink, I said, "Let's go out on the deck."

I motioned for him to take a seat at the round umbrella table and grabbed a chair across from him. It was after six, and the sun had already retreated behind the hills on the west side of the valley so the portion of the deck where we were sitting was in shadow. A cool breeze was blowing upstream, gently rustling the leaves on the alder trees that lined both sides of the river.

I raised my glass and took a healthy swig of the silky Scotch blend. "Oh, that's just what the doctor ordered."

Dave swirled the deep amber liquid in his glass before finally taking a sip. "Mmmmm, that's smooth." He then launched into what it was he originally came over to talk to me about. "So, after Spencer's accident, you asked me to find you a good used truck to replace your Ford Ranger. Is that something you're still interested in?"

"Yes, of course. I definitely need a truck for hauling stuff to the dump and getting firewood. But I don't want to spend a lot of money, and I don't need anything fancy."

Dave's face lit up. "Well then, I have some good news for you. A customer of mine is ninety and shouldn't be driving any longer. His kids finally convinced him to give up his driver's license and sell his vehicles. He's got a 1980 Toyota truck that would be just perfect for what you need."

"Is that the blue pickup I saw in your driveway when I pulled in?"

"Yeah."

"How much does he want for it?" I asked.

"Eight hundred bucks."

"Is that a good price?"

"Anything that runs is worth at least eight hundred bucks," Dave answered. "It's an old truck, so the body's a little beat up and has some coast cancer, but it runs great. It's a great buy!"

"OK, you sold me. Buy it, and I'll pay you back."

Dave laughed. "I already did. I had to strike while the iron was hot or somebody else would have snatched it up. You owe me eight hundred bucks."

"Thanks. I'll write you a check before you leave here tonight."

Just then, I heard the front door open. I looked in that direction and saw my nephew walking purposefully through the living room toward the deck. He had a scowl on his face. I smiled at him to see if that would soften his mood, but there was no change in his facial expression. It was obvious he had something he wanted to get off his chest, but I had no clue what it was. I looked down at my drink. *God help me,* I thought. *I just want to sit here and relax. I'm too tired to deal with teen angst right now.*

I took a large gulp of my drink and then looked back at my nephew. "OK, so tell me what's wrong."

"Why didn't you tell me when you came to the hospital to pick me up that somebody screwed with the truck and that's what caused the accident?"

"I didn't know it at the time. It wasn't until after Dave checked out the vehicle that we suspected somebody may have tampered with it."

"So why didn't you tell me then?"

"I don't know. I wasn't trying to keep it a secret. I guess I just didn't want to worry you."

Spencer gave me the stink eye. "I'm not a little kid. You should have told me."

"You're right. I should have. I'm sorry. So are we OK now?"

"No, we're not OK. Mom called while you were gone and said you told her about the accident."

"I did. I called the next morning after I brought you back from the hospital. I wanted her to know you were OK."

Spencer looked at me like I was a traitor. "You never told me you told her about the accident."

Dave grabbed his drink and started to get up. "Maybe I should go."

I grabbed his arm. "No sit. We're all friends here." Turning back to my nephew, I said, "She's your mother. She has a right to know that her son was in an accident. I told her you were fine and there was nothing to worry about. So what's the big deal?"

"The big deal is that Mom wants me to move back to Portland. She thinks it's too dangerous me living here with you after somebody sabotaged your truck."

Suddenly it dawned on me. "Wait a minute. I never told your mother anything about anyone messing with the truck. Someone else must have told her."

"I did," Spencer answered. "I told her what Jacob told me."

"And that was?"

"That somebody drained the gear oil out of the differential and that's why the rear end locked up. I said whoever did it was after you, and if he didn't want to kill you, he at least wanted to send you a message to stop sticking your nose in other people's business."

I was incredulous. "So you told your Mom that?"

"Yeah."

"Well, for fuck's sake," I yelled. "That's why she wants you to move back with her. You have nobody to blame but yourself. You know what a worrywart she can be."

Spencer was livid. "She was accusing me of being drunk or stoned when I had the accident. What was I supposed to do? I had to stand up for myself."

"This is my fault," Dave piped up. "I shouldn't have said anything to Jacob."

"Don't be silly," I countered. "You did nothing wrong. It's my fault for telling my sister about the accident in the first place. I know how she can get when she's upset. I should have known better than to say anything at all."

My nephew glared at me. "Why can't you stop playing detective and let the cops find the killer? Nobody cares about the people he offed anyway."

"Is that what you think?"

"Jacob says that's what everybody thinks."

I went ballistic. "Jacob says! Jacob doesn't know his ass from a hole in the ground. I know he's your friend, but you need to grow up and start thinking for yourself."

"I *do* think for myself," Spencer barked. "The difference between me and you is that I'm willing to listen to other people's opinions. You don't because you always think you're right. I should have known this would be a waste of time. I'm going out. I'll see you later." Spencer turned and stormed off the deck.

I wanted to tell him to come back so we could talk it out, but I knew he was so angry that it would have been a pointless exercise. Instead, as I watched him leave, I yelled, "Use your head. We'll talk when you get home."

I sighed wearily, grabbed my drink and pounded what was left in the glass.

"Well, that went well," Dave said sarcastically.

Looking into my empty tumbler, I said, "I need another drink." With my glass in hand, I got up and walked back in the house. Dave followed me into the kitchen and took a stool at the counter. As I grabbed the Scotch bottle and filled my glass, I turned to him and asked, "Are you ready for a refill?"

Dave shook his head. "No, I'm good."

I took a swig of Scotch and grabbed a stool next to Dave. "I probably could have handled that better."

Dave grinned. "You think?"

Getting my back up, I said, "OK, Mr. Know-It-All, so what would you have done differently?"

"Well, if you want me to be totally honest, I'd say pretty much everything. But for starters, I wouldn't have attacked Spencer's hero. You know he thinks Jacob is cool and loves hanging out with him."

"I know. I just lost it when he started parroting back what Jacob said."

"And that's because you were jealous."

"Of Jacob?"

"Well...not specifically, but in a way, I guess." Dave hesitated a moment to try to clarify his thoughts. "You're jealous of the way

Spencer looks up to him. You resent the fact that he blindly idolizes his friend but seems to have no problem recognizing your shortcomings."

"That's bullshit. I didn't give a damn about winning a popularity contest when I was a snot-nosed kid in seventh grade, and I sure as hell don't give a damn about that now."

"Cool your jets! You should see yourself. Your eyes are all bugged out, and your face is beet red. You need to calm down. Look, I know it's hard for you to accept it, but Spencer is at that age now where he's going to question authority...and that means you, old man."

I took a big gulp of Scotch and a deep breath. "You're probably right. I never had any kids of my own. I'm in uncharted waters here."

"I hate to break it to you, buddy, but it's probably going to get worse before it gets better. So you better get used to it."

"Oh, that's comforting." Staring contemplatively in my glass of Scotch as if I was looking in a scrying mirror, I said, "You know, maybe my nephew going back to live with my sister wouldn't be such a bad idea after all."

Dave frowned. "You know you don't mean that."

Still looking in my glass, I sighed. "No, you're right. It would tear me up if he left."

"So what are you going to do about it?"

"I'll use my powers of persuasion to convince my sister he should stay here with me."

Dave chuckled. "Good luck with that. Maybe we should start packing his bags now."

FORTY-ONE

After Dave left, I grabbed my phone and called my sister. I knew I had to undo the damage my nephew had done by telling his mother the truth. I had to convince her that her son was in no danger and would actually be better off by continuing to live with me. The irony of this did not escape me. Just a year ago, when she called to tell me she wanted Spencer to come live with me, I struggled unsuccessfully to come up with an argument why this would be a bad idea. As I listened to the phone ringing now, I thought to myself, *How things change.*

When my sister finally answered, I said cheerfully, "Hey, sis. It's good to hear your voice."

"Well, hello big brother. I wondered when you would finally get around to calling me."

I raised my eyes in disgust. *Oh, not the long suffering sister routine again.* "I just got home a few hours ago and talked with Spencer. He told me you want him to move back to Portland."

"Yes, that's right."

"Well, I thought the plan was for him to stay here until he went off to college. Scholastically, he's really turned around since he got here. He did great this year. His GPA is 3.88. Can't get much better than that, am I right?"

"It's not his grades I'm worried about. It's his safety. Spencer told me somebody did something to your truck and that's why he had the accident. Is that true?"

"You've met my neighbor, Dave, haven't you?"

"He's the mechanic friend of yours."

"Yeah, that's right. Well, Dave looked at the truck after the accident and said there wasn't any gear oil in the differential. He thought maybe somebody might have drained the oil out and that's what caused the accident. But it was just a theory, and the cops discounted it. They said there was no proof that anyone had tampered with the vehicle. They thought the most plausible explanation was that the vehicle was old and had a lot of miles on it. I hate to admit it, but I think they're right. I probably should have gotten rid of that truck years ago."

"But Spencer said somebody messed with your truck because you have been nosing around, trying to find the person who murdered your neighbors a year ago. Is that true?"

"No, it's not. Spence was just repeating what he heard from his friend, Jacob. He's a young mechanic who works in Dave's shop. Jacob is kind of a loudmouth and doesn't know what he's talking about. I admit I did talk to my neighbors. I thought I might be able to uncover some information which might be useful to the authorities, but nobody told me anything. It soon became obvious to me that I was just wasting my time, so I quit doing it. It's nothing you need to worry about."

Before she could grill me further on this, I changed the subject. "But what we *do* need to be concerned about is Spencer's emotional and psychological well-being. He's at that age where his peers mean everything to him. Ripping him away from them right now could do irreparable harm, and I don't think you want to take that chance."

"I only want what's best for my boy."

"So we're in agreement then that he should stay here as long as he's happy and continues to do well in his studies?" I held my breath and waited for her verdict.

"I guess so. I mean…yes…of course. He's doing so well. We don't want to do anything to jeopardize that. Do we?"

I pulled out all the stops to seal the deal. "No, of course not. Sis, you're such a good mother. Spencer is so lucky he has you." I felt like I wanted to vomit, but it worked. My sister fell for my bullshit hook, line and sinker.

"Oh, that's so sweet of you to say," she gushed. "Is Spencer there now? I'd like to tell him what we've decided."

"He's out with his friends. I'll tell him when he gets home. Well, look, sis, I still have to make myself something to eat. It was great talking to you, as always. Love you. Bye now." I quickly ended the call before she had a chance to change her mind.

I put the phone down on the kitchen counter and waited apprehensively for several minutes to see if my sister would have second thoughts and call me back. When she didn't, I was relieved, but I also knew I wasn't out of the woods just yet. I knew she would keep badgering Spencer for details, at least for several weeks, and if she even had the slightest inkling that I was still playing detective, she would have him on the next train to Portland.

My only recourse was to continue the lie. I had to make everyone believe that I had run out of leads and had finally abandoned my quest to find the killer once and for all. That meant I had to lie to Dave as well. While I felt bad about this, I couldn't take the chance that he might slip and say something to Jacob or Darwin. If he did, it would surely get back to Spencer, and it would only be a matter of time before my nephew unwittingly revealed it to his mother.

Just then, the phone rang, and I tensed up. *Oh, no, don't tell me it's her.* I glanced down at the screen and immediately relaxed. It was Mason calling.

When I answered the call, I must have let out a sigh because Mason asked, "Is everything OK?"

"Yeah, I'm fine. I just got off the phone with my sister. I was afraid she was calling me back. I'm just relieved it wasn't her. What's up?"

"Well, I talked to my ex-girlfriend, and it's a no go. She read me the riot act for even asking her to divulge any information about a student. I knew the privacy of student education records was protected, but I didn't think it was that big a deal. I mean, it's not like I'm some pervert stalking a kid or something. I just wanted to know if some kid transferred to our School District. What's the big deal? It wasn't like I was asking her for the kid's address or phone number for Pete's sake."

"What did she say to that?"

"She about ripped me a new asshole. She said there's a federal law that restricts disclosure of information from student records. It's called FERPA, the Family Educational Rights and Privacy Act. She said she'd lose her job and probably go to jail if anyone found out she told me anything."

"Did you tell her that there is a real possibility that this information could help us identify the serial killer the cops are looking for?"

"Yeah, she didn't care. She told me to tell the cops what we know. She said finding the killer was their job, and if they thought the information was important, they'd be able to get it legally."

"It's obvious your girlfriend's never met the sheriff," I said flippantly. "Well, shoot. That sucks. So we're at another dead end. I don't know where to go from here. Do you?"

"Do you still have that yearbook you borrowed from the football coach at the high school?" Mason asked.

"Oh shit. I think I do. I promised the coach I'd return it when I was through looking at it, but it totally slipped my mind. I'll have to look for it. Why?"

"Well, now that we have a name, you could at least go through the pictures of the students again. Who knows, we could get lucky. Maybe you'll find there *was* an Allyn Wilkes or at least an Allyn in the senior class the year Hutchinson graduated."

"Wouldn't that be nice?"

"Look, I know it's a long shot, but it's all we got."

"I can't remember where I left the yearbook," I said. "I'll have to check around. I know it's here somewhere. I'll let you know what I find out."

I ended the call, set the phone down on the counter, hopped off the stool and went upstairs to my study to see if I could find the yearbook. As always, the only section of my desk which was visible was the area immediately around my laptop and printer. To the left of the printer were reams of copy paper and stacks of books. To the right of my mouse, were mounds of articles I had downloaded from peer-reviewed science journals and popular nature magazines. Scattered on the floor around my chair was a clutter of discarded drafts of an article about Pacific tree frogs I was still working on.

I scanned the tower of books to confirm that the yearbook wasn't in the stack and then dug through the piles of printed journal and magazine articles to make sure it wasn't hidden among them. I then stepped on the papers on the floor surrounding my chair to be certain the book wasn't buried there either.

Satisfied that the yearbook wasn't in my study, I sat down at my desk to think and gazed out the large picture window which overlooks the river. By now it was pitch-dark, so nothing was visible outside, but with the light from the floodlights over my desk, reflecting off the glass, the window became a black mirror, and I could see my face staring faintly back at me.

Looking at my ghostly image, I asked myself, *If the yearbook isn't here, where is it? Where was the last place you remember seeing it?*

I sat there in silent contemplation for several minutes, and then it came to me. It was when I gave the yearbook to Vic Dyer to see if he could identify the girl Hutchinson took to the Prom. When I left Vic's place I threw the yearbook in the back seat of my KIA. *It's got to still be there!*

I jumped off the chair, went down the stairs, opened the front door and ran to my car. I opened the rear door on the driver's side and rummaged through the pile of clothes that were on the back seat. It didn't take long for me to find the yearbook. I grabbed the book and took it upstairs to my study.

The first thing I did was go to those pages of the senior portraits section that had students with last names starting with W.
I found a student whose last name was Wilkey but no one with
Wilkes as his surname. I then went to the beginning of the student pictures and ran through all the male students in the senior
class to see if there was any kid with Allyn as his given name. I
found two Alans and one Allen, but no Allyn.

I can't say I was surprised. Over the past year, none of the
leads I had uncovered had amounted to anything. So, although
I was admittedly disappointed, I wasn't deterred. I turned my
attention to learning more about Stacey Atwood. I realized that
when I had first looked at the yearbook, Stacey wasn't even on
my radar. I went back to the beginning of the senior portraits
and found her picture. I already knew she was attractive. I had
seen her photo when Vic identified her as the girl Hutch had
taken to the Prom. What I hadn't paid any attention to at the
time were the sports, extracurricular activities, hobbies and future career goals that were detailed below her picture. I now
read these for the first time with great interest: Girls Track…
Football games…Reading… Music… Good Times… College
bound.

I leafed through the book until I came to the sports section
and found pictures of the girls track team. Stacey was in two of
the photos. One was just a team photo (she was in the third row),
and the other was an action shot of her running the hurdles.
However, what caught my eye was a photo of the girl's track
coach. It was Emily Crick, the English teacher I had talked to
when I had visited the high school a few months earlier. I knew
I would have to pay her another visit. I wanted to learn more
about Stacey, and I thought Emily might just be the person to
provide the information I was looking for.

Suddenly, the sound of an approaching car broke the still-
ness outside. I recognized the sound of the engine and knew it
was Spencer's Honda. I watched the light from his headlights
dance across the walls of my study as he approached. As soon

as he turned into the driveway, he cut his lights. I looked at the clock on the wall to see what time it was. It was after eleven.

I heard him close his car door, walk up the stairs and open the front door. I knew he had to have seen the lights on upstairs when he pulled into the driveway. I waited to see if he would yell a greeting, but he just walked through the living room and went to his bedroom without uttering a word.

I toyed with the idea of going downstairs to talk to him but decided against it. He obviously knew I was still awake. If he wanted to talk to me, he would have done so. He was avoiding me, which could only mean one thing—he was still angry. Confronting him now would only make matters worse. If I did go downstairs, he'd probably accuse me of waiting up for him. He'd say I was treating him like a little kid, just like he did earlier in the evening. I shut off my laptop, went into my bathroom, brushed my teeth and went to bed.

FORTY-TWO

When I woke up at eight the next morning, I looked out the front window and saw that Spencer's car was gone. I put on my robe, went downstairs to the kitchen and made a pot of coffee. On the counter was a note from Spencer written on a paper plate: Went fishing with Jacob.

Well, it's not much, I thought, *but at least he's still communicating with me.*

I poured myself a cup of coffee and went out on the deck. Since the sun was only now beginning to rise above the ridge on the other side of the river, the warmth of its rays had not yet had a chance to warm the air, and the river was still shrouded in a dense layer of fog. I took a seat and sipped my coffee. I wanted to appreciate the beauty and serenity of my surroundings, but I was too antsy to sit for very long.

I went inside, grabbed my phone and called Emily Crick. It was late August, and although it would be another week yet before the kids returned from summer break, the teachers had already returned to their classrooms. I told Emily I was planning on coming to the high school that day to return a yearbook I had borrowed from the football coach and asked her if we could possibly meet while I was there. She agreed and suggested we meet at ten-thirty that morning.

When I got to the high school, I checked in at the office

and then went directly to the gym to return the yearbook. Even though school was not in session, the players on the football team were there, and they were heading out to the field to practice when I arrived. I caught Coach Benson just as he was leaving his office to join them. I gave him the book, apologized for not having returned it sooner and then headed straight for Emily's classroom. When I got there, I stopped briefly at the door to check my watch. I was right on time.

As I entered her room, she got up from her desk and walked over to greet me. Shaking my hand, Emily said, "It's good to see you again, Grady. I've been working on lesson plans all morning, so this is a welcome break. I could really use a cup of coffee. The teacher's lounge is just down the hall."

When we entered the breakroom, there were a few teachers sitting around a table talking, but they were some distance away and showed no interest in us. I didn't recognize any of them. Emily gestured for me to take a seat at an empty table while she walked over to the Mr. Coffee that was on the table near the door. She grabbed the pot, which was half full, and inspected the contents. "Looks like it's been sitting here a while," she said. "So I can't say how good it is, but I'm desperate. Would you like a cup?"

Laughing, I replied, "I'm game if you are."

Emily filled two Styrofoam cups and handed one to me. Taking a sip from hers, she said, "Well, it's not Starbucks, but I've had worse."

I took a swig of my coffee and concurred. "It's actually a lot better than I expected it to be."

Emily took a seat at the table across from me and chuckled. "That's the advantage of having low expectations. You're rarely disappointed."

Trying to steer the conversation back to the matter at hand, I said, "Well, I know you're busy getting ready for the new school year, so I don't want to take up much of your time. As I mentioned on the phone, I just have a few questions I'd like to ask you about Stacey Atwood. I know she was on the girls track team and that you were her coach."

"Yes, she was also a student in my Writing 121 English Composition class her senior year."

"What can you tell me about her?"

"Stacey was a lovely girl, and she was very bright. She wanted to be an English teacher and was attending Western Washington University in Bellingham when she died in that horrible accident."

"I heard from one of her classmates that she went to the Senior Prom with Dane Hutchinson. Do you know if that's true?"

Emily furrowed her brow. "Yes, why do you ask?"

"It may not be important, but it's been rumored that Stacey had already committed to going to the dance with another boy when Hutch asked her to go as his date. If that's true, the boy she dumped would certainly have had a reason to hate Hutchinson."

"So you think this boy may have been the one who framed Hutchinson?"

"I don't know. Right now, I'm just trying to determine whether this information is accurate or not. I was hoping you could tell me."

Emily thought for a minute before answering. "Yes, it's true. After Hutchinson asked Stacey to go to the Prom with him, she came to ask me what I thought she should do. It was obvious she wanted to go to the dance with Hutch, but she knew she had made a commitment to that other boy and hated the thought of having to dump him and hurt his feelings. I think she wanted me to tell her it was OK, but I couldn't do that."

"So what *did* you tell her?"

"I told her she should listen to her conscience, and if she did, I knew she would make the right decision."

"But she went to the Prom with Hutchinson anyway."

Shaking her head slowly, Emily answered, "Yes, rather than listening to her conscience, she let her libido be her guide. Oh well, she was young. I know it's unfair for me to judge, but I have to say I was disappointed in her decision nonetheless. This is going to sound terrible, but I thought she was too good for Hutchinson."

"Is that because of his behavior toward women?"

"Partly that," Emily admitted. "But also because Stacey wasn't vacuous like the other girls Hutch typically hit on. She was an intelligent, young woman. She deserved someone who could connect with her on an intellectual level."

"So you thought she was selling herself short."

"Absolutely. Don't get me wrong, I know Hutch was handsome, and that was a powerful attraction. But he had no substance. He was a Neanderthal. Hutch and Stacey were about as suited for each other as oil and vinegar. Even if you could take Hutch's proclivity for womanizing out of the equation, and that's a big if, there was no way their relationship was going to last once the physical attraction between them lost its luster."

"Did she tell you the name of the boy she sent packing?"

"No, she never told me his name, and I didn't ask."

"Did she tell you anything about him at all?"

"Stacey never mentioned his looks, so I'm guessing he was just average looking. I'm sure he was intelligent. She said he was well-read and loved books as much as she did."

"Can you think of anything else?" I asked.

"Yes, from what she told me, I'd say he was the quiet type."

"So you're saying he was shy?"

"No, I'd say he was reserved. I think he was a very private person. Stacey said he didn't like talking about himself and whenever she asked him something about his family, he'd say it wasn't important and change the subject. I think she found him mysterious, and maybe that's why she was attracted to him."

"Maybe he had some deep dark secret he was hiding," I observed.

Emily's eyes twinkled, and her lips curved upward in a wry smile. "Don't we all?"

FORTY-THREE

After my meeting with Emily, I went straight home. I hadn't eaten anything all morning, and I was hungry. I took some cold cuts, cheese and condiments out of the fridge, and as I grabbed for a loaf of rye bread, which was on the countertop, I accidentally knocked over one of the rocks glasses which was still sitting there from the night before. As soon as it hit the tile floor, it broke into several pieces.

After uttering a few choice expletives, I brought the garbage can out from the cabinet under the sink, grabbed a broom and dust pan, swept up the shards of glass and threw them in the trash. I then washed my hands, ripped some paper towels from the holder to dry them and tossed the used sheets in the garbage on top of the broken glass.

I was just starting to make myself a sandwich when Spencer walked in. There was an awkward moment as both of us stood there, staring at each other, waiting for the other to be the first to speak. I could see that Spencer was clearly uncomfortable. I wanted to be the first to break the silence, but he spoke before I could say anything.

"Uncle G, I'm sorry for what I said last night. I was out of line."

"No worries. We all say things in the heat of the moment that we later regret. I said some things last night I wish I could take back as well."

My nephew nodded his head slowly and looked down. It was obvious he had something else he wanted to get off his chest.

"Uncle G, I need to ask you something, and you have to promise that you'll be honest with me."

"Of course, buddy. What is it?"

"Did you tell Mom about the accident so she'd make me go back to live with her?"

"I don't understand. What do you mean?"

Spencer started to tear up. "Do you want me to leave? Is that why you told Mom about the accident?"

My mouth dropped open, and I muttered, "Where did you ever get that crazy idea?"

Spencer thought for a minute. Still staring at the floor, he said, "I guess it was after I told Jacob that Mom was making me move back in with her. He said, 'Did you ever think maybe that's what your uncle wants?'"

I did my best to hide my anger. I wanted to say something disparaging about Jacob, but I remembered the reaction I got from my nephew last night when I criticized his hero of the day. Instead, I bit my tongue and asked, "Have I ever done anything to make you think you weren't welcome here?"

Spencer's lower lip started to quiver. "No...but what Jacob said got me thinking. That's why I'm asking."

With tears now welling in my eyes and my voice cracking with emotion, I said, "Spence, look at me. Nothing could be further from the truth. I love having you here. It would tear me up if you left."

Spencer looked up at me, and a tear ran slowly down his cheek. "Really, Uncle G? You're not just saying that?"

"Really, Spence. If you don't believe me, ask your mother. I called her last night after you left and talked her out of making you move back to Portland." I smiled at him reassuringly. "You don't have to leave unless you want to. She agreed that you can stay."

Spencer's eyes grew big, and a beaming smile spread across his face. "That's killer! How did you get her to change her mind?"

"Your Mom was concerned that by me snooping around and asking questions, I was pissing somebody off and, in the process, putting you in harm's way. I gave her my word that if she let you stay here, I'd stop tilting at windmills."

From the confused look on my nephew's face, I knew what I had said had gone over his head.

"Have you ever heard of Don Quixote?" I asked.

"Who?"

"Never mind, it's not important. What I'm trying to say is that I'm not going to waste any more time fighting a losing battle. I've given up trying to find the killer. I'm done playing detective."

"That's awesome!" Spencer ran over to me and gave me a big hug. "I love living here."

Hugging him back, I responded, "You don't know how happy it makes me to hear you say that."

When we ended our embrace, I said, "I was just starting to make a sandwich. Are you hungry?"

"No, after I left Jacob's place, I drove down to Waldport and got a burger at Chubby's food cart."

"What did you get?"

"What I always get. Their pastrami burger and crispy fries"

As I loaded ham, turkey and cheese on a slice of rye bread, I said, "I bet it tasted a lot better than this week-old lunch meat. So how was fishing?"

"We got skunked, but we're going out again later this afternoon."

"Well, don't get discouraged. It's not even September yet."

"I know," Spencer responded. "It's still way early in the run."

"Where were you fishing this morning?"

"Just a little down river from Jacob's place. But with the rain we had earlier this week, we're thinking that the fish have probably moved upriver, so we're going to give it a try up here tonight."

"Well, good luck," I said, as I spread mustard and mayo on my sandwich.

Spencer glanced at the full garbage can. "Heck, if I'm still going to live here, I guess I should make myself useful. I'll take the trash out."

He grabbed the ends of the bag, lifted it slightly until he had enough plastic to cover the opening of the can and then pushed down on the garbage with both hands.

Just as he did this, I remembered the broken glass. I started to warn him, but I was too late.

"Ouch!" he yelled, as he drew back his right hand and blood started dripping from his middle finger.

Grabbing his hand, I said, "Let me see how bad it is."

I placed his hand under the faucet to wash off the blood so I could see the cut clearly. The cut was about a half-inch long, but luckily it wasn't deep, and the edges weren't ragged. I knew by looking at it that it wouldn't require stitches.

My nephew pulled his hand back and grabbed a paper towel from the holder to dry his hand. "It's no big deal, Uncle G."

"There are bandages in the medicine cabinet," I said. As I started to walk toward the bathroom to retrieve them, Spencer grabbed my arm and stopped me.

"Don't bother, Uncle G. I've got it covered."

Spencer opened the top drawer on the end of the kitchen counter, which is our junk drawer. I watched him as he rummaged through the rubber bands, refrigerator magnets, thumbtacks, playing cards and other odds and ends that were in there until he found what he was looking for. He grabbed a roll of black electrical tape out of the drawer, peeled off the end and wrapped the tape around his finger several times until he had the cut sealed off. He then pulled the vinyl tape tight until it broke from the roll.

As my nephew tossed the roll of tape back in the junk drawer and closed it, I asked, "So when did you start using electrical tape as a bandage?"

"When I saw the mechanics doing it at Dave's shop."

"I'm sure they must get a lot of busted knuckles working on cars."

"Yeah, they're always getting cut up. Everybody has electrical tape in their tool boxes. It's handy, and it works great. If a cut bleeds a lot, you might have to put a piece of shop towel over it before wrapping it, but for most scrapes, all you need is the tape."

"But surely they must have a first aid kit there somewhere," I added.

Spencer started to snigger. "I guess, but nobody at the shop uses it. Dave says Band-Aids are for pansies."

Shaking my head slowly in disbelief, I asked, "Why am I not surprised by that?"

Ignoring what I had said, my nephew asked, "Hey, does Dave know I don't have to move back to Portland?"

"No, I called your Mom after he left last night. I haven't talked to him since."

Spencer grabbed the garbage bag and headed for the front door. "I'll dump this in the can outside on my way over to Dave's. I want to be the one to tell him the good news. See you later, Uncle G."

FORTY-FOUR

As I mentioned earlier, when I decided to lie to my sister and tell her I had abandoned my quest to find the killer, I knew it would only work over the long haul if I made everyone else believe the same thing. And what better spokesman to initiate my disinformation campaign than a fine, upstanding young man like my nephew? I now had Spencer believing the lie, and he was now over at my neighbor's, unwittingly misleading him as well. I knew if Dave believed what Spencer was telling him, Jacob and Darwin would buy into it as well.

Later that afternoon, several hours after Spencer and Jacob had left to go fishing, I went over to Dave's to see for myself whether he believed what my nephew had told him. I brought a couple of Coors Lights with me and put one in the fridge. Opening the one I kept, I sat down on the couch next to the stove and took a big gulp of my beer.

"So did Spence tell you the good news?" I asked.

"Yeah, he was stoked. He's a great kid. I'm happy he's staying."

"No more than me."

"I bet," Dave said. "So did you sell your sister a bill of goods or is it for real?"

"What do you mean?"

"I know you. Once you get something in your thick skull, you're as tenacious as a pit bull. I have a hard time believing you've really given up trying to find the killer. Is that just something you told your sister so she'd agree to let Spencer stay here?"

"No," I lied. "It's true. Because of the blow up with my nephew yesterday, I never had a chance to tell you about my meeting with the retired sheriff up in Raymond. The trip to Washington was a humongous waste of time. He couldn't remember anything. I finally had to face the facts. Every lead I've followed so far has turned out to be a dead end. It's time for me to move on."

Trying to be supportive, Dave said, "Well, you always knew it was a long shot. At least you tried."

Satisfied that Dave was now a believer, I changed the subject. "So I hear you think Band-Aids are for pansies."

"Who told you that?"

"Spence did."

Dave cracked a smile. "Well, Spencer got it wrong. I said Band-Aids are for pussies."

"Oh, that's a lot different," I said facetiously.

Just then, I noticed Dave had a fire going in his wood stove. "For fuck's sake," I yelled. "It's the end of August. Why do you have a fire going now?"

"Why do you care?" Dave asked defensively.

"Because I have the windows open upstairs in my bedroom. The smoke from your stack is going to come in and make the place smell like a campfire."

"Then maybe you should go home and close your windows."

"It's not going to get below fifty degrees tonight," I argued. "Are you doing this just to piss me off?"

"Why does everything always have to be about you?" Dave groused.

"You're the one who's being inconsiderate. There's no good reason for a fire."

"Yeah, there is. I like staring at the flames."

"That's it? That's your reason?"

"Yeah, I find it relaxing."

"Look, if you're stressed out, maybe you should smoke some CBD or get some Prozac," I countered.

"I already smoke more weed than I would if I didn't have to deal with you on a daily basis."

At that moment, we heard the sound of a boat approaching. "That sounds like Jacob's outboard," Dave said. Walking over to the window, he looked out on the river. "Yeah, that's them. Let's go out and see if they caught anything."

I followed my neighbor outside, and we watched as Jacob eased the boat in next to Dave's dock while my nephew tied the boat off to a couple of cleats.

"Any luck?" Dave asked.

Jacob and Spencer reached down below the gunwale and each came back up, holding a good-sized fish. As they got out of the boat and carried their salmon to the fish cleaning station up on the bank, Dave ran up to his house to get some knives. I went to get the garden hose, which was attached to an outside faucet on the side of the house. I turned on the water and brought the hose down to the fish cleaning station.

Unlike most fish cleaning tables, Dave's does not have a sink. It is just a stainless steel table with a back splash, but he has it angled in such a way that the water from the hose hits the back splash and runs off the table on the left side, carrying with it the blood and fish parts into a five-gallon bucket. While the entrails remain in the bucket, the water and blood inevitably overflow onto the ground. During fishing season, the cleaning station gets a lot of use. Consequently, the soil around the table rarely has a chance to dry out, and it is always muddy.

Using a handheld hanging scale, Jacob and Spencer each weighed their fish. My nephew's Chinook weighed twenty-two pounds; Jacob's came in at just over eighteen. I used my phone to take pictures of them holding their catch.

Grinning from ear to ear, Spencer raised his right hand in front of his forehead and formed an L with his index finger pointing straight up and his thumb out to the side at ninety degrees. "Loser," he said as he looked directly at Jacob.

Jacob laughed loudly. Seeing the confused look on my face, he explained, "After Spence and I each caught our fish, we argued whose was bigger and made a bet. I obviously lost, so I have to clean and package the fish while Spence just sits on his ass."

My nephew walked over and patted Jacob on the shoulder. "Don't feel bad, buddy," he said in a patronizing tone. "You gave it your best shot." Spencer then turned and walked to the garage, chortling the whole way.

I burst out laughing, but it was obvious that Jacob didn't see the humor in my nephew's remark. Gritting his teeth, he snapped, "Just remember, little buddy, every dog has his day."

Jacob then walked up to the cleaning station, turned on the garden hose and started to rinse the fish. When Dave returned with butcher and fillet knives and a box of freezer bags, Jacob snatched the fillet knife from his hand and started to gut the first fish. He inserted the blade in the vent on the underside of the salmon and ran the knife forward along the belly until he got to the base of the gills. He then used the butcher knife to sever the spine behind the head and removed the head and entrails.

Losing interest in the cleaning process, I left Jacob alone to complete his task and headed back to the garage. Dave followed me in, and as I retrieved my last Coors Light from the fridge, I turned to him and asked, "Do you need a beer?"

Dave sat down in his recliner and grabbed the open Hamm's can that was on the small table next to his chair to see if it was empty. "Yeah, this one's a dead soldier."

I handed Dave a beer and took the same seat I had on the sofa before we went outside. My nephew was on the couch to my right, but I don't think he was even aware that I was there. He was staring down at his phone and didn't bother to look up or say anything. He just sat there like a slug, playing some mindless video game.

Dave grabbed the remote and surfed through the channels

on the TV. I just sat there chugging my beer while the stations flitted by on the flat screen. Eventually Dave found a preseason NFL game, but by then I had finished my beer. I got up from my chair and was ready to leave for the evening when Dave asked, "What are you doing for dinner?"

"I don't know. Why?"

"Chloe's at her sister's in Philomath, and I'm making my own dinner. I already invited Spencer and Jacob to join me. We're having chili. If you don't already have something in the works, you might as well stay here and eat with us. I've got a case of chili, so there's more than enough for everybody. Go home, get more beer and come back."

I tried to think of a good excuse to bow out, but I couldn't think of one. "Sure," I heard myself say. "That sounds great."

Dave got up and retrieved four cans of chili from a cupboard over his workbench. He opened all four with a can opener and placed them on the wood stove. As I headed for the door, he said, "If you have an onion and some cheese, bring them back with you. I'm all out."

When I got home, I diced a Walla Walla sweet onion and shredded a chunk of Tillamook medium cheddar. I placed the toppings for the chili in a couple of Ziploc bags, grabbed a six-pack of beer out of the fridge and headed back to Dave's.

When I got back to the garage, I saw that Jacob had finished his task and had appropriated my spot on the sofa next to the wood stove. I was annoyed but didn't say anything. I handed Dave the storage bags with the onion and cheese, removed a can of Coors Light from the six-pack and placed the rest of my beer in the fridge. I then sat down in an arm chair behind the stove.

From my vantage point, I could see that Spencer was still completely immersed in his video game. Jacob was watching the football game on the TV. He had a NAPA Racing baseball cap turned backwards on his head and was wearing a black Thrasher hoodie with the classic Skate and Destroy logo printed in white on the front. His jeans, which were ripped at the knees, were tucked inside his black rubber boots. He was slouched down on the couch, his right leg was off the floor and the sole of his boot, from the toes to the ball of his foot, was up against the side of the stove.

Just then, I heard a spitting sound. Dave heard it as well and got up from his chair. Sauce from one of the cans of chili was starting to bubble over the rim and fall onto the top of the stove. Dave grabbed a spoon, and as he started to stir the chili, he looked down and saw that Jacob had his foot on the stove. "Jacob," he barked. "Take your boot off the stove. I don't want to smell burning rubber all night long."

Jacob quickly withdrew his foot and sat up straight. I could tell by the look on his face he was embarrassed and that this probably wasn't the first time Dave had called him out on it. "I think it's this damn couch," Jacob stammered. "The seat cushions are too soft. There's no support. I sink down, and with my long legs, I can't get comfortable."

"Whatever," Dave said. "I just didn't want you to ruin your boots." Dave grabbed a shop rag and removed the cans of chili from the stove. "OK, guys, I'm not your mother. Get off your asses and grab yourselves spoons. There's cheese and onions on the workbench, if you want it."

I waited until my nephew and Jacob got off their chairs and began loading whatever toppings they wanted on their chili. When I was sure no one was paying any attention to me, I got up and walked outside, ostensibly to take a piss. In reality, I wanted to inspect the footprints Jacob had left in the mud around the cleaning station. As I walked down the bank, I glanced over my shoulder several times to make sure no one had followed me outside. Satisfied that I was alone, I went over to the table and looked down at the tracks in the mud.

What I saw made my heart race and my hair stand on end. Just as I feared, the tread pattern on the upper half of the right footprints was missing. It was only evident in the back half of the tracks. In contrast, the tread design was clearly visible in the left footprints. While I couldn't be certain, I thought these tracks looked just like the ones I had seen in the mud at Ryder's place the day I discovered his body.

Checking over my shoulder one last time to be sure no one was watching, I grabbed my phone from my pocket and took several photos of the tracks. I then stuffed the phone back in my pants and headed quickly back to the garage.

Before entering, I stopped briefly at the door to consider my options. I realized I didn't have any. Until I could come up with a plan, I had no choice but to keep my mouth shut and act like nothing was out of the ordinary. I took a deep breath, arched my back and rolled my head around on my neck in an effort to release the tension I felt. When I was as relaxed as I was going to get, I put on the best poker face I could muster and walked in.

To my relief, when I entered the garage, everyone was eating, and no one bothered to look up or ask me where I had been. I assumed they all thought I had just gone outside to urinate. Without saying a word, I walked over to the workbench, claimed my can of chili and took it back to my chair. I kept my head down, didn't say a word to anyone and just stuffed my face.

I wanted desperately to go home, but I didn't want to call attention to myself, so when I was done eating, I just sat where I was and stared at the TV, pretending to be interested in the football game. I watched the plays, but I had no interest in who was winning. My primary focus was on the time clock. When the fourth quarter came to an end, I got up and made my exit.

FORTY-FIVE

It had been a long day, and I was tired, but I knew if I went to bed now, I'd just lie there, tossing and turning. I couldn't get the image of Jacob's tracks out of my head, and my mind was racing a mile a minute. Could Jacob really be the killer?

I tried to convince myself this was a crazy notion and that I was just letting my imagination run amok. But something was eating away at me. At first, I couldn't put my finger on what it was, but then it came to me. It was the electrical tape. My nephew said all the mechanics at Dave's shop use it instead of Band-Aids. I remember him saying that for most cuts, all you need is the tape, but if the cut bled a lot, you'd want to put a piece of shop towel over the wound before wrapping it.

After I had found Harlan's body and the cops had arrived, I recalled that Deputy Darby had found what looked like a small wad of black tape with something blue stuck to it. I remembered that he had it in a plastic evidence bag. I now realized it was probably electrical tape and that the "blue something" attached to it was probably a piece of shop towel. Jacob could have cut his finger working at the shop and used tape and a piece of paper towel as a bandage. It's conceivable that this homemade Band-Aid could have come off in a struggle when Jacob ambushed Harlan and slit his throat.

Once I started to seriously consider the possibility that Jacob might be the killer, I began to think back to see if I could recall any other clues I might have failed to pick up on at the time. That's when it dawned on me that Jacob had also been in the garage when I first came over to Dave's to see if he knew who Skid was. It was only a few days later that someone sabotaged my truck and my nephew had his accident. I found it hard to believe that this was just a coincidence.

I suddenly realized I had been going about it all wrong. A good sleuth, like an accomplished poker player, keeps his cards close to his vest. I, however, had been shooting my mouth off the whole time and had carelessly revealed who I had talked to and what I had learned. I had given Dave a status report almost daily, and Jacob had been present at many of these meetings.

When my nephew first came to live with me, I was initially thrilled that Jacob had taken him under his wing. But I now had to consider the very real possibility that Jacob might have had an ulterior motive in doing so. It would have been an excellent way for him to get inside information regarding how far along I was in my investigation.

I suppose, at the back of my mind, I always knew there was a chance the killer could be someone I knew, but the prospect was so chilling I probably just didn't want to face it. I couldn't deny it any longer. Everything I knew pointed to Jacob as being the killer.

I wanted to contact the sheriff, give him the photos of the footprints and tell him who I thought was the killer, but I was reluctant to do so and with good reason. The last time we talked, I had assured the sheriff I had stopped "playing detective." As soon as he realized that was not the case, I knew he would launch into a diatribe, castigating me for interfering yet again in his investigation. Given our past encounters, I questioned whether he would even seriously consider anything I had to say.

I could take a bruised ego. If that was the only thing stopping me from calling the sheriff, I would not have hesitated, but I had a greater concern. I knew I had a lot to lose if word got out that

I had contacted the sheriff. Despite all my denials, it would be obvious to Spencer and Dave that I had lied to them. My sister would eventually get word of it. And this time, there would be nothing I could say to change her mind. She would have my nephew back in Portland before I knew it, and Spencer would never forgive me for that.

I asked myself: *If the sheriff is going to dismiss me out of hand, why take the chance?* I didn't have a good answer for this question, and until I could come up with one, I made up my mind that I wasn't going to do anything.

As fate would have it, something happened just two days later that changed my mind.

FORTY-SIX

It was mid-morning on Sunday, and I was on the deck enjoying my second cup of coffee. The weather couldn't have been any more perfect. A scattering of cumulous clouds floated lazily overhead in a powder blue sky. As I sipped my java, I watched with interest as evening grosbeaks, American goldfinches, pine siskins and purple finches vied for space at the ports on the thistle feeder I had hanging from the edge of the roof of my garden shed.

Spencer was next door at Dave's, helping Darwin get his car ready for an upcoming autocross race in Reno. Jacob was there as well. I didn't want my nephew spending time with Jacob until I was certain he wasn't the killer. But what could I do? In the year since my nephew had been living with me, he'd become a permanent fixture in Dave's garage. He loved going over there and hanging out with the guys. I knew there was no way I was going to be able to keep him from fraternizing with Jacob without a good reason, and I didn't have one. I had my suspicions, of course, but no concrete proof he was guilty. I had to admit, even after all these years, I knew almost nothing about him. He was as much of an enigma today as when I first met him.

I reminded myself that the same was true of Darwin as well. When Dave first introduced me to Darwin, we shook hands, and after that we hardly ever talked. On those nights when I came over to Dave's garage and Darwin was there, he'd typically either be on the computer, searching for auto parts or playing Guitar Hero. He'd be facing the workbench and have his back to me the whole time I was there. He wouldn't bother to turn around and acknowledge my presence. For the longest time I thought he was either stuck-up or intellectually disabled.

I remember when I finally asked Dave about this, he thought I was crazy. "Are you kidding me? Darwin's not a snob, and he's certainly not a retard. He has an IQ of 140. He's smarter than me and you combined. He doesn't talk because he's consumed by whatever it is he's doing, whether it's looking for car parts or playing some computer game. He's not interested in football, old TV shows or the other inane stuff you and I talk about, so he doesn't get involved. Ask him something about cars, motorsports or computers and you won't be able to shut him up."

I told myself I had misjudged Darwin in the past. Maybe I was wrong about Jacob as well.

Since I was deep in thought, I didn't hear someone coming up the steps, and I nearly jumped off my chair when I suddenly realized someone was behind me.

Dave nearly busted a gut laughing. "I thought you heard me coming. Don't tell me you were nodding off already. It's not even noon yet."

"I wasn't sleeping. I was just thinking."

"I thought I smelled wood burning."

"What do you want?"

"Spencer said you were going into town today." Giving me a sly sideways glance and sniggering, he asked, "Are you going to see Jim again?"

Dave never got tired of asking me this whenever he knew I was going to the gym. It was his backwater idea of a joke. He was implying I was gay.

Shaking my head and speaking very slowly as if I was talking to a child, I said, "No, I'm going to the gym, not to *see* Jim. As I've told you a million times before, gym is a place, not a person."

Speaking normally again, I said, "I must admit I'm surprised you even know what homophones are."

"I'm not stupid. They're people like me who hate fags."

"Those are homophobes. Homophones are words like gym and Jim, which are pronounced the same but...oh, never mind, I'd just be wasting my time."

"So when are you leaving to go to the gym? Wink wink, nudge nudge, say no more, say no more."

"I give up. You're incorrigible." Raising my cup slightly, I added, "I'm leaving as soon as I finish my coffee."

"Can you shop for me?"

The nearest store is twenty miles round trip from home. On weekends, Dave is as sedentary as a barnacle and rarely leaves the comfort of his man cave. When he's running low on one or both of his staples, which are beer and cigarettes, he asks me to pick them up for him, so I pretty much knew the answer to my question before I asked it.

"What do you need?"

"A thirty-pack of Hamm's and two packs of smokes."

"You bought a case on your way home from the shop on Friday," I argued.

"I know, but I forgot Darwin and Jacob were coming over to work on the MR2. We'll need more beer."

"You got money?"

"I don't have any cash on me. I'll have to pay you back."

"You still owe me for the beer and cigarettes I picked up for you at the store last week."

"You know I'm good for it. You don't need the money anyway."

Laughing, I said, "I'm glad you know so much about my finances. Alright, I'll shop for you, but it's going to be at least three hours until I get back."

"We should be fine until then. If we get desperate, we'll raid your fridge."

I chugged the last of my coffee and got up to go into the house.

"Wait, I got one more favor to ask," Dave said.

Pretending to be exasperated, I sighed heavily. "What now?"

"Can you stop by my shop on your way back and pick up my toe plates? We need them to adjust the front end alignment."

"I don't even know what toe plates are or what they look like."

"They're two flat pieces of metal with slots at both ends. You put two tape measures in the slots and measure the difference between the front and back of the tire. They're in a flat white cardboard box in the top of my tool box."

Dave stuffed his right hand in his front pocket and withdrew a large metal O-ring with at least a dozen keys. He searched through the keys until he found the one he was looking for and then removed it from the ring. Handing it to me, he said, "This is the one for the front door of the shop."

As I grabbed the key, I had a light bulb moment.

FORTY-SEVEN

After my workout, I drove to Dave's shop and picked up the toe plates. I then stopped at the convenience store and bought the items Dave asked me to pick up for him. When I got home, I grabbed the toe plates, beer and cigarettes and took them over to my neighbor's garage.

Jacob was the first one to see me coming. "Hooray! The cavalry has arrived." Running up to meet me, he snatched the thirty-pack out of my hand. "What took you so long, old man? We ran out of beer about an hour ago. If you didn't get here soon, we were going to have to resort to drinking water."

"I have Coors Light in my fridge," I replied.

"I know. That's what I was talking about."

Dave grabbed the cigarettes and the toe plates. "Thanks, Cramps. How's Jim?"

Giving him a dirty look, I said, "Don't start."

Jacob ripped open the thirty-pack and passed out beers to Darwin, Dave and me. After taking one for himself, he placed the rest of the beer in the fridge and took a frosty Mountain Dew out and handed it to Spencer. "Here you go, little buddy. It's break time."

With his beer in hand, Jacob walked over to the couch and plopped himself down. Spencer followed and sat next to him on the sofa. Dave took his usual place in his recliner, and I claimed the chair behind the stove. Darwin walked over to the work bench and, with his back to us, started drinking his beer while searching through a stack of CDs.

I tried to make small talk. Without addressing anyone in particular, I asked, "So when's the big race?"

Without turning around, Darwin answered, "Next weekend."

"It's in Reno, right?" I asked.

"Yeah, it's being held at Stead Airport, just north of the city."

"I thought you ran on loose surfaces, like dirt or gravel."

"You're thinking of rallycross," Darwin said. "Autocross is run on concrete or asphalt. The course is laid out with traffic cones in large parking lots or airport tarmacs."

"Darwin's lucky I'm giving him the time off," Dave interjected. "I've already told Jacob if he wants to keep his job he better show up for work the days Darwin's gone."

Darwin found the CD he was looking for and put it in the player. Laughing, he turned around and looked at Dave. "Nice try, Chief. But you can't make me feel guilty. I asked for those days off months ago. If you didn't write it on the schedule, that's your problem."

Smiling, Dave turned to me and confided, "I was just giving him a hard time. I scheduled us light for the days he'll be gone."

The music began, and Jacob yelled, "Hey, crank it up."

I recognized the song immediately. It was AC/DC's "You Shook Me All Night Long."

Darwin turned up the volume, and Jacob started headbanging, playing his air guitar and singing the lyrics:

> "She was a fast machine
> She kept her motor clean
> She was the best damn woman I had ever seen"

Dave pretended to not know who the artist was. "Hey, who's singing that song?"

"Brian Johnson," Jacob answered enthusiastically.

"That's right, so let *him* sing it."

Jacob shut up, and everyone including Jacob started laughing.

When the laughter quieted down, Darwin finally looked at me and said, "Actually, I think I may have given you the wrong impression."

"What?" I was totally confused. I didn't know what the hell he was talking about.

"Rallycross races are usually run on loose surfaces, but that doesn't mean that they can't be run on asphalt. There have been rallycross races run on mixed surfaces and even some which were held on inactive airstrips."

Trying to being facetious, I replied, "That's really interesting."

Darwin seemed receptive to my response and became even more animated. "Yeah, and the substrate the races are run on is not the only difference between autocross and rallycross. In autocross, it's your single-best run of the day that counts. In rallycross, it's your cumulative time for all the runs that day."

I thought to myself, *And I care about this, why?* I smiled and pretended his explanation was illuminating. "Wow, I guess you learn something new every day."

Dave thought I was serious and piped up. "I told you he was smart."

Looking at Dave in disbelief, I said, "Yeah, that you did, that you did."

The song ended, and "Thunderstruck" surfaced through the speakers. Darwin chugged the rest of his beer, placed the can down and grabbed the toe plates Dave had left on the work bench. Handing one to Jacob, he said, "Let's get this job done, and then we can party."

Dave stood up, grabbed two tape measures out of one of the drawers in the work bench and handed them to Jacob. "You'll obviously need these as well. While you guys are setting the toe, I'll go up to the house and make the pizza."

As Dave headed out the door, Jacob got off the couch, chugged the last of his beer and set the can down on the wood stove. With his toe plate and tape measures in hand, he walked back to the car. Spencer jumped up and followed him. "I want to help," he said. "What can I do?"

Setting his toe plate on the floor and placing it flat against the side wall of the left front tire, Jacob answered, "Once we're set up, you can get under the car and adjust the tie rods."

Darwin crouched down on the opposite side of the car and placed his plate against the right front tire. From his vantage point, I knew there was no way he could see me.

I got up and looked over to see what Jacob was doing. He wasn't looking at me either. He was running the tape measures under the car, one in front and one behind the tire, so Darwin could place the hooks on the ends of the tapes in the slots in his plate on the other side of the car. Spencer had his back to me and was watching what Jacob was doing.

I saw my chance, and I took it. I grabbed Jacob's beer near the base of the can and left mine in its place on the wood stove. I walked past Jacob as he was pulling the metal ribbons through the slots in his toe plate. He never even looked my way. As I walked out of the garage, I said, "I'm going home. I'll see you guys later."

When I got home, I placed the beer can in a paper bag and hid it in a desk drawer in my study. Now all I had to do was convince the sheriff to have it tested to see if Jacob's DNA matched that of the killer. *Oh, won't that be fun?* I thought.

FORTY-EIGHT

The next morning, I called the sheriff. I told him I had just uncovered some new information which I thought would be helpful in identifying the person who sabotaged my truck. I thought it best not to tell him the whole truth right out of the gate. I knew he would go ballistic if I told him the real reason for the call was that I thought I knew the identity of the serial killer. My plan was to eventually work up to this revelation during our meeting.

Whittaker agreed to meet, and we met at eleven at the City Hall in Waldport. He was already seated at the table in the conference room when I got there. I carried a file folder under my arm and had the paper bag with Jacob's beer can in my hand. Whittaker gestured for me to take a seat across from him.

I placed the file folder and the bag on the table in front of me and sat down. Whittaker placed his elbows on the table and folded his hands together under his chin. He stared down at the items I had placed on the table for a few seconds, took in a deep breath and then exhaled slowly.

Looking up at me, he flashed a false smile and said, "So, Mr. Riker, I'm a bit perplexed. The last time we talked, you assured me you were going to let us handle the investigation. Now you tell me you have some new information which you think will help us nail the perp who tampered with your vehicle. How is it exactly that you came upon this new information?"

I knew this would be his initial response, and I was ready for him. Speaking in a conciliatory tone, I responded, "When I said I had new information, I meant it would be new to you. When we talked last time, I was still traumatized by my nephew's accident, and I wasn't thinking clearly. After I had some time to calm down, I remembered some information which I now think is important but had neglected to tell you at the time. But before I get into that, can I ask you a question first?"

Whittaker didn't say anything, but pursed his lips slightly and shook his head affirmatively.

"Have you talked to my mechanic about the accident?"

"Yes. I questioned Mr. McConnell at length in his shop. He basically said the same thing you did, but he was more specific."

"Well, he's a mechanic, and I'm not."

"He also showed us paperwork which confirmed that you brought your truck in to his shop on a regular basis for routine check-ups. He was adamant that the accident was not due to poor maintenance. He said that when he inspected your vehicle after the accident, the drain plug in the differential was in but only finger tight. He said whoever drained the fluid most likely put the plug back in so that the driver wouldn't notice oil dripping on the ground when he backed out of the driveway. That made sense to me."

"So you believe me now that someone messed with my truck?"

"I think it's likely. If I didn't, I wouldn't be here. So let's cut to the chase. Who do you think tampered with your vehicle?"

"I think it was one of my neighbor's mechanics...Jacob Dietrich."

"And what makes you think it was him?"

"It's kind of a long story. Let's see, it—"

The sheriff cut me off. "Don't worry about that. Just begin at the beginning."

I struggled to keep from laughing. His response made me think of Lewis Carroll's *Alice's Adventures in Wonderland* and what the King said to the White Rabbit at the trial of the Knave of

Hearts: "Begin at the beginning and go on till you come to the end: then stop."

How appropriate that this reference should come to mind, I thought. *I feel like I fell down a rabbit hole when I stumbled upon Harlan's dead body.*

Looking at the sheriff with a straight face, I said, "I was just going to say that it all started when my nephew came home one day after doing yard work for Edwina Risley. She asked him to kill some rats that were living in her wood pile. When he completed the task, she told him to throw the dead rodents on the river bank and feed them to the turkey vultures. But she didn't say turkey vultures. Her actual words were 'feed them to your pets like you always do,' and she called my nephew 'Skid.'"

"Who's Skid?" the sheriff asked.

"Edwina has dementia. I think she mistook my nephew for the boy who did yard work for her years earlier, and I assumed his nickname was Skid. The fact that she referred to the vultures as *his pets* and said that he should feed the carcasses to them, *like he always did,* suggested to me that the boy she had working for her liked the birds and probably routinely fed them the nuisance animals she had him dispatch on her property. When I found Harlan's body on Edwina's property—the same place this kid used to work—he was being fed upon by vultures—the same birds this kid seemed to be fixated on and liked to feed dead animals to. I thought this was more than a coincidence. I thought this kid was connected to Harlan's murder in some way, so I went over to my neighbor's garage to ask him if he knew who the kid was."

"When you say your neighbor, you're talking about Dave McConnell, the mechanic?"

"Correct."

"Was he able to identify the kid?"

"No, but Dave said his grandmother was a friend of Edwina's, and he thought she might remember Skid and be able to tell us his real name. He agreed to set up a meeting for us the next day."

I could see the sheriff's eyes glazing over. "And this is important, why?"

"It's important," I said, "because Dave's two mechanics were in the garage, working on a car, while he and I were discussing everything I just told you. They both overheard everything we talked about. I never used my truck after that, and it was only a few days later that my nephew had his accident."

"Who was the other mechanic?"

"Darwin Nettles."

"So why is he not a possible suspect as well?"

"Because he's not Skid."

The sheriff's face instantly became crimson, and I knew he was nearly at his wit's end.

"Look, Sheriff, I know it's confusing. Please, just bear with me a little longer and give me a chance to explain."

He stared at me expressionless. Nodding and extending his hand, he said, "Go on."

I told Whittaker almost everything. I omitted the fact that Dave and I had conspired to illegally tape the old ladies' conversations at Edwina's tile rummy game. But other than that, I told the sheriff everything. I told him what I had learned from Liz Stoddard about Skid, his mother and his abusive stepfather. I opened the file folder I had brought with me and handed him copies of the newspaper articles she had given me, which dealt with the dual murders of Skid's mother and stepdad.

I recounted everything that Raymond's retired police chief, Virgil Sackes, had told me about the murders: that the stepdad beat Skid's mother to death; that he then went after the boy and shot two of his "pet" vultures; and that Skid then killed his stepfather in self-defense. I told the sheriff that Skid's legal name at that time was Allyn Wilkes but that he might have been adopted sometime after that and his name may have been changed.

When I finished my long explanation, Whittaker coughed slightly, gritted his teeth and grabbed a roll of antacids out of his pocket. Popping four tablets in his mouth and chomping down on them with his right molars, he said, "Well, that's quite a story, but it's all anecdotal. I don't think it merits bringing Dietrich in for further questioning."

"No, that's not all." I then told the sheriff the story about how I came to find Jacob's footprints. I removed the photos of the tracks from the file folder and handed them to the sheriff. "Look at these. I can't be sure, of course, but to me, they look a lot like the ones that were in the mud on the riverbank when I found Ryder Driscoll's body."

Whittaker examined the photos carefully for several minutes. "We'll compare these to the ones from the crime scene. If there's a match we'll bring him in for further questioning."

"No! That's just what I don't want. He'll know that you're on to him, and he could skip."

"So what do you want me to do?"

I slid the paper bag across the table. "The can in this bag has Jacob Dietrich's genetic material on it. I want you to have it tested and compare it to the serial killer's DNA."

Whittaker looked at me with saucer eyes. "How did you get this?"

"Does it matter?"

Whittaker scrunched up his face. "Of course it matters. If it was obtained illegally, it wouldn't be admissible in court."

"I didn't steal it, if that's what you mean. My neighbor asked me to buy him a thirty-pack of Hamm's, and this was one of those beers. I saw Jacob drink it. When he was done, he left it on the wood stove in my neighbor's garage, and I took it. I made sure I only grabbed the can near the bottom, so the rest of the prints on it will be his. Nobody else touched it or drank out of it. And I bought the beer, so the empty can is my property."

The sheriff seemed stunned by everything I had told him. He didn't say anything, so I continued my argument for why he should take what I was telling him seriously.

"Jacob spends a lot of time over my neighbor's place," I argued. "And two of the murder victims lived right next door. If

Jacob had nothing to do with the murders, then why would he want to sabotage my truck? There has to be something pretty bad in his past if he's willing to injure or kill someone to keep it hidden. I know you need more evidence before you can arrest him. I get that. That's why I'm giving you his beer can. If his DNA matches the killer's genetic material, case solved. If there is no match, then all it cost was the price of running the test. Hell, if it comes down to a budget issue, I'll pay for the test."

"That's not an issue."

"Then what's the problem? The way I see it, it's a win-win situation. If I'm right, you have your killer. If I'm wrong, it's no harm, no foul. You don't end up having egg on your face for arresting an innocent man, and my neighbors don't run me out of town on a rail for being the one who fingered him."

The sheriff still didn't say anything. He grabbed the roll of antacids, peeled the wrapper back and threw three more tablets in his mouth.

"Look, Sheriff, I know you're under a lot of pressure right now. The local newspaper has been critical of the way you've handled the investigation. The mayor and county commissioners are worried that they'll be the press's next target, and they're looking for a scapegoat to take the heat off them. I'm not your enemy. I never have been, and I've never criticized you in the press, but I'll promise you this. If you sit on your hands and do nothing and the murderer kills again and it turns out I'm right and Jacob is the killer, I'll go to the newspaper and spill my guts. I'll tell them about our conversation here today and how you had an opportunity to catch the killer but took a pass."

The sheriff started shaking with rage, slammed his fist on the table and barked, "I'm sick and tired of your insolence. Who do you think you're talking to? You can't intimidate me. This conversation is over. Good day, Mr. Riker."

I left the paper bag with the beer can and the file folder with the photos of the footprints and the newspaper clippings on the table and started for the door. Half way across the room, I turned and looked the sheriff in the eyes and asked, "What are you going to say to the family of the next victim when they ask you why you didn't have the can tested? I hope you have an answer for them that will let you sleep well at night. Good day, Sheriff."

FORTY-NINE

It was 8:00 am on Friday. Dave had just arrived at his shop and was surprised to see that Jacob's Jeep was not there. It wasn't like his young mechanic to be late for work. If anything, he was usually there early. When Dave arrived most mornings, Jacob would be sitting in the office, drinking coffee, eating his breakfast sandwich and looking at pictures of nude girls on the internet.

Shaking his head, Dave laughed to himself. Every time he got a virus on his computer, he would blame Jacob for it. "How many times do I have to tell you not to get on porn sites on my laptop? The next time I get a virus, you're fired!"

Dave knew he was a pushover. He was like a permissive parent who made threats his kids knew he'd never enforce. After Jacob had committed the same infraction several times without any penalty being imposed, he realized Dave's threats were idle and he'd suffer no consequences for his actions.

Dave grabbed his dog, Roscoe, off the front seat of his truck and lowered him to the ground. As he unlocked the door to the shop and removed the CLOSED sign from the front window, Roscoe shuffled slowly to his bed under the desk.

Dave checked the phone in his office to see if there were any messages. There were none. He then grabbed his cell out of the front pocket of his jeans. No text or voice messages.

Yesterday after work, Dave and his two young mechanics had

gone to the Flounder Inn for an impromptu, little send-off party. Darwin was leaving in the morning to drive to Reno to participate in the autocross race on the weekend. Nobody planned on staying very long. Dave was there for no more than an hour and only had a couple of beers. When he left, Jacob and Darwin were in the middle of a game of eight ball. Their pitcher was nearly empty, and he assumed they would be leaving as soon as their pool game was over.

Dave felt his blood pressure rising. *Jacob had better not have picked last night to tie one on. If he calls in sick today, I'm going to kick his ass. He knows Darwin's on his way to Reno, and it's only him and me today.*

Dave started a pot of coffee, and while he waited for it to finish brewing, he cleaned up the shop and jockeyed cars around. He moved three vehicles outside that had been left in the shop overnight and were scheduled for pickup today.

When he was done, he poured himself a cup of joe, sat down at his desk in the front office, grabbed his cell and called Jacob. As he listened to it ringing, he sipped his coffee. No one answered the call, and it went to voicemail. Looking at the clock over his desk, he said, "Hey dickhead, it's eight forty-five. Where are you? You better be on your way in. Let me know what's up."

Just as he ended the call, a car pulled up in front of the shop. Dave craned his neck to look out the front window. A little old man was just getting out of his 2004 white Cadillac Seville. Dave recognized him immediately. It was Charlie Evers, the retired grocery clerk who lived just a few blocks from his shop. He had a fedora straw hat on his head and was clad in a colorful Hawaiian shirt, white elastic waist slacks and white loafers.

Dave checked the appointment book that was open on his desk to make sure Charlie was on the schedule. "Yep, there he is, nine o'clock appointment for an oil change."

Dave liked the old guy, but he knew Charlie loved to shoot the breeze, and he didn't have time for that today. If Jacob was going to leave him high and dry, he had to get his customers in and out as quickly as possible.

The shopkeeper's bell on the front door jingled as Charlie entered the office and shuffled to the front desk.

Dave greeted him with a smile. "Hi, Charlie, your Caddy due for an oil change?"

The old man handed Dave the key. "Yep, and I'm here right on time, as per usual."

"Good man, Charlie. Punctuality is a virtue. Do you want to wait in the customer lounge or are you going to walk home and come back later?"

"I'm going to walk to the Flounder to get some breakfast. They have a new bartender that's caught my eye. She's a real looker."

"You're talking about Roxie?"

"You know her?" Charlie asked.

"Not personally, no. I saw an attractive older woman working behind the bar last night when I stopped in after work. I thought that might be who you were talking about."

"How did you know her name?"

"Oh, I don't know, maybe because she was wearing a nam-etag with Roxie printed on it. Look, Charlie, I'd love to chat with you, but I'm all by my lonesome today, so I got to get a move on. You can pick up your car in a half hour."

"Who're you kidding? The way I walk it will take me at least that long just to get to the Flounder."

"Well, Charlie, your Caddy will be waiting for you here when-ever you get back." Without waiting for a response, Dave left the shop, got in the Seville, and drove it into the garage.

Charlie shook his head in disapproval as he shuffled out the door. "Young people today are always in such a hurry."

After Dave completed the oil change, he did a safety check on a 1990 Toyota Motorhome RV, completed a used car inspec-tion on a 2008 Toyota Sienna and replaced a headlight on a 2003 Ford Escort. None of them were big jobs, but they took longer than they normally would have because he was constantly being interrupted by customers either coming in to drop off their vehicles or calling on the phone to make appointments for the following week.

Dave looked at the clock in his office. It was eleven-ten, and he was already running behind schedule. If Jacob didn't show up soon, he was screwed. There was no way he was going to be able to complete all the jobs today by himself before closing. He glanced down at his desk and saw that he had inadvertently left his cell phone sitting there and had missed a call. He had been in and out of the office repeatedly dealing with customers, so he couldn't say when he had set it down. He hoped the missed call was Jacob calling in to tell him he had overslept and was now on his way in.

Dave accessed his voicemail and waited anxiously to hear the message. To his dismay, the caller wasn't Jacob. It was Grady: "Hey Dave, I just discovered that we have no water. The pressure's not just low. We have no water at all. I'm going up there now to find out what the problem is and see if I can fix it. I just wanted to let you know what was going on. Don't worry about me. I'll be fine. See ya."

Dave played the message over and over again. Furrowing his brow, he thought to himself. *It's early September. We shouldn't have a problem with the water system at this time of the year. The water pressure was fine when I took a shower this morning. And now Cramps says we have no water at all. I guess a tree could have come down and busted the water line, but the weather's been great. It hasn't rained in two weeks, and we haven't had any strong winds. It makes no sense. What else could explain it? I suppose somebody could have purposely fucked with our water, but why would anyone want to do that?*

Suddenly, the thought of Spencer's accident flashed through his mind. Dave's eyes grew large and owl-like. "It's a trap!" he yelled.

He looked to see what time it was that Grady had called…just a little over ten minutes ago. He tried calling Grady back but got no answer. Stuffing his cell in his pocket, he grabbed a piece of paper from the notepad on his desk and scribbled the following message: Had a personal emergency. Be back as soon as I can. Go next door to the Hair Salon and ask for Tammy. Sorry for the inconvenience.

Dave taped the note to the front door, grabbed Roscoe from his bed under the desk and placed him on the bench seat of his truck. He then locked up the shop and ran to the hair salon, which adjoins his business, to talk to the owner, Tammy.

Dave and Tammy were good friends, so he knew he could trust her. "Something's come up, and I have to leave for a couple of hours. Here's the key to the shop. If someone comes by to pick up their vehicle while I'm gone, can you go next door and get them their keys?"

"Of course," Tammy said. "Is everything OK?"

"I don't have time to explain right now. I'll fill you in later. I left a note on the door telling customers to come here and see you. Tell them I'll give them a call as soon as I can and they can settle up with me later. You're a sweetheart."

Dave ran out of the beauty shop, jumped behind the wheel of his truck and started the engine. As he raced upriver, he took his cell out of his pocket and tried calling Grady. The call went straight to voicemail. Dave didn't bother to leave a message. He threw his phone down in the center console and cursed Grady out loud for being so pigheaded. "He knows we have a rule about no one going up to the water system alone. What was the big hurry? Why couldn't he just wait until I got home tonight?"

Thirteen miles up the highway, Dave took a right, crossed the bridge over the river and navigated the winding Forest Service roads for several miles before coming to the gate that separates the government land from the private property where the water system is located.

Dave hopped out of his truck and unlocked the gate. He then got back in his vehicle and headed up the dirt road for a few miles more. When he was within a quarter-mile of the water system, he found an open space on the side of the road where he parked his truck. Grabbing Roscoe by his muzzle, he looked into his dog's cloudy eyes and kissed him on his head.

"You have to stay here, old friend," Dave said. "I'll be back soon." Since Roscoe was deaf and blind, it was no surprise that he didn't show any response. Dave grabbed his 30-06 off the rack on the back of his cab and walked briskly up the road.

FIFTY

Since Dave was the one in charge of maintaining our water system, I called him at work as soon as I discovered we were out of water. I knew it must have been a recent occurrence because Spencer had taken a shower before he left for school today, and everything at that time was just fine. Dave didn't answer my call, which didn't surprise me since I knew he was shorthanded today with Darwin being gone. I left him a voicemail message to let him know I was going up to the water system to see if I could figure out what the problem was. It was nearly eleven when I got in my truck and headed up to the water system.

When I got to the site, I got out of my vehicle, exchanged my sneakers for rubber boots and walked toward the wire fence, which kept elk and domestic cattle from defecating in our water source. Before I even opened the gate, I saw the problem. The volume of water, coming out of the eight-inch flume, was robust, but someone had placed a cover over the holding tank, preventing the water from filling it. Someone had sabotaged our water system.

Suddenly, something tore into the back of my right leg, sending a sharp, stabbing pain shooting up my spine and radiating down my leg. As I collapsed on the ground, I grabbed my limb and saw that I had been shot with an arrow from a crossbow. The bolt had traveled through my thigh, and the razor-sharp broadhead was sticking out of the front of my leg.

I instinctively looked up in the direction from where I thought the attack had come. I scanned the canopy of trees on the riverside of the road and saw a man about thirty feet away from me, dressed in lightweight camo clothing, sitting twenty feet up in a tree stand on a western hemlock. His face was covered in black make-up, and he had moss and sticks tied to the camo baseball cap he wore on his head. At first, I didn't know who it was, but then he spoke.

"You know it didn't have to be this way."

I recognized his voice immediately, and it all suddenly made perfect sense to me. It was Darwin. Unless a miracle happened, I knew I was going to die. I couldn't hide the pain I was in, but I was determined to hide my fear. I tried to affect an attitude of self-confidence and acknowledged him with a flippant response.

"So, Skid, how did you get your nickname anyway?"

Chuckling, he asked, "Does it matter?"

"Not really, I'm just curious."

"Not a good trait to have. It often gets you in trouble. Just ask Harlan and Ryder...oh, wait...you can't."

"So you admit it was you who killed them?"

"Among others," Darwin said smugly. "And soon you'll be the latest member of the club."

"When do I get to learn the secret handshake?"

Darwin started laughing in an exaggerated, halting manner. "That's a good one. Even in adversity, you still have a sense of humor. I like that."

Squeezing my leg in a vain attempt to alleviate the burning pain, I said, "I think it was Charlie Chaplin who once said: 'To truly laugh, you must be able to take your pain, and play with it.'"

"Well, if he was right, by the time we're done here today, you'll be positively giddy."

"I can't wait."

Chuckling, he replied, "Oh, trust me, you won't have to wait long."

"You can kill me, but you won't get away with this," I retorted.

"Before I left to come up here, I left a message on Dave's cell phone. You know, your boss and mentor? I told him I was coming up to fix the water system. He's probably on his way up here right now. Are you going to kill him too?"

Darwin laughed. "Dave's not coming up here, at least not until he closes the shop at the end of the day. And you'll be long dead by then. He and Jacob are all by themselves today. I'm supposed to be on my way to Reno for a race, remember?"

"I know you won't believe this," I said truthfully, "but I actually feel sorry for you."

Darwin looked at me with genuine remorse. "Why couldn't you learn from what happened to Ryder? I didn't want to kill him either, but he wouldn't let it go. He had to keep stirring the pot and asking questions...just like you're doing now. Why did you have to get involved in all this anyway? You hated Harlan like the rest of us. You should be happy he's gone."

"Yeah, he was a pain in the ass, but I never wanted him dead."

"He was trying to californicate the river," Darwin argued. "If Cali was so fucking great, why didn't he stay down there where he belonged? Why did he have to come up here and try to change the way we live?"

"That's bullshit, and you know it," I countered.

"You're telling me he didn't try to change things?"

"No, I'm saying that's not *why* you killed him. Harlan started looking into the Hutchinson case. He believed Hutch was innocent and that somebody set him up. How close he was to figuring out it was you, I don't know. But I know you didn't want him dredging that case back up. You couldn't take the chance he might learn the truth: that it was you who killed the drug dealer, not Hutch. That's the real reason you killed him, isn't it?"

Darwin's lips curved upward in a twisted grin. "Yeah, that's right."

Taking a conciliatory tone, I asked, "So why did you hate Hutchinson so much?"

"He was an arrogant piece of shit. He disrespected me in high school, and I swore I would get even."

"He stole your girlfriend, didn't he?"

Darwin became defensive. "He did it to everyone. Not just me."

"You were going to take Stacey Atwood to the Prom, but she ended up going with Hutchinson instead. That's why you framed him."

Darwin seemed self-satisfied and chuckled. "Yeah, I killed two birds with one stone. I got rid of a meth head who was selling poison to the kids in our schools, and I made sure Hutch got what was coming to him. It was a stroke of genius, if I do say so myself."

"But Stacey wasn't blameless in all this," I argued. "She was ultimately the one who dumped you. So you made sure she eventually got what she deserved as well. You sabotaged her car, and she ended up going off the cliff at Cape Foulweather."

Darwin smiled broadly and giggled in delight. "It couldn't have worked out any better if I had planned it that way."

"So who gave you the right to play God?"

"Oh, don't give me that holier than thou bullshit. I just had the guts to do what needed to be done."

"Your victims were human beings for fuck's sake!"

"They were human garbage: a drug dealer, a sex offender and an animal abuser. Are you going tell me the river isn't better off without them?"

"Yeah, in your warped mind, I'm sure you see yourself as an unsung hero. You like to think that you're providing a valuable service by cleaning up the river, just like the turkey vultures you love so much."

"Don't try to psychoanalyze me." Darwin shook his head slowly in disgust. "Boy, you really do have an inflated image of yourself, don't you? You think that you're better than us river rats, that you're morally superior."

"Well, I haven't murdered anyone if that's what you mean."

Darwin had obviously run out of patience with me. He placed his crossbow on its stirrup on the foot platform of the tree stand, pulled the cable up and cocked his bow. He grabbed a bolt and placed the odd-colored, fletching of the arrow in the rail with the end of the bolt firmly against the cable.

As he did this, I used my forearms to feverishly drag myself backwards on the ground in a futile attempt to find cover behind my pickup. But the burning pain in my right leg severely hindered my progress, and I was only able to move a few feet before Darwin had his bow ready to fire.

Turning his attention back to me, he barked, "Don't move any further or I'll kill you right now!"

I knew he was serious and stopped dead in my tracks.

"I want to know what you know and who else you've shared this information with."

Looking up at him, I said, "And I should give you this information, why?"

Sneering down at me, he said, "Because I can make it easy or hard on you before I kill you. I would think that would be ample motivation."

"Your argument would be a lot more compelling if one of the options was me leaving here alive."

Darwin's lips turned upward in a contemptuous sneer. "Not gonna happen."

Closing my eyes and dipping my head slightly, I said, "OK, I'll tell you what you want to know, but only after I get answers to the questions I still have."

"Why should I tell you anything? You don't have any leverage."

Looking up at him defiantly, I said, "Oh, I think I do. I know a lot more than you realize."

"You're bluffing! I know everything you know and who you've talked to. From the very beginning, you've shared everything you know with your buddy, Dave. Either me, or Jacob, was present when most of those conversations took place, either in the shop or in Dave's garage at home. That was your big mistake."

"Yeah, you're right. In the beginning, it was. But when Edwina dredged up Skid out of her memory, and I came over to ask Dave about him, you and Jacob were in the garage and overheard everything we talked about. I never used my truck after that, and it was only a few days later that Spencer had his accident. I knew the person who sabotaged my truck had to be somebody close. I knew it wasn't Dave, so that left only you and Jacob. From that moment on, I kept my mouth shut and didn't say anything to anyone, not even Dave. But I kept on digging and finally discovered that you were Skid and found out everything about you."

Darwin looked down at me with a scowl on his face. "You're lying! You're trying to buy time. That's what all my victims have done at the end. Even though they know death is inevitable, they'll say or do anything if it will extend their lives for just a few precious minutes more."

"If you're so sure, than why didn't you kill me right off? You shot me in the leg intentionally to incapacitate me so you could force me to tell you what I know."

Darwin was obviously flustered. His eyes danced around erratically as he tried to decide whether to kill me right then or to answer my questions first.

I took advantage of his moment of indecision to further argue my case. "Look, we both know that you're in the catbird seat. You're going to kill me, so anything you tell me will go nowhere. So what have you got to lose? Let me satisfy my curiosity and die a happy man. I really just want to understand your motivation. I want to know why you did what you did."

I could see in his eyes that Darwin had made a decision. He had regained his confidence. "Yeah, you're right. I have nothing to lose, so I'll humor you. Ask your questions."

"Ever since you killed the sex offender, you've left DNA at each of the crime scenes. I know it's not yours. So whose is it?"

"You're the detective. You tell me."

"It's Jacob's."

"Very good, you get a gold star. What else do you want to know?"

"Why would you throw Jacob under the bus? I don't understand. I know you guys don't have a lot in common, but you were friends and housemates. You always seemed to get along."

"It was nothing personal. Jacob just happened to be a ready source of DNA. Since we worked together and shared a house, I had ample opportunities to collect his genetic material. A pop can, cigarette butt, used Kleenex, beer bottle or roach, you name it. I knew the cops didn't have his DNA on file, so the only way his identity would be discovered would be if he became a prime suspect and the cops got a warrant to get a DNA sample from him. If I thought the cops were ever getting close to closing in on me, I'd just plant some incriminating evidence on him or in his car and make an anonymous call that would lead the cops to him."

As Darwin was talking, I caught sight of Dave walking stealthily down the right side of the road with his rifle in hand. We made eye contact, and Dave brought his finger to his lips, signaling me to remain silent. I knew Darwin couldn't see him since he had his back to him. I quickly looked away from Dave and fixed my eyes on Darwin so as not to tip him off.

When Darwin finished talking, I said, "It's basically the same thing you did when you set Hutchinson up. You left the murder weapon in his truck and then made an anonymous call to the cops claiming to have seen his truck at the crime scene when you murdered the drug dealer in the marsh."

Shaking his head, Darwin said, "Exactly. Why reinvent the wheel? It worked like a charm then, and it will again."

"That's where you're wrong. If you were going to kill me, you should have done it sooner. By doing it now, the cops will know for sure that you're the killer."

Darwin contorted his face in disbelief. "That doesn't make any sense."

"Oh, but it does. I originally thought Jacob was the killer. So last weekend when you guys were working on your car in Dave's garage, I stole Jacob's beer can off the wood stove and gave it to the sheriff to have his DNA tested. They have his DNA now. If you try to pin my murder on Jacob, it won't work. How could he leave his DNA up here if he was working at the shop with Dave all day? The cops will know he was framed, and they'll eventually figure out that it was you who's been setting him up all along."

Darwin exploded in anger, "You meddlesome piece of shit! You fucked everything up!"

He raised the crossbow to his shoulder and was about to shoot me when Dave yelled out, "Darwin stop!"

The sound of Dave's voice startled Darwin, and he swung around to face him. Wild-eyed and shaking, he lowered his bow and moaned, "Oh, no...no...no. It wasn't supposed to be like this. This isn't what I had planned."

Dave had a determined look on his face, but it was tempered with a sadness that dwelled deep in his eyes. "It's over, Darwin. No more killing. Please...just drop the bow now."

Darwin hung his head in silence for what was only seconds but seemed to me like an eternity. Raising his head, he looked at Dave and pleaded, "I can't go to jail. Just let me kill him, and everything will be OK. I'll stop. I won't kill any more. I swear."

"It's too late for that. You're not going to kill anyone. It's over! Make your choice. If you try to kill him, I'll shoot you."

Darwin looked away and started to cry.

Dave tried to be firm, but his voice was cracking with emotion. "Look at me, Darwin. Look me in the eyes. You know I'm serious."

Sobbing and choking, Darwin was convulsed with grief. He looked at Dave like a kid who just realized his hero was a mere mortal, no different than himself. "I thought you were on my side. You and Pop-Pop were the only ones who ever really cared about me. And now you're siding with this infected piece of shit!" With tears streaming down his face, he looked Dave in the eyes and said, "I don't have to make a choice. You already made my decision for me."

Darwin raised his crossbow to his shoulder and placed his cheek on the rest. I froze, thinking he was going to kill me. But instead, Darwin pointed his bow at Dave, put his finger on the trigger and fired.

I heard the loud crack of a rifle shot echo across the valley and saw Darwin's body jerk backwards as the bolt from his crossbow sailed just feet above Dave's head. A Douglas squirrel let loose with a high-pitched alarm call, and a murder of crows, frightened by the rifle shot, took flight from surrounding trees and squawked incessantly as they flew across the river. Darwin fell backwards off his perch and plummeted to the ground, landing on his back. Dark red blood was pouring from his chest and running down his sides.

Dave ran over to Darwin and knelt down next to him. Looking down at his friend's lifeless body, Dave started crying uncontrollably and shaking his head slowly from side to side. "You stupid kid, why did you make me do it?" Choking on his tears, he asked over and over again, "Why, buddy, why?"

FIFTY-ONE

Dave's grief was palpable. I knew he regarded his two young mechanics as his kids, and now he had just killed one of them. I couldn't begin to know what was going through his mind. I wanted to say something which would alleviate his pain, but I knew anything I said right now would ring hollow. He had killed Darwin in self-defense, saved my life and, most likely, prevented other people from being murdered in the future. Maybe in time he could find solace in that but not now, so I said nothing.

I stripped the belt from my jeans and used it as a tourniquet to stop the bleeding in my leg. I then reached into my pocket, retrieved my cell and dialed 911. The phone was dead. No service. I had no choice. I wanted to let Dave grieve, but I desperately needed his help now.

"Excuse me, but I'm dying here."

Dave jumped up, wiped the tears from his eyes and said, "Oh, shit! I'm sorry, Grady."

As he ran over to me, I said, "I tried dialing 911, but my phone doesn't work."

"You don't still have Verizon do you?"

"Yes."

"Well, that's why it doesn't work," Dave barked. "I told you the last time we came up here that AT&T owns the cell tower.

Verizon doesn't have access to their network. I told you to change your provider, but you didn't listen to me."

"I just forgot."

"No, you're just stubborn and lazy."

"For fuck's sake," I shrieked. "This is no time to argue. Use your phone and call 911."

"I can't. I left it in my truck."

"Where's your truck?"

"About a quarter-mile down the road."

"Well, help me over to my truck, and we'll go get the phone from your vehicle on our way out."

Dave dragged me over to the back of my truck and helped me stand up. "Why are you always so angry?" he asked.

"Maybe the fact that I've got a fucking arrow sticking out of my leg has something to do with it. Do you have anything in your truck we can use to cut the tip of the arrow off so we can pull the bolt back out?"

"We don't have to cut the shaft," Dave answered. "The tip unscrews." He bent down, grabbed the shaft with his right hand, placed his left hand on the broadhead between the blades and unscrewed it. He threw the tip on the ground and said, "I don't think we should remove the shaft. I'm afraid you'd start bleeding more if we did."

Dave jumped into the back of the truck and started to pull me into the bed. I squealed in pain as he lifted me up.

"Stop being such a baby," he said. "It's just a flesh wound."

"Flesh wound? I'm bleeding like a stuck pig!"

"Stop being so melodramatic, you're not bleeding that badly."

"That's because I've already lost so much blood, there's not that much left in me to drain out," I retorted.

"That's stupid, and you know it. If you had lost that much blood you'd be unconscious, and I wouldn't have to hear you whining like a little bitch."

Dave jumped into the cab, started the truck and drove up the road to the wide spot where we usually turn around to go home. I saw that Darwin's car was parked there. I reached up and pounded on the back window of the cab. Dave reached back and opened it.

"When the cops search Darwin's vehicle," I said, "I'm willing to bet anything that they'll find something inside it with Jacob's DNA on it. Darwin's been leaving Jacob's DNA at each crime scene to frame him."

"I know. I heard you guys talking about that when I came up."

"Darwin also admitted to killing the drug dealer and framing Hutchinson."

"I know. I heard that too."

Dave raced down the dirt road as fast as he could go and still maintain control of the vehicle. When we got to his truck, he jumped out of the cab and grabbed his cell from the center console. Petting his dog on the head, he said, "Be patient, Roscoe. I'll be back for you, buddy."

Dave handed me his phone and hopped back in the driver's seat of my pickup. As he put the truck in gear and stepped on the gas, he yelled, "I'm glad I didn't lock the gate behind me when I came in. I had a bad feeling that something wasn't right."

"You're a smart man," I yelled back.

"Wow, I've never heard that before," Dave countered. "Are you willing to put that in writing?"

"You can't hold me to anything I say right now. I'm probably delirious."

Dave chuckled. "So, you're no different than normal."

As we raced down the winding Forest Service road, I dialed 911. "It's ringing!" I yelled.

The dispatcher answered. "Lincoln County 911. What is the address of your emergency?"

"We're on a Forest Service Road up Boundary Road," I answered. "I've been shot in the leg with a crossbow."

"Sir, I need an exact location."

"I can't give you one. We're on an unmarked Forest Service

Road. We're in a blue '80 Toyota pickup, heading toward Boundary Road. Please send an ambulance."

The road was littered with potholes, and at the speed we were going, I had to cling to the side of the truck to keep from being battered about. The pain in my leg was excruciating.

Dave yelled out, "Tell the dispatcher to send the paramedics and the cops to the Tidewater Post Office. We'll wait for them there."

I relayed that information to the dispatcher.

"The EMTs and police are on their way," she responded. "Please stay on the line until they get there. What's your name, sir?"

"Grady Riker."

"Can you spell that for me?"

"R-I-K-E-R."

"How old are you, Mr. Riker?"

"What difference does that make?"

"Please calm down, sir. I have to ask these questions."

Sighing heavily, I responded, "I'm sorry. I understand. It's just that every time we hit a bump I get a huge jolt of pain, shooting up my spine. I'm 61."

"OK, what is your emergency?"

"I've been shot in the leg with a crossbow."

"You're breaking up. What part of the body did you say?"

"My leg…my right leg…in my thigh."

"OK, got it. Are you bleeding badly?"

"I'm using my belt as a tourniquet, so I'm not bleeding that badly right now."

"How long ago were you shot?"

"I don't know, maybe an hour ago. I really don't know. That's just a guess."

"OK, was this an accident?"

"No, the person who shot me wanted to kill me. He's the serial killer the cops are looking for. He was going to kill me, but my neighbor shot him in self-defense. He's dead."

"Where is the person who shot you?"

"Up in the woods. I can't give you an exact location. My neighbor, who's driving right now, can show the cops where it is when they meet us at the Post Office."

"OK. What's the name of the person who shot you?"

"Darwin…Darwin Nettles."

"Do you know how old he is?"

"Mid-twenties, I think."

"OK. And you said you think he's dead."

"Yes. He was shot in the chest."

"OK. Tell me exactly what happened."

As I continued to answer the dispatcher's questions, we reached the main road and turned left, heading west on Highway 34. Dave punched it, and in no time we were sailing down the road at eighty. In comparison to the washboard we had been on, the highway seemed as smooth as silk.

The dissonant chorus of emergency sirens, which at first was barely perceptible, grew ever louder as we traveled the last few miles to the Tidewater Post Office. As we turned into the Post Office parking lot, fire department and police vehicles came careening around the bend in the road. With their lights flashing, they screeched to a halt behind us.

EMT firefighters ran over to attend to my injury, and the sheriff and his deputy went over to question Dave. As I was being loaded into the ambulance to be taken to the hospital, Dave got in the back of the sheriff's car, and they headed back up to the water system. The sheriff's deputy and another team of paramedics followed closely behind them in separate vehicles.

FIFTY-TWO

I opened my eyes and saw an attractive Hispanic woman in turquoise blue scrubs, looking down at me. Smiling broadly, she said, "I'm Anna, your recovery room nurse. How are you feeling?"

"I'm OK, I guess."

"Still feeling a little groggy?"

"Yes…and my mouth is really dry."

Anna smiled reassuringly. "That's normal. You're doing great. My job is to monitor your vital signs and to do everything I can to make sure you're as comfortable as possible while you recover from the effects of the anesthesia. Are you in any pain?"

"No. I feel good."

"I'm not surprised," Anna said. "We've got you on an opioid, which is being delivered through the IV catheter in your arm. It's highly addictive, so we have you on what's called a PCA, a patient controlled analgesia. If you start hurting, you can give yourself a fixed dose of the drug by pushing this button here. You'll hear a beep when you press the button. It means you're receiving the pain med. You don't have to worry about overdosing because the pump will only deliver a set amount of medication within a set period of time. Do you have any questions for me?"

"When can I go home?" I asked.

"In a day or two, if all goes well. I can assure you, there's nothing to worry about. The doctor just wants to make sure you don't get an infection. Once you've fully recovered from the anesthesia and your condition is considered stable, you'll be transferred to an inpatient room."

Anna continued to closely monitor my condition, and after about an hour, I was moved to a private room on the second floor of the hospital. When I glanced out the window, I was happy to discover that my room was on the west side of the building. I watched as a sea of fog, coming off the ocean, slowly made its way over the Coast Highway. It had a calming effect on me, and the only thing which could have made it more perfect was if there was some Native American flute music playing in the background.

A young RN, who looked like she was fresh out of nursing school, entered the room and smiled at me. "Hi, I'm Brandy. Are you comfortable?"

"Yes, I'm fine."

"I'm glad. Are you up for some visitors? Your nephew and neighbor are in the waiting room. They're anxious to see you."

"Of course, please send them in."

Within a couple of minutes, Spencer and Dave's girlfriend, Chloe, came in the room. Spencer ran over and gave me a big hug.

"How are you doing, Uncle G?" Spencer asked. "Are you OK?"

Patting my nephew on the arm, I said, "Yeah, I'm fine. I'm ready to go home."

"The doctor talked to us after your surgery. He said you have to stay here at least overnight. He wants to make sure you don't get an infection."

"I know," I said. "The nurse in the recovery room told me the same thing."

"The surgeon showed us the X-rays they took of your leg when the paramedics brought you into the ER," Chloe interjected. "The arrow went through the muscles in your leg but missed your femur. The doctor told us you were lucky that the arrow didn't hit the main artery in your thigh. If it had, he said you could have bled out before you got to the hospital."

I smiled weakly. "I must be living right."

Chloe smirked. "Yeah, I'm sure that's it." Getting serious again, she asked, "Are you in any pain?"

Raising my arm with the IV catheter, I responded, "No, I feel good. It's amazing what drugs can do for you."

Looking at my nephew, Chloe said, "See, I told you your uncle would be fine." Turning back to me, she explained, "Spencer was worried about you. He wanted to bring a six-pack of Coors Light to make you feel better, but I told him the nurses wouldn't be too happy about that."

"Oh, Spence, that was really thoughtful of you," I gushed. "Thanks for looking out for me, buddy, but I'm not supposed to have any alcohol while I'm on this medication." Looking at Chloe, I asked, "When did you guys get here anyway?"

"I don't know, probably a couple of hours ago," Chloe responded. "You were still in surgery. Dave called me after he was done dealing with the sheriff and told me what happened. It blew me away."

I grimaced. "Tell me about it."

Spencer piped up, "Chloe was there when I got home from school. That's how I found out about it. I could have driven here myself, but Chloe was afraid I'd be too upset, so she insisted on driving."

"Well, she's a good friend," I responded. "I'm glad she did, and I'm really happy to see you both." Looking at Chloe, I asked, "Where's Dave, by the way?"

"He's probably still at the shop trying to smooth it over with the customers he ditched today when he closed the shop early to come up to the water system to save your ass."

"Well, once he explains what happened, I'm sure they'll understand," I rationalized.

"I'm not so sure. You know how people are. I'm sure there will be a few who won't be satisfied until they've raked him over the coals."

"I'm sorry about that. Hey, what time is it?"

"It's almost seven."

"Have you eaten anything?"

"No, we came straight here," Spencer said.

"Well, you two should go get something to eat. I think visiting hours are over soon anyway, and I probably should get some sleep. Hopefully, I can come home tomorrow. Thanks for coming. You don't know how much it means to me."

I opened my arms and gave each of them a hug. As they made their exit, I suddenly felt very tired and was eager to get some sleep. I didn't know if my extreme drowsiness was due to the narcotic I was being given or from the stress I had endured today. I suspected it was probably a combination of both. I closed my eyes, and within minutes I was fast asleep.

FIFTY-THREE

I woke up the next morning at seven-thirty and was hungry. The nurse brought me the breakfast menu, and after I had made my selection, I occupied my time until my meal arrived by staring out the window and watching the stream of cars as they traveled haltingly in both directions along the Coast Highway.

I've lived here long enough to know why the traffic was moving so slowly at this time of the year. It was because of the influx of seniors. Every year, they wait until the kids go back to school in September, and then they make their annual pilgrimage to the Coast. I knew by mid-October, most of them would be gone, and the traffic would be light again until the advent of the holiday season in November.

Since I hadn't eaten much yesterday, I was famished. I know hospital food is not supposed to be very good, but to me, the scrambled eggs, toast and fresh fruit I was given tasted great, and I scarfed down my entire meal in ten minutes.

Just as I was done eating, the nurse entered the room. "Do you feel up to having a visitor? Sheriff Whittaker is here and is anxious to talk to you. I told him visiting hours usually begin at eleven, but he said it was important."

Sighing heavily, I said, "Sure, send him in."

Within a few minutes, Whittaker came in. "I know you've

been through a lot, Mr. Riker, but I wanted to talk to you while the events of yesterday are still fresh in your mind."

"You're not going to charge Dave are you? He killed Darwin in self-defense. There was nothing else he could do."

"I don't anticipate him being prosecuted, but it's too early in the investigation to say definitively. So far all we have is his testimony. That's why I need to get your version of what happened."

I told the sheriff everything. I told him that Darwin had confessed to being the serial killer and leaving Jacob's DNA at each of the crime scenes to frame him. I also told him that in addition to the victims the cops had already identified, Darwin was also responsible for murdering the drug dealer Hutchinson was convicted of killing, framing him for the murder and sabotaging Stacey Atwood's vehicle. I told him that if it hadn't been for Dave, I would have been Darwin's next victim.

When I was done, the sheriff smiled and shook his head. "Well, you're a very lucky man, Mr. Riker. Your neighbor told us he suspected something was wrong when his mechanic, Jacob Dietrich, didn't shown up for work yesterday and you called to tell him your water system was on the fritz. If we hadn't taken Dietrich into custody yesterday morning, he would have reported for work, and Mr. McConnell would not have thought something was amiss and closed his shop to come up to your water system to check up on you. You'd be a dead man."

"You arrested Jacob?"

"Yes, we picked him up just as he was leaving for work. We didn't want to go inside the house until we had a search warrant signed by a judge."

"So, I assume you had the beer can I gave you tested and that Jacob's DNA matched that of the serial killer."

"Correct. And the footprints you gave us also matched those that were left at the Ryder Driscoll murder scene."

"There's probably something with Jacob's DNA in Darwin's car," I said.

"We found a Rolling Rock can in a paper bag on the floor on the passenger side of Nettles' vehicle. We're having that tested."

"Rolling Rock is Jacob's favorite beer," I responded. "I'm sure his genetic material will be on the can."

"That's what we suspect as well."

Just then, the nurse came in and said, "I'm sorry, Sheriff, but the doctor is doing his rounds and will be in shortly to examine the patient. I'm afraid you'll have to go back to the waiting room if you still have more to discuss with Mr. Riker."

Whittaker smiled thinly at the nurse. "That won't be necessary." Turning back to face me, he added, "I think we're done for now, anyway. We'll obviously want to question you in greater detail and get a sworn statement from you once you've been released from the hospital. Thanks for your time, Mr. Riker."

It wasn't long after the sheriff had left that a short, clean-shaven man with a mid-length crew cut walked into my room. He was wearing a white lab coat and had a stethoscope hanging around his neck. He had a youthful face, but I suspected he was older than he looked.

He walked briskly to my bedside and shook my hand. "I'm Doctor Wilson. I'm the guy who removed the arrow from your leg. How are you feeling?"

"I feel fine."

"That's what we like to hear. I'm here to check your surgical site for signs of bleeding or infection."

As he went around to the other side of the bed, he asked me to pull down the sheets and roll over on my left side so he could examine the front and back of my right thigh.

When he was through, he said, "OK, you can lie on your back again and pull up the sheets." He waited for me to get comfortable. "Well, everything looks great. The sutures are intact, and there's no sign of infection."

"When can I go home?"

The doctor smiled. "You can go home today. Let the nurse know who you want us to contact to pick you up. It should take a couple of hours to complete the discharge process. Before you leave the hospital, the nurse will come by to discuss with you the medications you'll need to take at home and tell you when you need to schedule a follow-up appointment with your family physician. Do you have any questions for me?"

"No, I don't think so."

"Well, if you should think of something, please don't hesitate to ask your nurse." The doctor extended his hand. "It was a pleasure meeting you, Mr. Riker."

We shook hands, and he left.

FIFTY-FOUR

A couple of hours later, Spencer and Dave entered my hospital room. Spencer ran over to me while Dave stood in the background, holding a small, gift-wrapped box under his arm.

Spencer gave me a hug. "We're here to take you home."

Dave piped up, "Well, not just yet. The nurse just told us they're running a little behind schedule, and it will still be a while before she can come in and review your discharge instructions with you. She took my cell phone number and said she'll call me when we can come back to pick you up. Spence and I are going to run some errands in town while we wait, but we wanted to pop in for a few minutes first to see how you're doing." Dave walked up to me and extended his hand. "How are you doing, Cramps?"

I grabbed his hand and said, "I'm fine. What I want to know is how are *you* doing?"

Dave smiled weakly. "I'm OK."

"What happened with the cops? They're not going to arrest you are they?"

"I don't think so, but I'm not worried about it."

I became visibly agitated. "What do you mean you don't think so? What did they say? It shouldn't even be an option. I told Whittaker what happened. He was just here a few hours ago to get my version of events."

263

Dave raised his hands and spread his fingers wide. "Calm down! You're going to pop a head gasket."

"I just want to know what Whittaker said."

"He didn't say anything," Dave barked. "The cops asked me a million questions. For fuck's sake, I killed a man yesterday! They were just doing their jobs. I think they believed what I told them. If they didn't, I wouldn't be here talking to you now, would I?"

I got my back up. "You don't need to bite my head off. I was just worried about you."

Dave lowered his head and closed his eyes. "I'm sorry. We've both been through a lot." After a long pause, he said, "Let's go back to my original question. How are you doing, Cramps?"

I looked at my nephew and saw he was upset. I realized I had to lighten the mood. Turning back to Dave, I said, "Oh, I'm hunky-dory."

Remembering an earlier conversation, Dave laughed. "I'm glad you still have a sense of humor." Changing the subject, he asked, "Did the nurse tell you yet what drugs the doctor prescribed for you? I bet he'll give you a prescription for Percocet."

"I don't want any drugs," I countered.

"Don't be stupid. Take anything they'll give you. If you don't want the drugs, you can give them to me."

"I didn't know you were in pain."

"I'm always in pain," Dave retorted. "You're my neighbor. I have to deal with you every day."

"I'm glad to see nothing's changed."

"A lot's changed, Uncle G," Spencer interjected. "The phone's been ringing off the hook all morning. You got a call from that *News-Times* reporter who came to the house."

"Mason Fowler?"

"Yeah, I think that was his name. And there have also been calls from reporters from other papers, local radio DJ's and all three of the Portland TV stations."

I hung my head. "Oh no, that's all I need."

Dave groaned in disbelief. "Who are you kidding? You know

you're going to love every second of your fifteen minutes of fame. You love being the center of attention. Me, me, me! Look at me!"

Bringing my arms up to my chest and pulling my hospital gown away from me as if I was holding broad lapels on an expensive suit jacket, I smiled smugly and replied, "Well, I was the one who flushed out the serial killer after all. I wonder how long it will be before I get the $5K reward."

Dave burst out laughing. "Are you kidding me? You taking credit for finding the killer is like a nightcrawler, skewered on a hook, taking credit for catching the fish that ate him. You didn't find the killer. He found you. You were the bait."

I tried to pretend I was offended, but no one seemed to care. Pointing to the gift box, which was still under Dave's arm, I asked, "So is that for me?"

Handing it to me, he said, "Oh yeah, I forgot. I got you this get well gift."

"Wow, I'm impressed. I don't think you've ever given me a present before." Playing on Dave's homophobic tendencies, I asked, "Are you sure it's OK? I mean, one dude giving another dude a present. That's not gay, is it?"

Struggling to keep a straight face, Dave said, "Not in this case, no."

Curious to see what he had brought me, I ripped off the wrapping paper and opened the box. There was a red tomato pincushion with just one lone hatpin sticking in it. Looking at Dave, I asked incredulously, "Are you kidding me?"

He bit his lower lip to keep from laughing. "When I saw this, I thought of you."

Shaking my head slowly from side to side, I said, "You really don't have any filter do you? You don't know what's inappropriate."

Pretending to be innocent, Dave deadpanned, "I'm sorry. Is it too soon?"

Spencer cracked up laughing. "Dave, you're too much!"

"Don't encourage him, Spence. He'll think he's funny."

FIFTY-FIVE

When I got home from the hospital, I soon learned that Spencer hadn't been exaggerating about the number of calls that had come in from the media. There were probably twenty names on the list of people asking me to return their calls. However, there was only one reporter I was interested in talking to, and that was Mason Fowler. I gave him a call and invited him to come over the next day.

When Mason arrived, Spencer answered the door and ushered him through the living room and out onto the deck where I was feeding the Steller's jays and chipmunks. Mason had a six-pack of Hamm's in his hand.

"Spence, can you take the beer from Mr. Fowler and put it in the fridge?" I asked.

"Sure, Uncle G." Spencer grabbed the beer and went into the kitchen.

I started to get up to greet Mason, but he quickly motioned for me to sit.

"Don't even think about getting up," he scolded.

I sat back down, and we shook hands.

"The weather's a lot nicer here than it is on the coast," Mason observed. "It's got to be about eighty degrees up here, and it's still fogged in and windy in Newport."

"That's the best part about living ten miles upriver. It's at least ten degrees warmer here and sunny every day in the summer."

There were a group of mergansers, floating lazily on the river. There was no wind, and it was slack tide so the water was flat and mirror-like. The birds and the trees on both sides of the river were reflected perfectly on the water's surface.

Looking out on the river, Mason said, "I forgot how beautiful it is out here. What kind of ducks are those? They're not mallards, are they?"

"No. They're common mergansers. They're tree-nesting ducks, and they eat fish. The ones with the brown heads that look like they've got punk rock haircuts are the females. The ones with the dark green heads and white bodies are the males."

Mason chuckled. "I wasn't expecting a nature lecture, but thanks anyway. I forgot who I was talking to."

Smiling, but slightly irritated by his comment, I said, "I'm sorry. Am I boring you?"

"No, not at all," Mason insisted. "I actually envy your love for what you do. I can't say I've ever experienced that kind of passion in my line of work."

"Speaking of your line of work," I segued, "I want you to know you're the first person I've called since I got home. I want to make sure you get the scoop before I talk to any other reporters."

Removing a digital recorder from the front pocket of his shirt, Mason made the sign of the cross over me and said, "Bless you, my son."

Grabbing his arm, I said, "Before you attempt to give me absolution, I need a beer. How about you?"

Mason looked at his watch. It was four in the afternoon. "Why not? By the time I leave here, I'll be off the clock."

I started to get up, and Mason held up his hands. "Sit back down. I've been here before. I know my way around. I'll go get the beers."

"I want a Coors Light," I said.

Mason looked confused. "Then why did you tell me to bring the Hamm's?"

"We'll get to that in due time," I answered.

Mason returned with two Coors Lights in hand. He gave me my beer, opened his and started the recorder.

I thought back to what Dave had said in the hospital. *You're going to love every second of your fifteen minutes of fame.* I smiled and asked myself, *Why not have some fun with Mason?*

I scratched my head. "Let me see. Where should I begin? I guess it's always best to start at the beginning. I was born a poor black child—"

Mason raised his eyes and cut me off. "Unless you have some abiding need to imitate Steve Martin in *The Jerk,* maybe we can just jump past that and start at what happened when you discovered you had no water at your house and went up to your water system to investigate."

"I guess we could do that," I said facetiously. "I'm just afraid if I'm rushed, I might forget something that's important. I'd hate to leave it out when I'm talking to you and remember it later when I'm being interviewed by *another* reporter."

Mason shook his head and snickered. "I'm willing to take that risk."

I got serious and recounted everything that had transpired. Throughout the process, Mason interrupted me to ask questions, seeking clarification of those aspects of my narrative he found confusing.

When I was through, Mason couldn't contain himself. "So Harlan and I were right after all. Hutchinson was framed! And Nettles told this to you and your neighbor?"

"Well, to be accurate," I said, "Darwin confessed this to me after he shot me in the leg. My neighbor Dave was coming down the road, and Darwin didn't know he was there. My neighbor just happened to be close enough to overhear it."

"Same difference," Mason argued. "You're telling me two people can testify they heard the killer confess to murdering the drug dealer and framing Hutchinson. That's huge! You said you told Whittaker about this. Do you think your neighbor would be willing to confirm this is what he told Whittaker as well?"

I cracked a half smile. "Oh, I'm sure he would…for a price."

Mason was deflated. Shaking his head, back and forth, he said, "We don't pay for information."

I chuckled. "You already have. That's what the Hamm's is for." Patting Mason on the arm, I said, "Come on. I'll take you over to meet my neighbor."

I grabbed the Hamm's out of the fridge, and we went next door to Dave's garage. Predictably, he was rooted to his recliner, watching a NASCAR race on TV.

It was late afternoon, but that didn't matter. Seeing me, Dave grumbled, "Good morning, dickhead." He was doing his best to sound like Walter Matthau in *Grumpy Old Men.*

"Hello, moron," I answered, reciting Jack Lemmon's response to Matthau in the same movie.

Squinting at Mason, Dave asked, "Who's the stranger? I would have said who's your friend, but I know you don't have any."

"This is Mason," I responded. "He's a reporter from the *News-Times*. Mason, this is Dave. He's my asshole neighbor."

Mason started laughing. "Are you guys always this friendly to each other?"

"Only when we're getting along," Dave replied. "You caught us at a good time."

"Mason is interviewing me for a story he's writing," I explained. "He just wants you to corroborate what I told him."

"Nothing against you, Mason," Dave replied, "but I don't talk to reporters."

I held up the six-pack. "That's too bad because Mason brought these just for you."

"Maybe I should clarify my statement," Dave said. "I don't talk to reporters, but friends bearing gifts are always welcome here." He looked at me, held up his right hand and opened and closed his fingers repeatedly, indicating he wanted me to give him a beer.

I grabbed a can out of the six-pack, handed it to Dave, gave another to Mason and kept one for myself. I put the remaining

three cans in the fridge, opened my beer and motioned for Mason to sit on the couch. I took a seat next to him.

Dave looked at Mason with a thin smile on his face. "So what do you want to know?"

"I just want to hear your version of events. Tell me what happened from your point of view."

Dave looked at me to see what I wanted him to do.

"He's on our side, Dave," I said. "Be totally honest with him."

Dave then went on at length and confirmed everything I had told Mason earlier.

When he was through, I said, "So now it's our turn, Mason. Tell us what you've learned from your sources. I'm sure the cops have searched Darwin's house by now. What did they find?"

"Nothing incriminating, if that's what you're asking. There weren't any scrapbooks that contained news articles related to the killings, and they didn't find any pictures of his victims, hanging on the walls, like trophies or anything like that."

By the look on my face, I'm sure Mason could tell I was disappointed.

Mason chuckled to himself. "But I didn't say the cops didn't find anything of interest either. There was a photo album with pictures of Darwin and his grandfather and cards and letters that the old man had sent to his grandson when the kid lived in Washington. In most of these, the grandfather referred to the kid as 'Skid' and rambled on about how he was looking forward to them spending the summer together on the Alsea. The old man also mentioned them watching a TV show called *Hardcastle and McCormick*. It seemed to be a big deal to both the old man and the kid for some reason. Do you know the show I'm talking about?"

"When was it on?" I asked.

"It was on ABC for about three years in the early to mid-eighties. Brian Keith and Daniel Hugh Kelly were the stars of the show."

Shaking my head, I said, "No, it's not anything I ever watched. I probably thought it was dumb."

"Well, that's because you were already farting dust by then," Dave interjected. "I was in my teens when that show was on. It had a cool looking car, and there was a lot of chasing and racing. I loved it. It was awesome!"

I looked at Mason with a puzzled look on my face. "So what's so important about this show?"

Mason smiled broadly. "I wondered the same thing so I went to Chuck's Waldport Video and rented a few VHS tapes of the first season of the show. One of the two main characters is a race car driver. His name is Mark "Skid" McCormick."

"Are you shitting me?" I exclaimed. "So that's where Darwin's nickname came from."

Dave leaned forward abruptly and nearly jumped out of his chair. "That's right! I remember that now!"

You could tell by the look on his face that Mason was enjoying himself. "Oh, and there's more. When the sheriff's detectives questioned Darwin's father, he confirmed that Darwin was adopted and that Felicia Longbough was the kid's biological mother." Turning to Dave, he said, "I know Darwin was a mechanic in your shop and that you and he were close friends. Did you ever meet his father or did Darwin ever tell you anything about him?"

Dave shook his head. "No, I never met the man, and I don't remember Darwin ever mentioning his folks at all."

"That's not surprising. Apparently they were estranged and hadn't talked in years. After I learned that the cops had questioned Mr. Nettles, I called him to request an interview, and he agreed. We met for about an hour this morning."

"Did he tell you why he wanted to adopt the kid?" I asked.

Mason smiled broadly. "Oh yeah, he was very forthright once I assured him everything he told me would be off the record. He told me he was the kid's biological father. He said he was only eighteen when he got Felicia pregnant and didn't want to get hitched and be trapped in some dead end job. He tried to convince her to have an abortion, but she refused. He said for years he felt guilty for not doing the honorable thing and marrying her. When he found out she was murdered and that the kid, his son, was up for adoption, he said he and his wife contacted DSHS and said they wanted to adopt the boy. He admitted to being the kid's biological father, and DNA testing confirmed it. He and his wife got custody of the kid."

"So you're telling me Darwin Nettles is *definitely* Allyn Wilkes," I said.

"Yes, there's no question about it. The father said that after what had happened, he and his wife thought it best to change the kid's name to protect his privacy and give him a fresh start. He said the kid liked the idea of a name change and that he and his wife let the boy choose the name. Darwin was the name he chose."

"You said Darwin and his folks hadn't talked to each other in years. Did his father tell you what caused the rift between them?"

"Yes. He said he and Darwin got along great for about a year or more. Then one day, when they were out fishing on the Alsea, he confessed to the kid that he was his real dad. I asked him why he did it, and he said he thought it would strengthen the bond between them. Unfortunately, it had the opposite effect. The kid started to hate his father for having abandoned him and his mother. Their relationship just continued to go downhill, and when the kid turned eighteen, he moved out of the house. His father said that was the last time he and Darwin spoke to each other."

"So what happens now with Dane Hutchinson?" I asked. "I'm sure his conviction will be overturned."

"Oh, he'll definitely be exonerated," Mason replied. "I'm sure the sheriff and the district attorney are already racking their brains, trying to figure out how to put the best face on their Hutchinson case fuck up. They know he was convicted based on weak evidence, and they're worried he'll sue them for wrongful conviction."

"How much could Hutchinson get?"

"That's hard to say," Mason responded. "Oregon doesn't have a wrongful conviction compensation statute, but that doesn't mean he can't seek compensation. He can still file a lawsuit in state court or lobby the legislature to pass a private compensation bill. I'm sure Hutchinson will have no problem getting a high-priced attorney from Portland to represent him."

"Well, he deserves everything he can get," I said. "The justice system failed him miserably. His wrongful conviction robbed him of a chance to have a lucrative pro football career, and he wasted the best years of his life in prison."

Changing the subject, Dave asked, "I'm curious, Mason, can we go back a minute? Did the father ever tell you why the kid picked Darwin as his name? I mean it's not that common."

Mason nodded. "I know. I asked the father the same thing. He said the kid told him he liked the name because it was different, like he was. The father said he and his wife considered vetoing the kid's choice because the first thing they thought of when they heard the name was Charles Darwin and his theory of evolution. But then they looked up the meaning of the name and found out it meant 'dear friend.' They thought that was sweet, so they went with it. They kept the kid's original name as his middle name, so his full legal name is Darwin Allyn Nettles."

"Dear friend...how ironic? I'm sure Jacob would take exception to that," I observed.

"Yeah, tell me about it," Dave added. "When Jacob found out he was being scapegoated by Darwin, he went ballistic. If Darwin wasn't already dead, I'm sure Jacob would have killed him."

"Well, I think it's a sad story all the way around," I said. "I know it's hard to believe, but I actually feel sorry for Darwin as well. Through no fault of his own, he was dealt a shitty hand right from the start. I'm not a psychologist, but I have to think that had something to do with the way he turned out. Nobody's all good or all bad. I didn't know Darwin that well, but I know my nephew liked him. Dave was close to Darwin and probably knew him better than anybody else. What do you think Dave?"

"There's no way anybody could condone what Darwin did," Dave said. "But I'd like people to know he also had his good side. It's going be difficult after what happened, but I'm going to try to remember the good things I liked about him. It's true he had a hard time relating to people, but if you got to know him, he was an interesting guy. He was smart as a whip, he could make you laugh and was the best there ever was at Guitar Hero." Tears started to well up in Dave's eyes, and he looked away from us, pretending to see something of interest out the window.

I wasn't the only one who saw it. Mason saw it too. He stood up and turned to me. "Well, thanks you guys. I better get back to the office and start writing my story so I can make the deadline for Wednesday's paper."

I knew Dave was uncomfortable showing his emotions and needed some time to compose himself. I got up as well and said, "I'll be back in a minute, Dave. I'm going to walk Mason to his car."

When we were outside, Mason turned to me and said, "You and Dave have been through a traumatic experience. It's understandable that both of you would have trouble coping with that. Are you going to be OK?"

"I'm not going to lie to you," I said. "I'm already starting to have flashbacks. It's been tough for both of us, but things will get better. It will just take time."

Mason nodded his head slowly. Without saying anything, he reached out and gave me a hug, got in his car and left.

As I turned around to head back to the garage to see how Dave was doing, it suddenly dawned on me that I had never thanked him for saving my life. When I walked through the door, Dave looked up, smiled at me, held up his hand and asked, "Can you get me another beer?"

I opened the fridge, grabbed a Hamm's and gave it to him. Extending my hand, I said, "I'm going home, but I want to say one thing before I leave. I know I should have told you this sooner, but thanks for saving my bacon."

Grabbing my hand, Dave replied, "Don't mention it."

"Are you kidding me? If you hadn't shown up when you did, I'd be a dead man."

"I'm not trying to be polite," Dave protested. "I'm serious. I don't want you to tell anyone I'm the reason you're still here. Most of our neighbors aren't too fond of you, and I'd hate to have them think less of me."

I laughed and thought to myself, *Yeah, we'll be all right. It will just take time.* I turned to leave but stopped at the fridge and got myself another beer. "Oh hell," I said, "I guess I have time for one more."

ACKNOWLEDGMENTS

I extend my heartfelt thanks to my friend and neighbor, Dave McClellan, for serving as my technical advisor for all things automotive and backwater.

I also want to thank my good friend, Don Wilder, for designing the book's cover. His black and white photo captures perfectly the sense of foreboding and mystery I wanted the cover to convey. Don also provided insightful comments and suggestions, which improved the manuscript.

I am also grateful to Danielle McKinnon, who drew the provocative illustration found on the back cover, and to Connie Andrews, who wrote the intriguing book description.

Made in the USA
Columbia, SC
10 May 2019